The Caress Was Unexpected and Startlingly Gentle.

"Don't"

The word burst from Aloise's lips, but he ignored it. "Never fear, maiden. I mean you no harm."

"I only wished to ascertain th[illegible]ent of the damage."

"Neverth[illegible] touch me. I don't like [illegible]

He watche[illegible], black eyes. A distinct gleam of sa[illegible]tion entered their depths. "Then, obviously, you've not been properly touched. Not yet, anyway."

Aloise gasped. "A gentleman would never say such a thing to a lady."

"Ahh, but I never claimed to be a gentleman."

The hair prickled at the back of her neck.

"Who are you? . . ."

Books by Lisa Bingham

Silken Dreams
Eden Creek
Distant Thunder
Temptation's Kiss
The Bengal Rubies

Published by POCKET BOOKS

THE BENGAL RUBIES

LISA BINGHAM

POCKET BOOKS
New York London Toronto Sydney Tokyo Singapore

This book is a work of fiction. Names, characters, places and incidents are either products of the author's imagination or are used fictitiously. Any resemblance to actual events or locales or persons, living or dead, is entirely coincidental.

An *Original* Publication of POCKET BOOKS

POCKET BOOKS, a division of Simon & Schuster Inc.
1230 Avenue of the Americas, New York, NY 10020

ISBN 978-1-4767-1574-2

First Pocket Books printing August 1993

10 9 8 7 6 5 4 3 2 1

Cover art by Lisa Falkenstern

Printed in the U.S.A.

To Wade,
who never fails
to make me feel like a queen.
Love,
Mrs. Rampton

She is more precious than rubies;
and all the things thou canst desire
are not to be compared unto her.

Proverbs 3:15

Prologue

Cornwall, England
Spring 1751

"PLEASE, MATTHEW. PLEASE."

The words melted out of the awful silence which had cloaked the keeping room. Delicate, fine-boned fingers touched Matthew Waterton's wrist, but he didn't respond. He couldn't bear to look into Jeanne's luminous eyes and see her pain.

When he didn't answer, she stepped closer. "If you want me to beg . . . I *will* beg." Not allowing him time to speak, she sank to her knees on the worn rug. "I can't live another day in the company of that man. He doesn't love me. He never has." Her comments were interspersed with barely submerged sobs. "I've received word that he'll arrive within the week. Help me take Aloise away tonight! I can hire a skiff to row us to Judith-on-the-Sea and from there buy passage on a ship to Calais. I've a pair of maiden aunts who will shelter us. Oliver Crawford will never find out where we've gone!"

"Jeanne, don't do this." Slipping his arms beneath hers, Matthew tried to help her rise. But she lacked the strength to stand on her own, merely falling into his embrace. Supporting her weight, he caressed her hair, trying to infuse a measure of calm into her trembling frame. But the birth and subsequent death of her second daughter days ago had sapped Jeanne of her energies and filled her with an overriding panic. "You aren't well. Give yourself time to recover. Things will look brighter in a month or two when you've regained your health."

Jeanne grasped at his waistcoat, clumping the fabric in desperation. "No!" She shook her head from side to side, causing the pins of her coiffure to release a few precious strands of chestnut-colored hair. "Don't you understand? I couldn't bear him a son!"

"Crawford would never blame you for such a thing."

"But he will! He wants an heir. He won't rest until he has one. I disappointed him years ago by giving him a daughter, a girl he scarcely acknowledges as his own—your betrothed, Aloise."

Matthew still found it hard to believe that he—a mere commoner and the son of the local schoolmaster—had been contracted to marry a child born well above his station. But when Jeanne's husband had given her permission to form a match for their first daughter, Jeanne insisted that the girl not be doomed to a marriage of political and monetary "strategy." Therefore, she had approached Matthew Waterton. Her friend. Her confidante. A man she could trust to see to Aloise's happiness.

At first, Matthew had demurred. But after weeks of persuasion, he had learned that he was far from opposed to such an arrangement. Not because Aloise's father was a wealthy merchant, but because the girl was Jeanne's offspring. If little Aloise matured to look anything like her mother, she would be stunning. Dark-haired, dark-eyed, with skin as rich as cream and a body as delicate as a sparrow's.

"The second child I bore wasn't a boy either." Jeanne's voice grew husky with suppressed emotion, betraying how deeply the baby's demise had affected her. "Oliver will never forgive me for failing to provide a male heir."

"He knows there can be other children."

"No." As if disclosing some painful secret she whispered, "Midwife Mackie informed me that I am no longer . . . capable."

Matthew's heart nearly broke at her strangled confession. He knew how much she'd longed for a houseful of babes. "Please, Matthew. *Help me.*"

If she'd asked for anything else, he would have come to her aid. Or if more time had passed and he knew she was acting rationally, not merely suffering from the exhaustion of labor and the grief of a mother's empty arms. But Jeanne's suggestion had several serious flaws. Oliver Crawford was a powerful man who was feared by many of the villagers—and with just cause. He might not be a part of the charmed circle of titled aristocracy, but he had important contacts in government as well as a great deal of wealth. He was fanatically possessive of his horses, his estate, and his wife. To tamper with any aspect of his household would not bode well for Jeanne—or for Matthew, who had no real money or contacts to speak of. Merely the cottage his father had left him after his demise, a vast collection of books, and a set of jewels that could not be exchanged for money without causing his father's ghost to haunt Matthew for the rest of his days.

"My plan will work. I promise!"

Matthew didn't respond. How could he? She thought she could escape her husband as easily as rowing across the inlet. Matthew had been Jeanne's close friend for nearly a year—since Oliver Crawford had impregnated her and sent her from his home in London to his estates in Cornwall, to "breed." In that time, Matthew had become intimately aware of the kind of man she'd married. Crawford might not actually live with her on a daily basis, but he would not let her go. If she tried to escape his iron reign, he would hunt her to the ends of the earth.

Matthew couldn't tell Jeanne such a thing, however. Her pallor proclaimed eloquently enough that she barely had the wherewithal to stand.

"Go home and rest, Jeanne."

"But—"

"Aloise relies upon you—to see you in such a state would frighten her."

"Will you help us?"

Matthew hesitated over his answer, finally touching the curve of her cheek. "We'll talk again once you're feeling better."

Bit by bit, Jeanne drew upright, an exhausted resignation covering her features. "Very well." Freeing herself from his support, she summoned as much dignity as she could muster. Halfway across the room she stumbled slightly, but when he offered his assistance, she waved him away.

Once in the doorway, she hesitated. "Good-bye, Matthew." There was an unfamiliar edge to her voice. A fathomless hint of sadness.

"Swear to me that you won't try anything."

The silence pulsed loud and keen.

"You've been a good friend. And remember . . . whatever happens, you have promised to marry my daughter, to see that she is happy."

"Jeanne, if you attempt anything foolish, I'll—"

"No." Her eyes shone with defeat and regret. "I think I'll take your suggestion and nap until supper."

With that parting comment, she disappeared, leaving Matthew feeling that he had failed her somehow. But what could they have done with her feeling so ill? She wasn't ready for a short rowing, let alone a channel crossing.

"Jeanne, wait!" He rushed outside, but she'd already gone. A wake of dust showed the haste of her departure.

"Damn." Ducking inside, he slammed the door

behind him, planting his hands on his hips and scowling at the cramped room with its dog-eared books and maps crammed in every available space. The shadows appeared thicker now. A growl of thunder mocked him for his impotence. Shrugging away his disquiet, he vowed he would visit her on the morrow. After she'd had a chance to sleep.

Little more than an hour had passed when he found himself pacing the floor. By nightfall, as the afternoon's brewing squall intensified into the makings of a full-fledged storm, he was filled with frustration, knowing that Jeanne had come to him as a friend and he'd turned her away.

"Master Matthew?"

Matthew looked up, even though, at one-and-twenty, he had long since abandoned his childhood title. In the past few years—after the death of his father—he'd spent most of his time at the university, then had returned home to assume his father's position as schoolmaster. He'd grown accustomed to responding to "Mr. Waterton" and "sir." But he hadn't been called "master" in some time.

"Yes, Miss Nibbs."

The old woman who had served as his father's housekeeper for over a decade hesitated, obviously thinking what she had to say might be rather forward.

"Out with it," Matthew barked, then regretted his curtness. It wasn't her fault that he was ill-tempered.

"There are lights on the old sea road."

"Lights?"

"Lanterns of some sort." She chose her words carefully, "I thought I heard a woman's screams."

Matthew felt the blood drain from his face. *Jeanne.*

He brushed by Miss Nibbs, lunging outside. One of the draft horses used for tilling the upper meadow was just being led into the mews next door. Matthew jerked the halter rope out of the farmer's hands. Ignoring the man's cry of surprise, he swung on the animal's broad back, and dug his heels into its side.

As Mrs. Nibbs had said, there were lights flickering and bobbing on the old sea road. From a distance of half a mile, the wavering dots of brightness conveyed a certain panic. Maybe even a scuffle.

Damn it! Why hadn't she heeded him? Why hadn't she stayed at home? He had no doubts whatsoever that Jeanne had ignored his warnings and tried to escape. Tried and failed. The faint feminine cries of grief and outrage told him as much.

When he rounded the bluff, approaching the spot where the lights had been, there was nothing to greet him but churned-up earth and the lash of the sea below. Matthew reined the steed to a halt, cocked his head, and strained to hear the intermittent shouts that had led him this far. Jeanne was close. She had to be. He could feel her presence—her horror.

"Jeanne?" His call shuddered through the night. He waited, heart pounding. But even as he labored to hear a response, the breeze gusted, mocking him by snatching away any retort she might have made.

"Jeanne! Answer me, damn it!"

Just when he was about to lose hope, another shriek came, louder and to the right. This sound was higher pitched and filled with a childish fear. *Aloise.*

Matthew spurred his horse into a gallop, charging the length of the rocky trail. The wind clutched at his clothing. Huge drops of rain began to plop into the dust, lazily at first, then harder, faster, stinging his hands, his face.

The horse heaved from the effort of galloping uphill. Urging it on, Matthew silently prayed. *Dear God, let them be safe.*

Finally, he reached one of the uppermost knolls of the seaside cliff. Rounding the bend, the sight he encountered caused his stomach to knot in terror. *"Jeanne!"*

In the light of a single lantern, he saw her fragile form huddled between a pair of boulders precariously balanced on a narrow ledge. She was no match for the hulking man who held her wrist and grappled to pull her free, but she fought with all her might—obviously desperate about the five-year-old girl shielded behind her body.

"Maa-theew!"

The ruffian glanced away from Jeanne and Matthew recognized the man as Ruban Brannigan, one of the village blacksmiths. The gap-toothed fellow had a reputation in the county for his meanness as well as his greed. Another servant waited beyond, holding aloft a pair of flickering lanterns, the same pinpoints of brightness that had alerted Miss Nibbs.

Lightning flashed, rain pounded in icy torrents. Jeanne sobbed and backed Aloise against the rocks to form a crude protective blockade. Brannigan sneered and yanked at her wrist, clearly intent upon retrieving them both.

Growling deep in his throat, Matthew swung from his horse. He'd taken only a few steps when Brannigan saw him and whipped a knife from his boot, holding Jeanne and brandishing the weapon in Matthew's direction. "Get back, y' little whelp. This is none o' yer concern."

"Let her go!"

Brannigan ignored him and turned away as if Matthew were no more than a minor irritation. Speaking to Jeanne, he said, "Come along, Missy. The master has asked us pretty like t' bring ye home. He's promised us a guinea or two if we can do it without causin' a fuss that might rouse the village."

"No." Her knuckles gleamed white where she gripped Aloise. The girl whimpered, not understanding what was occurring, but frightened nonetheless.

Matthew stalked forward. "The woman is ill, can't you see that? Leave her. I'll see to it that she gets back to Crawford's estates." His words were a gamble he knew, but Jeanne imperceptibly wilted. *This time* he would help her.

Brannigan shook his head. "She's coming with us.

Now. Otherwise, I don't get me coin." He shook the knife in Jeanne's direction. "Do as I say! Come along—and bring yer little brat!"

Again lightning flashed, and the blade glinted as Brannigan waved it menacingly. Peeking behind her mother's skirts, Aloise saw the weapon, shrieked, and wriggled free, running toward Matthew. Startled, Brannigan caught the child with one arm.

"Aloise!" Jeanne bolted forward to claim her daughter. From his vantage point, Matthew saw Brannigan's instinctive reaction, saw it, but couldn't prevent it. His body seemed filled with lead as the man swung the knife. Too late, Jeanne lurched against him, driving the weapon into her stomach.

Aloise screamed. The servant above dropped the lanterns and—muttering a litany of half-uttered prayers—scrambled to drag the child away.

Unable to believe the evidence of his own eyes, Matthew staggered toward his friend. "Jeanne?"

She looked in his direction. Her mouth gaped in disbelief and her expression grew haunted, brimming with a potent mourning. "Mat-thew?" His name was a poignant whisper on her lips, a wistful farewell. Then her limbs lost their strength. She wavered, teetering closer to the edge of the cliff.

Matthew ran to her, trying to catch her—and for a moment he thought he'd succeeded. She clutched at him, her hands becoming anxious talons that bit into his skin, clawed at his cheek, drawing blood. Matthew caught at her gown, nearly securing her balance, but the fabric rent and she screamed, falling back, back . . .

Horror washed over Matthew as he heard the sickening thud of her body landing on the rocks below. Sinking to the ground, he peered over the ledge.

She lay so still, her arms and legs curiously twisted. The wind and rain caught at the heavy strands of her hair, plastering them across her cheeks in such a way that Matthew expected her to rouse, swipe the tresses away in impatience, and continue her flight.

She didn't move.

The clatter of hooves echoed in the distance. Looking above him, Matthew saw the impressive silhouette of a rider coming to a halt on the promontory.

He didn't need the stab of lightning to tell him who the gentleman was. He'd seen Oliver Crawford only once and from a distance, but he recognized him immediately.

The man swung from his horse, standing arrogantly with his back to the wind, looking down at the scene with cold eyes. Slapping his quirt against his thigh, he descended the slope and peered over the ledge. Not by so much as a flicker did he give away any signs of remorse. In fact, the man looked more irritated than grieved.

His next words punctuated such an attitude. "I see you've made a mess of a simple errand, Brannigan." He turned to frown at the man he had hired to retrieve his wife. The *spat, spat* of his quirt became slower, more deliberate.

The blacksmith cringed. "I didn't mean . . . to . . ."

"For that you and your assistant will have to be punished." The statement was uttered matter-of-factly, but there was no disguising the chill buried deep in each word.

Brannigan blanched, the bloodied knife dropping from his trembling fingers. "No. Please! I didn't mean to hurt her! I didn't—"

Crawford waved aside his protests. "Such an accident is of little consequence. You merely saved me from disposing of the woman myself. I've already discovered that she's become useless to me. Completely useless." He used the same tone one might employ if Jeanne had been little more than a quill that refused to write. "However, you have provided me with several unfortunate witnesses to her demise." His steely gaze flicked to the servant who still held the wriggling child. "My daughter, I can control. But as for *that* gentleman . . ."

All attention turned to Matthew who had pressed his back against one of the boulders. He froze in sheer disbelief at the casual venom flickering deep in the man's gaze.

"Take care of him, Brannigan."

"But, sir—"

"The man is a murderer." Crawford's tone became hard, implacable. "Can't you see the blood on his hands? His shirt? He killed my wife. We can all testify to that fact—and the authorities would never dare to dispute my word. I pay them enough to see to that. Take care of him."

Brannigan's eyes widened. "But, sir, I've never killed a man. Miss Jeanne was an accident, I swear. But this!"

Crawford frowned and cut his protests short with a wave of his hand. "Fine. If you haven't the stomach for such tasks"—he dropped the quirt and bent, retrieving the blade—"then I shall have to see to them myself."

Matthew shrank into the shadows, his boots scrabbling against the rocks. But Crawford sought another goal. The blade lifted, gleaming for a fraction of an instant, then plunged into Brannigan's throat.

Aloise screamed again, squirming free. Swiping at her shoulder, Crawford threw her to the ground. The sound of her head hitting a rock reverberated in Matthew's consciousness. He tried to dodge to her, then saw Crawford draw a pistol from the waist of his breeches. In an instant, there was an explosion, the smell of spent powder, and Brannigan's assistant lay in a pool of his own blood, having managed to run less than a yard.

Crawford turned, peering into the darkness. "Only one remains . . ." he murmured, squinting slightly, obviously trying to determine Matthew's identity midst the rain and the intermittent lightning. "Tell me . . . have we met?"

Matthew shook his head, scraping his hands against the granite at his back as he sidestepped the rocks. Beyond Crawford lay his only opportunity of escape. If he could get by the man and make his way down the slippery path, he could mount the plow horse and gallop away. But the small cruel smile Crawford displayed made it quite clear that he knew Matthew would try such a thing.

"What a pity that you aren't willing to make the proper introductions. I generally prefer to assign a name to those who are about to die."

The words were said so calmly, so coolly, that they held more of a threat than if they'd been shouted. Tucking the spent pistol back into his breeches, Crawford stooped, yanking the blade from the blacksmith's throat. Rising, he inched forward, his knife dripping with rain and more.

Stunned, horrified, Matthew eyed his assailant, the horse waiting behind him, and then the unconscious child. Blood trickled from a gash at her temple, yet her father hadn't bothered to give her a second glance.

"You may as well submit to your fate, young man. You really have no recourse."

But he did. Crawford had only a knife. Matthew was younger, stronger, he could outrun him. In doing so, however, Aloise would be left alone. Defenseless. His heart wrenched at her plight—but he couldn't stay!

He couldn't stay!

Closing his mind to her situation, he scooped a rock from the ground, throwing it at Crawford's horse. The stallion reared, crying out. Crawford swore, instinctively turning to see the steed racing into the night. Matthew dodged past him and tore down the slippery path.

A curse erupted behind him, but Matthew didn't

pause. Running to the plow horse, he swung on its back.

Only once did he chance to look behind him. Crawford stood with his feet braced apart, staring in his direction. The rain whipped at his clothing, but he remained impervious.

"Such an escape is useless, you know!" he shouted, the words a statement of fact, not a boast. "I will discover your identity. It is only a matter of time. Say what you will to whomever you wish, but at the first breath of scandal . . . *you* will be the one to hang."

Matthew wanted to refute the man's cocky assurance, his all-out gall. But even as he opened his mouth, he knew what Crawford said was true. From this night on, Matthew would never be safe unless he could find a way to completely escape the realm of Crawford's power. It would only be a matter of time before the man discovered his true identity. Within hours, Crawford would see to it that Matthew Waterton had been framed as a murderer and branded an outlaw. The authorities would be scouring the countryside by morning. And if Crawford were ever to find him . . .

Matthew could consider himself lucky if the local officials only hanged him.

A tightness gripped his throat and he blinked at an unfamiliar wetness gathering in his eyes. *Damn the man. Damn him all to hell!* Matthew Waterton must cease to exist. He would have to find a new world, a new identity. One that could bear no resemblance to the peaceful life he had enjoyed up to now. He would become a man without a home, without a name, without a past.

A loneliness and guilt such as he had never known possible settled into his bones. He should have helped Jeanne when she came to him at the cottage. He'd had the power to avert this tragedy, and in his youthful inexperience with such matters he failed them all.

Swiping at his eyes, he stared hard into the darkness, imprinting the scene on his consciousness for all time. Jeanne's body lay broken on the jagged boulders at the base of the cliff. Little Aloise had collapsed on the ground, her arms outstretched in her mother's direction. And in the howl of the wind, the tumble of the rain, he thought he heard a fragment of Jeanne's voice: *Remember . . . whatever happens, you have promised to marry my daughter, to see that she is happy.*

Someday, he would be forced to reckon with the vow he'd made to Jeanne. If it took the last bit of strength to be wrung from his body, Matthew would be back. He would see to it that Crawford paid for his crimes. He could only pray that Aloise would survive the intervening years. From this night on, the girl was out of his reach, firmly imprisoned beneath her father's rule. He prayed she would somehow manage to survive his cruelty. Otherwise, she would become his creature. His effigy.

God help her.

God help them both.

Drawing on the reins, he urged his horse into a gallop, plunging into the blackness of the night. The shadows of the unknown.

1

France
September 1766

WILLIAM CURRY DAMNED THE FACT THAT PARIS NEVER truly settled. Long after the sun had set, long after midnight cloaked the streets in an inky stain, a subdued activity lingered in the deep alleys and twisted paths. Even at this late hour, people lurked in the patches of blackness, some scurrying for the safety of a warm fire, others stumbling drunkenly over the rain-slicked cobblestones in search of another tavern and another pint of grog. Such activities made a quick, unnoticed flight through the streets nearly impossible.

Gesturing to the men who followed him, Will abandoned all caution and quickened their pace. The news he had to convey was far more important than the risk of rousing the neighborhood—even though if any of these men were spotted by the wrong sorts of people, they might all end up swinging at the end of a rope. The odd contingency of roués, rakes, and outlaws had been dodging the mistakes of their pasts for years.

Such a fact only intensified the import of Curry's mission and he leaned a little closer to his horse's mane. After a quarter mile of traveling, he pointed to an inn on the far corner.

"There, up ahead!" Signaling to his companions to surround the entrance, he reined his animal to a halt. "Wait here. As soon as Slater has joined us, we ride."

The gelding had scarcely come to a jittery stop when Will swung from the saddle and loped toward the stoop. Flinging the door open, he headed directly for the stairs, taking them two at a time.

There would be hell to pay for his sudden arrival. Curry might have the advantage of being known as Slater McKendrick's closest friend, but the man had left specific orders not to be disturbed. To have trespassed beyond his wishes did not bode well for Will's reception.

Once at the upper landing, he hurried to the appropriate quarters. He stood with his feet braced, his fist poised, ready to issue a secret combination of knocks that he hoped would gain him entrance.

"Aagh!"

The sound, sharp and high-pitched, came from within, followed by a low, guttural moan.

"Slater?" Will pounded on the weathered boards. "Slater, are you ill?" When he received no answer, Will clasped the doorknob only to discover that the lock had been bolted on the other side.

Another cry came, higher this time. His friend was in trouble. Obvious trouble. Will slid his saber from its sheath. "Hold on, Slater. Hold on!"

He slammed his shoulder against the wood, but the barrier held true. Backing away and lifting his sword free from his body, he charged toward the portal full force. "Slaaaa-terr!"

Mere seconds before he would have connected with the solid planks, the door whipped open. Unable to stop, Will stumbled headlong inside, tripped on the rug, and fell face-first onto the bed. His sword clattered uselessly to the ground as he floundered, sinking deeper and deeper into a sea of coverlets and feather beds. When his struggles only intensified his predicament, he sputtered and grew still.

Bit by bit, his senses relayed to him the true extent of his folly. Satin and linen rubbed at his hands and slid against the leather of his shoes, but it was not only the covers that embraced him. To his astonishment, he became aware of the exotic scent of Arabian musk and the friction of sweat-beaded skin. Firm breasts cradled his cheeks, the fragrant mounds rising and falling in a quick pattern of breaths that caused the honeyed valley to press against him again and again.

Dear Lord, he had interrupted an evening of frolic! For this, the other man would accept no glib excuses for attempting to break down the chamber door. Taking a peek at the creamy breasts that had been nestled against his cheek, Will couldn't blame him.

"Explain yourself, Curry."

The low phrase slid out of the ensuing silence, accompanied by the cold kiss of steel pricking Will's neck.

"Slater, please, I had no idea." He lifted his head, connecting with the startled gaze of the woman he'd sprawled upon. "My humble apologies, mademoiselle," he offered, groping for a safe location to provide him with enough leverage to rise.

The keen tip of the sword digging into the base of his skull prevented him from moving. Reminded again of the seriousness of his untimely interruption, he became quiet. The two men might have a special bond fostered by years of traveling together, but that did not extend far enough to excuse disturbing an apparent *liaison.*

"I trust you have an excellent reason for your unannounced arrival."

The voice that melted from the shadows had become as familiar to Will as his own, its timbre dark, gravelly, with the almost imperceptible lilt of a well-educated man. Will had followed the evocative cadence through the densest jungles and fiercest deserts with the attitude of a devoted servant attending his master. He'd also noted the way the passage of time had added an edge, a bitterness, to the inflection.

"I told you I didn't want to be disturbed."

"I know, but—"

"Has my ship sunk?"

"No, I—"

"Has a plague swept France?"

"No—"

"Is the inn on fire?"

"No."

"Then what are you doing here, Curry?"

Will's fingers curled into the duvet. The news he had to relay was important, yes. But there was no telling how Slater would react. No telling at all.

"Well?" The man behind him demanded, the sword point pressing more distinctly against its mark.

"She's on her way to England," he uttered quickly.

For several minutes, Will's statement hovered in the air about them. He'd mentioned no specific name, but he knew his friend understood the import of his words by the quiet intensity that began to pulse in the limited space of the chamber. The man's weapon eased away and Will dared to breathe.

"Get up."

Will was more than happy to comply. "A thousand pardons, mademoiselle," he muttered when he finally managed to wedge his hands against the bolster and push himself to his feet.

The woman smiled as he tugged at the hem of his vest and smoothed his hair. Her gray eyes sparkled in amusement and more. Curiosity. Interest. "It was entirely my pleasure. I assure you."

"Where is she?"

The cryptic demand for information caused Will to wrench his attention away from the nubile female. Although the thought should have occurred to him, he was not at all prepared for the sight of his friend, clad in no more than the steel of his sword. Even at nearly two score years, Slater McKendrick cut an impressive figure, one honed by battle and hardship and sheer strength of will. His hair and eyes were black as the night itself, his form tall and ruthlessly fit.

"Rudy and Louis just arrived from delivering our latest shipment. Earlier this week they saw Crawford's clipper, *The Sea Sprite,* at Calais. The ship was taking on supplies and passengers for a channel crossing. When they recognized the only female being led aboard as Miss Crawford herself, they bribed one of the seamen into telling them that *The Sea Sprite* will stop at a deserted spot in southern Cornwall—a small town known as Tippington. The passengers will disembark at dawn on the last day of the month."

"Excellent." Slater adopted the focused energy of a stalking panther. "What arrangements have you made for our departure?"

"Manuel has already prepared your ship. After taking us to Tippington, he will sail on to London. There, he will send word for your estates to be prepared and a coach to be sent to meet us. After that, he will wait for further orders should it prove necessary to leave England again."

Slater nodded in approval. In seconds, he had collected his scattered belongings and dumped two leather haversacks in Will's arms. Then he buckled his scabbard around his waist and proceeded to finish arming himself: a knife in his boot, a pistol beneath his waistcoat, a dirk up his sleeve.

"What time is it?"

"Just past twelve. We'll have to hurry if we plan to intercept them. Each hour is of the essence."

"The men?"

"Assembled and waiting."

Slater McKendrick's normally sober features lightened somewhat. "Let's ride. Come the last day of the month, we'll be ready to meet her ship." The crisp edge to his tone deepened. "Her father should arrive in Tippington soon after—if he hasn't already."

Will watched in avid fascination as Slater bent low

over the bed and scooped the woman hard against his chest. The kiss they shared was openly carnal, a meshing of mouths, tongues, and desires. Will shifted in discomfort, feeling distinctly like a bawdy-peeper as the embrace continued long past what he would consider proper.

He was not surprised by the dazed look the woman wore when Slater backed away. She seemed to have completely forgotten that they were not alone in the room as she rose, her bosom heaving. She clutched a coarse sheet to her neck. The swathe of fabric draped enticingly over one breast and flowed past her hips to tangle under her knees, leaving most of her evident charms completely and brazenly bare.

If a woman had looked at William Curry with half her evident passion, he would have stripped naked and stayed for a month, but Slater appeared entirely unaffected.

"Let's go."

"But—" Will had not the time to voice his protest as McKendrick moved into the hall, the length of his stride attesting to his newfound purpose. Rousing from his own stupor, Will followed.

"Shouldn't we leave her a coin or two?"

Slater didn't pause. "My dear friend, the Marquise du Laque does not accept money for her favors."

Will's jaw dropped. A *marquise*—and a married one at that. Great bloody hell, the man had nerve.

Outside the inn, Slater McKendrick strode toward a riderless steed being led out of the crush of attendants and animals. Behind him, Curry gave the carryalls to one of his companions and quickly mounted a lathered horse.

A rush of energy began to infuse Slater's veins as he swung into the saddle and gathered the reins in one fist. This night had been a long time in coming, but now that it was here, he felt no regrets for what he was about to do.

Aloise Crawford was about to return to England.

After nearly a decade and a half of waiting, Slater had finally found her. The time had long since come to liberate her from Crawford's care and exact his revenge against the man who had branded him a murderer and outlaw.

Inhaling the warm coal-tainted air, Slater could almost believe he caught a wisp of the country buried in its scent. Clover, sea mist, and rich loam. His frown grew fierce. Damnation, how he'd missed his home. Missed the sky hanging over his head like an endless azure bowl and the cool kiss of the surf come dawn.

Fifteen years ago, he'd been forced to abandon his birthplace and his identity in haste and despair. He'd journeyed pell-mell across the width of England, obtaining a position on the first ship heading anywhere away from his homeland. In all the intervening years, he'd never set foot in Britain, knowing that to do so would mean certain death. Crawford had seen to that. Just as expected, the man had wasted little time in ruining his name.

Slater straightened, squinting into the night, suddenly anxious for what was to occur. He'd traveled the globe and seen wondrous places, but his bones yearned to reside in Cornwall. At the thought of traveling back, the guilt and anger that he'd harbored in the very core of his soul began to intensify, burn, spurring him on.

It was past time to return.

It was past time to force a reckoning.

Signaling to his companions, he touched the horse's flanks. "Make your way to the ship as swiftly as you can. We're off to Tippington!"

England

Aloise Crawford waited until three in the morning to escape.

Mere hours ago, her father's ship had dropped anchor near the small village of Tippington and

Aloise knew without a doubt that if she didn't take this opportunity to run away, she would be taken ashore, bundled into her father's carriage, and driven directly to Briarwood where she would be forced to marry a man she didn't know and didn't love. It had happened twice in the past; she couldn't believe that he would do anything else.

Aloise had no intention of submitting to his plans. Lying stiff as a corpse on her narrow berth, she counted the passing minutes like beads on a rosary. One hour bled into two, then three, each moving with the inestimable laggardness of an inchworm measuring a stalk. To anyone who might have entered her cabin, she gave every appearance of sleeping. She kept her eyes closed and her features sweetly serene. But inside . . .

Inside, an unbearable tension coiled like a steel spring. Her mind centered on a single objective. She *would* manage to flee from her father. *Today.*

Her lashes opened and forest brown eyes probed the blackness, searching for any minute detail which might jeopardize her future freedom.

Aloise didn't know the precise moment she'd begun to formulate her plans. Surely, not the first time Mr. Humphreys had come to fetch her from Sacre Coeur Academy—an exclusive French school for young ladies of breeding. She'd been sixteen then and a little wild. Her instructors had referred to her as a "challenging" student, kindly omitting that the term had been awarded due to Aloise's lack of decorum and not to a lack of intelligence. However, until her father's secretary had arrived, Aloise hadn't realized how she'd grown so unaware of the realities of life.

Within moments, Mr. Humphreys had informed her that her father had begun to make arrangements for her to become a bride before the month's end. In the meantime, she was to prepare herself for such an event by being fitted for a wedding gown—a rather garish red wedding gown, in her opinion—that had been ordered by her father to set off a collection of jewels he'd chosen to be her only dowry.

Aloise supposed the seeds of her imminent escape had been sown that night. Her father had paraded enough of his own wives in front of Aloise for her to determine she was too young to be consigned to such sugar-coated imprisonment. Each time he'd remarried, she'd been summoned from Sacre Coeur, taken to London, and introduced to his new mate. Then she'd been sent back to France with her determination to avoid a similar fate intensified threefold. There were things she needed to do, places to see, adventures to experience.

Three weeks later, Mr. Humphreys returned to tell her a mate had been selected and she was to dress for the nuptials and don her dowry. At that moment when Mr. Humphreys had opened a slender velvet envelope to reveal the necklace she was to wear, Aloise had been more than a little suspicious about the jubilant news. At last she understood her father's motives for such a match. Apparently, Oliver Crawford had decided that she must marry into a title. And it wasn't her wit, her charm—or even her body—that her father used as a bargaining tool. Instead, he attracted her prospective mates like drones to a honey pot by promising that her dowry would include the famous Bengal Rubies. The same stones he had ordered her to wear.

Where her father had managed to land such a prize, Aloise couldn't even begin to imagine. All of England had become familiar with the intricate history of the gemstones as well as their supposed blessing—or curse, depending on how one viewed such matters. The huge collection of jewels was supposed to reward the pure in heart with riches beyond measure and damn all others. There had been rumors at one time that the stones had been given away by His Majesty to a commoner for faithful service, but Aloise knew her father could never be awarded such a prize.

Nevertheless, she hadn't openly complained when her father had essentially bribed a man to wed her, bed her, and claim her as his spouse. She reluctantly accepted the impending marriage, hoping that—if all else failed—at least she would be liberated from Sacre Coeur and her father's will. She'd journeyed to the outskirts of Dijon where Mr. Humphreys had rented several rooms at a local inn. By midafternoon she had been bathed, powdered, and perfumed in anticipation of her bridegroom's arrival.

She discovered the necessity of the precautions as soon as her husband-to-be arrived. At eight-and-forty, Lord Greenby's eyes were slightly crossed and horribly nearsighted. He couldn't see her clearly, but—to an amazing degree—he certainly managed to smell her. Once they'd been left alone he began stalking her like a hind after a rabbit.

Poor, poor, Lord Greenby. That night he'd choked on a chicken bone during their betrothal dinner. Within days, Aloise had buried her suitor and had herself been immured behind the high stone walls of Sacre Coeur.

After such a horrible experience, Aloise had known it was only a matter of time until her father found another groom for her. Therefore, she made every effort to take charge of her own life—attempting to escape so many times that her father was forced to hire bodyguards to reside at the school. She saw her own classmates graduate and leave, then the girls beneath her. Bored with courses she'd taken three times already, Aloise took to the library instead, filling her head with whatever information could be found. When that supply of reading material grew old, she befriended one of the elderly gardeners whose son-in-law was a bookseller and allowed her to preview his materials as long as she did not ruffle the pages.

On a mild April morning soon after her eighteenth birthday, Mr. Humphreys journeyed to Sacre Coeur again. Offering a shrug and a sigh, he repeated the same message he'd already given her once before. She was to be married. At dusk. Her father wasn't taking any chances that her groom would not survive the day.

She hadn't even been allowed to pack her belongings. Mr. Humphreys had bundled her into the carriage and driven her to a small church in the heart of Calais. Balking each step of the way, Aloise had tried reasoning with her father's secretary, threatening, pleading, but to no avail. He had his instructions and would see them carried out to the letter.

Stepping into the chapel, she'd peered up the aisle. Filled with dread and fury, she'd searched the gloomy interior for a decrepit old man who'd lost his hair, his teeth, his health, or all three.

To her amazement, a young gentleman eagerly awaited her arrival. An angel. A god! Cecil, Lord Kuthright was every bride's dream. Shining golden hair had been drawn against his nape and tied with a velvet ribbon. His blue eyes sparkled and his brilliant smile dimmed the gilded light spilling from the stained-glass windows over his head.

Aloise sighed, the sound melting into the night with untold regret. Cecil, dear unfortunate Cecil . . .

He'd only managed to take three steps when the doors at the rear of the chapel had burst open and a strange man had begun shouting in French about wives and cuckolds. Shoving Aloise onto one of the pews, he lifted his arm, brandished a pistol, and took incredibly accurate aim.

She buried Cecil too—in the same churchyard where the two of them were to have toasted their marriage with champagne and a picnic luncheon Lord Kuthright had so thoughtfully provided.

This time, Aloise had *not* been sent back to Sacre Coeur. She shuddered at the memory. Her father had decided her behavior had not improved at the ladies' academy. He'd thought she'd needed a reminder that her will was too strong. So he'd exiled her. Imprisoned her in a rotting farmhouse in the depths of the Loire Valley, isolating her from her scattered friends and—most tragically of all—separating her from her source of new books. Allowed to take only a few of her own she'd been kept in Loire for nearly two years. Until her father had decided to retrieve her again.

Aloise's tongue nervously swiped her lips. How many nights had she lain awake, plotting, planning, scheming to circumvent her father's strangling control? She'd tried to escape him—oh, how she'd tried. She'd become a master at picking locks, at scaling walls, at manipulating even the most hard-hearted guard into coming to her aid. But each time, Oliver Crawford had tracked her unmercifully, then had punished her for her disobedience.

By now, she would have thought he would pray to have her vanish into thin air. But after so many failed attempts at freedom, Aloise had learned one important lesson. Her father would never, *never,* release what was his. Not until he was good and ready. Therefore, Aloise was prepared to take destiny into her own hands.

Sweeping aside the covers, she slipped from the bunk and opened the sea chest bolted to the floor. Inside was the bundle of belongings she'd carefully gathered for her journey. Digging to the very bottom, she retrieved a small golden locket. Opening the clasp, she peered at the familiar miniature painting, experiencing the same confusing swirl of emotions that swamped her each time she looked at the portrait. Loneliness, betrayal, anger. Fear.

"Why, Mama, *why?* Why can't I *remember?"* Aloise's brow pinched in a frown of concentration and she fought to pierce the fog of confusion that had shrouded her mind for as long as she could remember. But try as she might, she had no memories, no memories at all, beyond the first morning she'd awakened at Sacre Coeur. She'd been five then. Even now, fifteen years later, those early years of her childhood were lost in a murky maelstrom of confusion. And pain. If she tried too hard to remember, a blinding pain settled into the base of her skull, so much so that she had given up all hope of piercing the blackness.

The girls at school—and the teachers as well—had been a little wary of Aloise because of her "malady." She supposed they feared she was a bit mad. Only Mr. Humphreys had dared to try and help her, relating a few scattered stories about Jeanne Alexander Crawford, including the fact that her mother had originally arranged a marriage between Aloise and a schoolmaster in Cornwall, Matthew Elias Waterton. Her father had reluctantly agreed to such a match, but had nullified the agreement upon Jeanne's death, offering Aloise no other explanation than the marriage was not suitable to her station.

As the succeeding months passed, Aloise's desire to wriggle far beyond her father's reach only intensified. She waited for the perfect moment—the next time Mr. Humphreys had come to collect her for another marriage attempt. Unfortunately, after the debacle with Cecil, Lord Kuthright, her wait had been a long one. As she cooled her heels in Loire, it became quite clear to her that most of the titled aristocracy considered her to be a bit of a risk as far as matrimony was concerned. After all, having a childhood betrothal severed was regrettable. Having a second prospective husband die on the eve of marriage could be counted as a misfortune . . . But a *third* such occurrence? She might bring with her a dowry rich enough to fill the coffers of even the most penniless duke or earl, but if one didn't live long enough to spend it . . .

Aloise closed the chest and lay her bundle of belongings on top. Over the past few days, she had taken careful stock of the guards Mr. Humphreys had chosen for the trip, and she had to give him credit for his selection. She had discovered that none of them could be bribed, threatened, or seduced. However, she had also determined that the gentleman who took his turn in the evening—a portly, balding man—tended to nod at his post. Because of this, he had taken to walking the length of the corridor. Twelve steps fore, thirty-two steps aft.

Pressing her ear to the door, she strained to hear more than the sound of the slapping waves and her own hammering heart. Within minutes her prayers were answered. She caught the creak of the chair, a grunt, a sigh.

One . . . two . . . The floorboards squeaked as he began his stroll.

Aloise's fingers trembled as she gathered her hair over one shoulder and wound it into a thick braid. Luckily, its dark chestnut color would blend easily into the shadows.

The guard began to pace toward the rear of the ship. *One . . . two . . .*

Flipping the plait out of her way, Aloise tugged at the buttons of her night shift. Only half of the ivory discs had been unfastened when she whipped the garment over her head, exposing the severe ebony gown she'd worn beneath.

Dragging the blanket from the top of the berth, she rolled it into a long coil, then stuffed it beneath the sheets in a way she hoped would pass for a body should anyone check on her. Moving quickly, she retrieved the items she'd managed to pack for her trip: a change of clothing, the locket, two precious travelogues, a novel, and several pouches of gold coins that she had "liberated" years ago from the school safe at Sacre Coeur.

She took a step, two, then stopped. Turning, she stared at the too-familiar trunk wedged in the corner beneath her own meager collection of baggage. Mr. Humphreys had brought her that container, one made of gold and mahogany inlay. He had told her that come morning, she was to don her best gown and adorn it with the Bengal Rubies. Rubies that were worth a fortune . . .

Did she dare?

No. Her father would surely kill her if she touched the collection. Mr. Humphreys only kept the stones in this cabin because of the security to be found with a guard constantly a step away.

And yet . . . even one small piece would provide her with the funds she would need to start a new life. Her father wouldn't discover the missing items for days. Days and days.

The temptation proved too strong. Kneeling, she tugged the case free and opened it.

This was her dowry. Her father's bribe. Nestled within the padded velvet lining lay a huge gold tiger, its mouth opened in a perpetual snarl. The glistening blood-red stones used in its eyes called to her, beckoned, as if they held a will of their own.

Aloise's fingers trembled as she reached to lift the tiger free of its protective container. She was surprised by the weight of it. The warmth. Her father had never let her see the entire collection. Setting it on the floor beside her, she released a catch on its side, opening the lid.

Dark black velvet cradled the exotic assortment of jewels, jewels so stunning that Aloise suddenly understood why so many men had been obsessed to obtain them. Why they were willing to marry a stranger of the middle class and trade their aristocratic titles with her father to own them. The jewels were alive. Glowing.

She reached out to touch the earrings first. Fashioned of a heavy antique gold, they were modeled after two tigers snarling and grappling together. Delicately cut stones dripped from the ends like a scarlet waterfall.

Next, she examined the necklace, nearly gasping at its beauty. The heavy band had been molded into the gamboling shapes of antelope and lions, exotic birds, graceful ostriches, playful hippopotamuses, and in the center, another signature Bengal tiger. The entire creation shimmered with the most stunning rubies she had ever seen.

The squeak of a floorboard outside reminded her that she didn't have the time to stare at the rest of the contents of the case. She had to go. Now!

Ignoring the other pieces, the brooch, a bracelet, a half-dozen rings, and a circlet, she snatched the huge necklace cascading with jewels. In her haste, a stone from the clasp dropped to the floor. Swearing under her breath, she tucked the gem under the binding of her stomacher, then hid the necklace in her haversack beneath the folds of an extra petticoat. Moving as quickly as she could, she returned the tiger to its trunk and shoved it back into place.

Tiptoeing to the door, she wondered if someone had heard the scuffling noises she'd made, but the pacing in the passageway hadn't altered. Soon she was able to determine the direction of the guard's steps. *Fore, aft, fore, aft.* Taking a deep breath, she waited until the footsteps passed her on their way to the rear of the ship.

The carefully oiled hinges made no sound as she crept out. Not bothering to look behind her, she ran toward the hatchway. Before the guard had finished his final turn, she dodged into the cool misty air.

The next few minutes would prove critical. The skiffs were anchored aft. Aloise had managed to disable all but one of the boats earlier this afternoon. She would have to climb into the remaining vessel and employ the well-oiled pulley system to lower it into the water, and pray that no one would see her. Under cover of darkness, she would row ashore and hide midst the trees on the upper bluff. She had studied enough maps of the area to know that, come dawn, she should take the back roads north to Dalton, and from there, a public coach to London. Once in that city, she was sure she could find employment with the groups of missionaries who were constantly looking for volunteers to travel to heathen lands.

Aloise offered a silent prayer of deliverance and darted away from the threshold. She had only taken a few steps when a huge sailor loomed out of the night. Gasping, she flattened against the bulkhead, hoping to make herself invisible.

"Guards! Guards, she's loose!"

All of Aloise's well-laid plans scattered beneath the need to escape. She would have to jump and hope she could swim ashore. Now. Before it was too late.

Hiking her skirts well above her knees, she threw one foot over the railing. The hollow thump of running boots behind her warned Aloise that she hadn't much time, but she still hesitated, peering down into the frothy sea below. In daylight, the drop into the ocean hadn't seemed so far, the waves hadn't seemed so high . . . and her courage hadn't seemed so false.

"Miss Crawford. Miss Crawford!" Mr. Humphreys ran toward her, his wig askew, a pair of breeches tugged hastily over his nightshirt, his shins bare and skinny in the moonlight. "Miss Crawford, please don't. You're to be a bride soon. Your father has chosen some wonderful prospects. I promise!"

Prospect*s? Prospects!*

"Not bloody likely," she muttered under her breath.

"Miss Crawford, your father will—"

Her father be damned.

Climbing the rest of the way over the beam, Aloise clung to the support for a fraction of a second. Then she jumped.

2

SLATER MCKENDRICK URGED HIS STALLION TO THE TOP of the bluff bordering the beach at Tippington, joining the group of men who waited for him there. The gutted shape of an abandoned church loomed behind them, cloaking their ebony-clad forms in the anonymity of its shadow. A full moon bathed the area in a dull pewter gleam. The sea remained fairly calm, rolling into shore with a mesmerizing lunge and burble while the land curled around the inky water like a velvet horseshoe.

Slater ignored the chill that feathered through his extremities. Tippington might be nearly thirty miles from his birthplace, but the bluff he waited on held an uncanny resemblance to the spot where Jeanne had been murdered.

The thought alone brought a wave of guilt, a rush of sadness. Not for the first time, Slater cursed the mistakes he'd made in his youth. Mistakes he feared he would never be able to atone for.

The burly Russian at his side shifted, muttering, "I don't like it, Cap'n. There ought to be someone here. It's far too quiet. I'm sure Crawford is at an inn somewhere, safely abed, but with the ship so close, he should have a man about."

"As I'm sure he does. Somewhere." Slater's eyes swept the area again. No figures waited below. A hundred yards away, the vague outline of *The Sea Sprite* bobbed up and down against the leash of its anchor, waiting for dawn before releasing its passengers. Slater could only pray that one of them would be Aloise Crawford. Otherwise, all of their efforts would be in vain.

The pummeling sound of hooves alerted the group to another rider's presence and they whirled, pistols raised, swords drawn, to confront the noise. After ten years of service on a trading vessel, Slater had earned enough money to buy his own ship. He had then begun gathering a crew from a motley assortment of outcast aristocrats and rakes who had looked to Slater for leadership and adventure, forming a tight group of allies whom Slater knew would remain true to the death. They relaxed when they realized it was Will Curry who rode hell-bent up the crooked trail.

"You're late."

Will drew his animal to a halt. "I was delayed in town. I stopped in the local tavern to inquire about the conditions of the roads and became embroiled in a game of whist with one of the guests. I soon discovered I was talking to none other than Crawford's valet. The man was quite in his cups and seemed determined to waylay someone for a little . . . conversation. I soon became privy to some rather titillating gossip concerning Aloise. However, I fear the news may astound you. Crawford's audacity is beyond description."

"I would believe Crawford capable of anything." Slater's words rang with a quiet intensity that revealed far more than he had intended.

"Even an auction?"

Slater sighed and shifted in the saddle. "I thought we were speaking about his plans for his daughter."

"We are."

"Do you mean to tell me . . ." Slater stared at his friend in disbelief.

"Dear Papa Crawford intends to auction his daughter to the highest bidder."

"You can't be serious."

"Deadly serious. He's invited a half dozen of the most eligible—and penniless—bachelors in all England to his country estates. Their ages range from seventeen to three-and-forty. Supposedly, the lucky gents are invited to Briarwood for a grand soiree—hunting, gaming, musicals, et cetera, et cetera . . ." His blue eyes twinkled. "But the lack of feminine companionship on the guest list is noticeably evident."

"You must have heard wrong, Will. Why would Oliver Crawford go to such lengths? With his money, Crawford could see to it that his daughter's dowry alone would far outweigh any wealth these men might bring."

"Not wealth. A title. I have it straight from the man's man himself. According to him, Oliver Crawford is quite determined to claim a berth in the aristocracy. Unfortunately, His Majesty is unwilling to forget past offenses. Seventy-five years ago, Crawford's grandsire absconded with one of the royal mistresses. The story still tends to crop up from time to time. Ergo, Crawford's only hope for joining the ranks of the nobility is to form an alliance."

"For that, he will virtually *sell* his daughter?"

"Precisely. Though why the fact should surprise either one of us, I haven't a clue. Crawford has done far worse to obtain his means."

"She's his own blood."

"She is a woman. Chattel. Property."

Slater frowned, stroking his cheekbone with his index finger, tracing the silver scar that formed a nearly invisible crease against the bronzed hue of his skin. The scar incurred on that night so long ago when Jeanne had grappled to save herself.

The vow to avenge Jeanne's death still churned in him like a bitter brew. *He should have helped her. Damn, he should have helped her.* But the thought proved useless now, just as it had for so many years. Mayhap he would never be able to banish his feelings of remorse.

His hands tightened over the reins he held. Nevertheless, he could see to it that Crawford was exposed for the villain he was. To do that, he needed the only other surviving witness to the events that had taken place that night. Aloise.

But Aloise had been kept hidden away for so long he'd feared he would never find her. Thank heaven that the diligence of his own men—and the kind eyes of Fate—had seen fit to allow him to become privy to Crawford's plans.

"Rumor has it that Crawford won't part from his daughter without a hefty reward," Will added when the silence grew overly long. "He intends such a reward to be in the form of favors which will land him a title of his own."

The rage Slater had stoked for two decades rose within him. He kept remembering Jeanne's body, bloodied and broken at the bottom of the cliff. Little Aloise pale and hurt.

"Title be damned. I'll see Crawford in hell first." As far as he was concerned, Crawford had lived far too long without paying for his sins. Slater McKendrick—alias Matthew Elias Waterton—was the only man with the power to bring them to justice. He had worked long and hard for this moment. Soon after leaving England, he'd taken a position as a seaman, then fabricated his own death, sending the body of a fellow sailor who had died of smallpox home to Cornwall to be buried in the family plot. He'd known that Crawford would have spies to relay such news to him, thus leaving "Slater McKendrick" free to make his own way in the world, build a fortune, important contacts, and a career that would ultimately be used against his nemesis.

"What do you intend to do?"

"Clayton, Rudy, take the far side of the clearing and wait in the copse of trees beneath the church. Keep to the shadows; we can't chance having you seen. Crawford has guards about the area, I'm sure."

"Aye, aye, Cap'n."

"Marco, Louis, take the lower area near the rocks where the road leads to the shore. I want to know the minute the old man makes his appearance. He'll come by coach, so he should be easy to spot."

Marco glowered, adopting a savage frown. The Frenchman at his side poked him in the ribs with his crop to lighten the Spaniard's mood. "Come, *mon ami*. Why so sour? We are about to embark on an adventure."

An adventure, indeed, Slater concurred silently. One that could result in a public execution if Crawford determined the true identities of these men and the crimes they had been unjustly accused of committing.

"Hans is already at the point with a spyglass. He'll let us know when activity resumes on the ship. Watch for his signal. Louis and Rudy are sure that Aloise is the only female passenger. As soon as you see any sign of the girl, I want you to follow her. Her father will most likely take her to Briarwood, but don't let her out of your sight in any case."

The men saluted and settled into place, leaving only Slater and Will to their vigil.

Slater touched the locket suspended by a heavy gold chain around his neck. An intricate design had been applied to the casing: a cross, a dove, and a griffin. The tracings were engraved as deeply in his mind as they were in the smooth metal. Slater never removed the piece. Inside, the miniature portrait of Jeanne Alexander Crawford continued to spur him on. Jeanne's death would be avenged.

"What do you intend to do, Slater?"

"What else can I do? I have to find a way to get her away from her father. Take her."

Curry shook his head, his expression becoming more grave. "According to Crawford's manservant, Aloise is heavily guarded. You will need a battalion to abduct her."

"Does Crawford know we're here?"

"Doubtful. More than likely, the precautions are due to Aloise herself. She's developed a streak of independence while on the Continent. She's tried to escape her father's clutches several times, but to no avail. Some people believe she means to avoid Crawford's attempts to marry her off to a title." He tipped his head to one side. "And yet, she would have married you—a commoner—if all had gone as planned. How extraordinary that you would have been given such a marital opportunity."

"It was Jeanne who pressed for our betrothal, not Crawford. Jeanne and I met in Cornwall prior to the birth of her second child. In those long months, we became . . . friends."

He changed the subject when dangerous memories knocked at the door of his consciousness. "At that time, I doubt Crawford cared who married his daughter. He must have thought that he would eventually have a son to carry out his plans, so what did it matter what happened to a mere girl?" Slater's mouth settled into a harsh line. "When I proved to be an inconvenient witness to Jeanne's death, quickly Crawford had to repair the untidy loose ends my presence caused. He branded me a murderer and annulled the agreement. From what I've heard he burned the contracts. Months later, he must have breathed a sigh of relief, thinking that I'd died."

"And yet, you live, *mon ami,*" Curry said with a grin. "He will learn to regret having tangled with you, I am quite sure."

Slater glared at the ship in the harbor, a searing

hatred settling in his gut. He'd lived with that hatred for so long it had become a part of him. A black, gnawing hole. "Damn Crawford to the ravages of perdition," he rasped. "He killed Jeanne as surely as if he'd knifed her himself. He murdered two men whose only crime was to witness her death. Then he proceeded to terrorize a host of women in pursuit of an heir. For that, he will pay dearly." The promise emerged in a low fervent tone, thereby conveying more power than if it had been shouted.

"What about the girl?"

"What of her?"

"I sense a buried thread of enmity on your part."

Slater's jaw clenched. He knew he shouldn't feel this way toward Jeanne's daughter, but deep inside his soul he resented her for continuing the lie, for never bothering to explain what really happened that night. She should have gone to the authorities. She should have found someone who would have listened to her tale.

"She's a sort of pawn in this affair, don't you think?"

"She could have told the truth."

"The girl was only five when her mother died."

Slater speared his friend with a steely gaze. "But she is an adult now. An adult who has chosen to cling to a lie and protect her father in the process."

Will grew quiet as he studied the ship in the distance. "Have you seen her since that night?"

"No."

"You never bothered to discover what she looked like after she'd grown?"

"Nay, Will," he responded impatiently. "I was a wanted man. I had other important things to consider —such as staying alive and keeping my identity hidden."

"Hmm."

"What is that supposed to mean?"

"Nothing, nothing." In the darkness, Will's sudden smile was difficult to conceal.

Slater found it irritating that Curry had found some amusement at his expense. "Perhaps you'd be kind enough to reveal what facet of my situation has you so amused."

"From all reports of those who have seen the girl, she is said to be quite pretty."

"A fact which means nothing to me."

"She may remember you."

"I find that very doubtful. My only contact with her were her weekly visits to the cottage. She spent most of her time thumbing through my father's books while Jeanne and I talked."

"In that case, you may be forced to win her trust. Seduce her tender feelings, as it were."

"Damned if I will."

"I assure you, you can be quite charming when you put your mind to it."

"Frankly, I'd rather throw a bag over her head and be done with it."

The noise of an approaching horseman alerted them. Both men had drawn their swords and pistols when Hans skidded to a halt a few yards away.

"Slater, there's trouble on the ship. It appears someone has jumped overboard. A woman." He laughed in evident triumph. "Since Aloise Crawford is the only female we've spotted, it must be your beloved bride."

"I'll be damned." Slater whipped the hood of his cape over his face to shield it from the betraying light of the moon. "The girl is about to deliver herself right into our hands."

"There's more. Her precipitous escape alerted Crawford's guards. As you suspected, three men were waiting at the point. We managed to take out two of them, but the third rode hell-bent for town—presumably to alert Crawford himself."

"Bloody hell!"

When Slater would have urged his mount into action, Curry caught the bridle. "What do you intend to do?"

"Find her."

"Then what?"

"See that justice is finally served." Pulling the reins from Curry's grip, he nudged the beast with his heels. "Capture the girl!" he shouted. "Then bring her to me!"

Dear God in heaven, she was going to drown.

Aloise fought to hold her breath as the sea swallowed her whole and dragged her down, down, ever down. Hampered by the fullness of her skirts and the bundle she refused to release, she wondered if she would be imprisoned forever in the bottomless blue.

Since dying would completely unsettle her plans, she began to fight in earnest. After much kicking and struggling, she freed herself of one heavy petticoat and the loss helped to reverse the direction of her dive. In seconds, she broke the surface of the waves.

Her head tipped to gulp huge drafts of briny air into her lungs. The rush of oxygen filled her body, easing the pounding of her head.

"There she is! Get her!"

Spinning in the water, Aloise managed to look up in time to see the entire crew of *The Sea Sprite* crowded around the railing. Spurred into action, she struck out toward shore. She knew most of the sailors had a distinct aversion to water—if the stench of their bodies was any indication—but it would only be a matter of time until one of them grew brave enough to follow her.

The pack she carried hindered her progress, so she rolled to her back and kicked while she clumsily fought to loosen her gown at the waist. Stuffing the bundle firmly into the folds of her skirts, she twined the laces around the knotted cloth and fastened her bodice again. With both hands free, she began to move toward shore with greater speed.

She could hear Mr. Humphreys's voice echoing through the night. "Stop her! She's getting away!"

Something popped behind her. A splash resulted at her right shoulder. Another pop. Another splash. A stinging sensation tore through her upper arm and her pace faltered when she realized they were shooting at her. At *her!*

"Damn it, man!" She heard Mr. Humphreys shout. "That's Crawford's daughter, not an escaped galley slave! What a fool thing to do! Lower the skiff. We'll go after her that way."

Aloise wasted no time to see if Mr. Humphreys' orders had been obeyed. Even if the sailors hadn't managed to stop her, the pistol fire would have alerted people on shore—and she had no doubts her father was staying somewhere nearby to ensure she did what she was told. Mr. Humphreys had said her father intended to oversee all of the arrangements himself.

Moonlight bathed the area, illuminating several avenues of escape. Using the spire of a distant church steeple as her guide, she swam toward land. The tide was working to her advantage, pushing her closer. The breakers crashed over her head, their rhythm coming more quickly, more forcefully. Rolling in the surf, she tumbled end over end and came to a skidding stop facedown upon the beach. Having put more than a hundred yards between her and the ship, she could only pray the night kept her hidden from her pursuers.

Her fingertips curled into the wet sand as the retreating ebb tried to tug her along. Coughing and gasping for air, she blinked against the sting of the seawater. Her limbs trembled in exhaustion, demanding a few minutes of rest, but Aloise knew her flight had only begun. She couldn't afford to hesitate. It would take the sailors at least a quarter hour to determine that she'd jammed the rigging to all but one of the skiffs. She needed that time to get away.

Preparing to rise, she braced herself against the ground, but it was not the grainy texture of sand that she encountered. Ignoring the runnels of water still streaming down her face, she saw that she had touched a boot. A man's boot.

No. No! Her eyes squeezed shut in denial. *Please,* she prayed, *don't let it be my father. Please.*

Slowly, ever so slowly, she followed the gleam of black leather as it stretched over firm calves and strong knees. In seconds, she knew it wasn't Oliver Crawford who watched her, but a stranger who had been attracted by the commotion on the ship.

Drat it all! How could her plans have gone so miserably awry? She'd meant to make a quick, quiet getaway, and instead had managed to rouse the entire ship and probably most of the seaside community of Tippington.

Making a small sound of distress, she gazed up at the man who'd caught her inauspicious arrival to England. An errant wind tugged at the bottom of the all-encompassing cape he wore. The hem flapped in the breeze, allowing her toying glimpses of the masculine form hidden underneath. Woolen breeches molded a set of muscular thighs and narrow hips. A white shirt billowed from his waist and had been left unfastened nearly to his navel, exposing a broad chest covered in black, black hair. In the center of his sternum, moonlight glinted against a round medallion adorned by an intricate gold and silver crucifix.

Her eyes skipped from the medallion to the church on the hill and she nearly wilted in relief. A friar. The furor of her escape had disturbed the holy man and drawn him from his sanctuary.

"Forgive me, Father, for stumbling into your good graces."

Aloise could have sworn she heard a faint guffaw, but when she peered into the shadows, she saw no one there. The beach was empty of anyone save the priest. And yet . . .

A niggling fear began to tickle the hairs at the back of her neck. They weren't alone. She couldn't see anyone else, but she was quite sure that someone was there.

Sitting back on her heels, she fixed her eyes on the man who loomed above her. "Father?"

The stranger didn't speak. Indeed, he stared at her with an intensity that was unsettling—as if he disbelieved what he saw.

She managed little more than a cursory inspection of a bearded jaw, and dark hair. Then he drew the cloth more firmly about his head. For long moments there were no sounds save the slither of waves against the shore and the distant din of Mr. Humphreys and the sailors. The water lapped at her shoes, but Aloise found she couldn't stand.

"Father?"

Her question was barely audible this time. She swiped at the chestnut-colored strands that had come loose from her braid and straggled over her cheeks, but the action caused him to glance farther down. The fichu that had been tucked into the daring neckline of her gown had been lost somewhere in the surf. Without the modest scarf, her breasts pushed against the tight column of her stays, the pale mounds gleaming in the platinum sheen of the moon.

"Father, please, can you help me?" When he didn't respond, Aloise wondered if she'd offended him by using an improper address.

For one flashing instant, the man's expression became strangely haunted. Tormented. Then, he jarred loose from whatever spell had been cast over him, and crouched down to her level.

An odd tingling began at the tips of Aloise's toes as the distance between them disappeared. The cloth of his breeches strained over the flesh of his thighs, pulling tautly enough for her to determine that it was lean muscle that pushed against the close weave. She caught a faint wisp of a scent that could only be described as masculine. Soap and leather and musk.

Aloise tried to retreat, but quick as a trap, he clasped her wrist.

"God has provided for your safety, my child. There's no need to fear."

There was—she knew there was. The priest might speak of God and salvation, but his voice eased out of the night like liquid velvet, rumbling low in his chest then emerging to stroke her senses. Far from soothing her, it caused a rash of chills to pebble her skin. The sensation of being spied upon intensified manyfold.

"I must go." When she twisted her arm in an attempt to free it, he held her fast.

"No." It was an implacable command.

"You're hurting me!"

"I apologize most sincerely."

He didn't sound sincere; and he didn't let her go. He pulled her closer. So close, she could feel the heat of his body mingling with the icy damp of her soaked clothes.

Aloise managed to struggle to her feet, but he followed just as quickly.

"Come with me, mistress. You're cold and damp and in need of a fire."

The gleam of a jeweled signet ring flashed, causing a renewed skitter of unease to wriggle up her spine at the apparent sign of worldly ornamentation. A blunt, faintly calloused finger hooked under her chin and lifted her face to the moonlight. He peered at her intently as if to memorize each facet of her appearance. A brief spark appeared in his gaze, burning her.

"Jeanne . . ."

Aloise couldn't be sure what he'd said. The word had been a bare puff of sound, but she had thought he'd called her by her mother's name.

"No," she whispered, her head shaking in disbelief.

It couldn't be. She'd been mistaken. The word she'd heard was the result of her pulse galloping in her ears.

Planting her palm on his chest, she tried to push free, but the impact of solid flesh and bone caused her efforts to falter. Inexplicably, a voice deep in her head argued that she did not want to retreat; she wanted to step closer. She felt so tired, so cold, so hungry, she wished she could lean into his strength.

Aloise thrust such a thought away as quickly as it had come, horrified by her inappropriate reaction. The hooded stranger must have sensed her chaotic emotions because his mouth tilted in an ironic smile. One that would have caused her to stumble had he not held her so firmly. There was something infinitely wicked about that grin. Something carnal. This was no priest, of that she was suddenly quite sure.

"I've come to help you."

The phrase fairly stroked her senses and the experience frightened her. "N-no. Please don't."

"Don't what?" He moved inexorably nearer. So near that his thighs pressed against the folds of her skirt. She could feel each corded muscle, the solid shape of his hips, the hilt of a sword digging into her side.

"Let me go. Please, let me go." She'd meant the words to emerge as a demand. They seeped from her throat in a wispy plea. Aloise despised herself for such a display of weakness.

As she grew skittish, trying to dislodge his hold, the bearded stranger cupped her cheek in his palm. "Shh. There's no need to fear me." He bent, his words brushing across her cheek like a butterfly's caress. "I promised her I would claim you."

His statement confused Aloise, terrified her. "No!" Choking back a cry of distress and confusion, she jerked free.

It was then the stranger noted the bulge of her belongings beneath the waist of her gown. A strange pallor flooded his cheeks and he grew still, silent. Although he didn't move, his manner overpowered her, causing her to become rooted to the packed sand. The waves tickled the hems of her skirts, bidding her to flee. But she couldn't.

The man prowled forward, his jaw growing rock-hard beneath the fullness of his beard. For some reason, Aloise divined that he was angry. Very, very angry. If she were to retreat, she would place herself in certain peril.

"Isn't it a little late in the evening to be swimming in your . . . condition, mistress?"

3

ALOISE TOUCHED THE BUNDLE HIDDEN BENEATH HER gown. He thought she was pregnant. *Pregnant.* And even that information had not dampened the determination in his eyes. However, she didn't intend to deny such a condition. It might prove to be a limited source of protection.

From far away, she could hear Mr. Humphreys and the sailors arguing and grappling with the skiffs, but since the tone of their voices had not changed, she prayed that they couldn't distinctly see her. She had to get away before they could untangle the rigging and row ashore.

But the stranger noted each movement she made with a blazing thoroughness. It would do no good to try and run; she knew he would follow.

Think, Aloise, think, she told herself sternly. Now was not the time to forget the methods she had learned over the years to escape her numerous guards. Blackmail, bribery, and seduction. A woman's three most powerful tools. One of them was enough to unarm a man. But which? As she reevaluated her captor, she realized her alternatives were few.

Seduction?

Staring at him, she castigated herself for even considering such an idea. But a faraway splash warned her that the sailors had managed to lower one of the skiffs to the water. Seduction was her only viable method to take him unaware. She would be subtle; she would be charming. She would be swift.

Clinging to her own weak spurt of courage, she tipped her face more directly to the moonlight and adopted a look of panic. "I was not swimming, sir . . . I f-fell overboard."

Unfortunately, the man did not appear in the least affected. In fact, he watched her quite suspiciously.

"You can't imagine how terrified I was." She touched her breast. "My heart is fairly pounding through my ribs. Feel how it throbs?" She took his wrist and pressed his hand to the bared flesh above the neckline of her gown. To her own surprise, the touch of his calloused skin caused a slight charge. Her pulse leapt, providing proof of her claim.

Her palm slid up his arm, and cupped his shoulder, then went behind his neck, pulling him down toward her. Closer, closer. As he bent, she felt a brief stab of disappointment that this man could be so easily wooed, so easily fooled. "Oh, Father, I was so afraid!"

His lips touched her own and the brief caress startled her to the very core. Rather than feeling her control over him strengthen, a frisson of excitement scattered like grapeshot through her body. A tiny voice in her head urged her to retreat, but she lingered, absorbing the taste of him, the quick rush of desire. Dear heaven, it felt so good to be kissed this way! As if he felt at least a spark of meaning to their embrace.

No!

Before the stranger had time to entrench her further in his spell—or worse yet, absorb the fact that the bulge of her middle was far too pliant to be a child—she lifted her knee, ramming it into the man's groin.

His breath escaped in an *oof!* of surprise and he doubled over, but to Aloise's infinite dismay, her aim was not entirely true. She'd managed to force her release, but she hadn't felled him completely.

Frantic now, she began to run. But she'd taken little more than a half-dozen paces when the stranger's arm snapped around her shoulders.

"Let me go, you warthog!" Aloise planted her heels in the sand and fought with all her might. By all that was holy, she was not about to gain her first taste of freedom, only to be surrendered to Mr. Humphreys. With all the commotion that was made on the ship, this man would have to be dense not to realize that the occupants of *The Sea Sprite* were determined to have her back. The stranger might even be tempted by the thought of a reward.

Desperate, Aloise bent her head, grasped the man's wrist and bit him.

"You little brat!" He whipped free, but when she would have dodged away, he yanked her back.

Aloise gasped, a fiery dart of pain shooting through her left shoulder. Seeing her reaction the man released her, lifting his palm to the vague light of the moon.

In an instant, Aloise knew what she would see. She told herself not to look. For some time now, she had ignored the heated moisture seeping through the fabric of her gown and the insistent ache. But in the sheen of moonlight, she saw it anyway. Gleaming. Thick.

Blood.

Her blood.

Damn, those sailors. They'd shot her. *Shot* her.

Her stomach roiled. Apparently disconcerted by her injury, the stranger let her go. Whirling, she gazed wildly about her, holding the wound to stem the flow of blood.

The beach seemed to lurch. Spin. "No, please, no." A buzzing began in her head. A fierce pain shot through her temples. She took a stumbling step, two, but four men loomed out of the darkness apparently willing to stop any sort of flight. All were dressed in black. All looked as fierce and unforgiving as a herd of brigands.

Aloise came to a weaving halt. Behind her, she could hear the rhythmic slap of oars and knew that Mr. Humphreys and the sailors had begun to row ashore. The bearded stranger looked at her much like a hunter regarded a cornered fox, pitying the animal, but willing it to surrender.

Panic-stricken, she searched for some sort of weapon, but there was nothing. A cold clamminess dotted her brow. Nausea blossomed in her gullet. Brackish memories burbled to the fore of her mind, indistinct yet insistent. A storm. Lightning. An overwhelming horror. The pain in her head intensified, becoming an ache, a pounding.

Uncurling her fingers, she chanced one peek, one glance.

Blood. She simply couldn't stand the sight of blood. As a child, she'd screamed each time she witnessed the crimson liquid. As an adult, such an occurrence invariably made her sick. Made her . . . faint.

"Oh." The single word slipped from her lips in a mere wisp of sound. The pain in her head became overpowering. Blackness gathered, her limbs trembled. Then the world was eclipsed by darkness and she wilted to the sand.

For a moment, the clearing throbbed in a stunned silence. Only Curry dared to nudge her wrist with the toe of his boot. When she did not react, he glanced up at Slater.

"I must say, Slater," he drawled. "You have an astonishing effect on women." He made a *tsk*ing sound. "She's been shot, poor mite—though I'd say it's little more than a flesh wound and hardly worth such a fuss."

"That 'poor mite,' as you call her, nearly emasculated me," he muttered, bending to rest his hands on his knees to relieve the ache in his groin. One which had not been entirely caused by Aloise's aim.

Curry chortled. "I know."

Sighing in impatience, Slater twisted to squint into the darkness. The men from *The Sea Sprite* were little more than a dozen yards from shore.

"Is the coach readied?"

"Louis has it waiting behind the church. But I think we would all be better off leaving her here for now. Those men will follow us if—"

The rattle of hooves and harnesses alerted them mere seconds before the distant shape of a coach appeared on the road from the village.

"Crawford has arrived!" Hans shouted, riding madly toward them. "We've got to leave. Now!"

Slater immediately snapped to attention, a rush of adrenaline surging through his body. "Rudy, take the young lady to the phaeton. Marco, join him inside the conveyance and *watch* her," he added forcefully. "I wouldn't trust her to refrain from biting your nose off if she rouses."

The huge Russian scooped Aloise from the ground, carrying her limp figure into the shadows. Aloise's head lolled over Rudy's beefy arm and her hair dripped to the sand, causing a curious sense of worry to settle into Slater's bones. He'd seen women faint in the past—usually through art more than through necessity. But never had he seen a woman grow so pale so quickly. At the sight of her own blood, she'd gone positively gray—perhaps due to her . . . family condition. For a moment she'd looked just as fragile as her mother on that fateful night she'd come to beg for his help.

He should have helped her. Sweet heaven, why hadn't he helped her?

Curry, who had been checking the pistols tucked into his belt, glanced up, then followed Slater's regard. "Quite a scrapper, isn't she?"

Slater didn't comment, resolutely shaking away the

eerie sensations of déjà vu. But then, the sight of this woman, this *pregnant,* unconscious woman left him stunned nevertheless.

Pregnant! Damn it all to bloody hell!

"She didn't appear to recognize you a'tall."

"Fifteen years have passed since the last time we saw each other. We have both changed dramatically I would venture to wager."

"Yet, she knew you once."

"As a child."

"A child to whom you were betrothed."

"It's dark, Curry. Perhaps she did not see me well enough to prick her guilt." Pushing away his own disquiet at the woman's reaction, Slater chanced one last glance at the men who'd tumbled from the skiff and now tugged it onto shore. A gleaming coach had come to a stop on the beach nearly fifty yards away. A swarm of seamen clambered to surround the conveyance as the door opened and Crawford stepped out, standing arrogantly on the water-packed sand.

Slater felt the years drop away. In an instant, he experienced the same burning anger, the same lust for revenge, the same horror that had filled his chest fifteen years ago. Staring at the man who had destroyed his life as well as Jeanne's, he committed to memory the changes that had occurred in his fleshy face. One day soon, that man would fall at Slater's feet and beg him for mercy.

Will tugged at his sleeve. "Damn it, Slater, this isn't the time to gawk. We've got to be leaving!"

Heeding his friend's warning, Slater turned and ran toward his mount.

"I still maintain it's a bad idea to take the girl this way."

"So you've said."

"Wait awhile—a day or two. At least until we've had a chance to see the extent of Crawford's power in the area."

"No. We take her now."

"They've probably seen us, you know," Curry added as they swung into their saddles.

"Not distinctly."

"No doubt they *will* follow us."

Plans began to sprout and Slater's lips twitched in the beginnings of a rare rakehell grin. "For a time. Only for a time, my friend." Uttering a bark of laughter, he urged his stallion into action. "Come along, Curry."

The two men galloped toward the carriage which had already turned onto the upper road. They were nearly a mile away from the church when Will asked, "May I inquire what nefarious plots you're hatching?"

Slater gazed ahead at the rocking phaeton. Inside was his onetime betrothed. Crawford's daughter.

His eyes crinkled slightly and a note of pleasure tickled his reply. "Why, Willie, whatever do you mean?"

"I've seen that predatory expression many times in the past. It never ceases to make me nervous."

"Then by all means trust your instincts, Curry. After all . . . the hunt has just begun."

"The hunt for what?"

Slater threw back his head and laughed, allowing the wind to tug at his hair and clear his brain. Urging his retinue into greater speed he shouted, "Us, my friend. Us!"

Crawford glared at the horsemen and the glittering phaeton rushing away from the beach. Damn, damn, *damn!* How, by all that was holy, had his daughter managed to thwart his will *this* time?

"Humphreys!"

The stooped-shouldered man snapped to attention. "Yes, sir."

"What did you tell her?"

"N-nothing, sir."

"You must have said something about our plans—where you would dock, the time I would arrive.

Otherwise, how could she have arranged such an escape?"

Mr. Humphreys clutched his hands together, cowering in that way Crawford had always despised.

"I don't know if she . . . planned this, sir."

A chill of warning crept into his bones, one which Crawford had learned in the past to trust. "What do you mean?" he drawled, his tone deliberate, silky. Dangerous.

"I . . . I mean that I thought I saw Aloise struggling. As if she did not want to go with those men."

Crawford's hands tightened around the head of his cane, his knuckles gleaming white in the darkness. The foreboding he felt intensified, growing so strong that he fought to breathe. In the past, he had fostered many important allies—allies closely connected to His Majesty himself. In doing so, he had also made many enemies. Enemies who would dearly love to see him publicly disgraced. How better than to take his daughter mere weeks before her own wedding, leaving him with a houseful of guests and a half-dozen prospective grooms waiting to bid for her dowry?

He whacked the cane against the coach wheel, causing his secretary to jump.

"Who else knew of our plans?" The query dripped with ice.

"N-no one, sir."

"Damnit, someone must have known! Otherwise why would they have taken her?"

Mr. Humphreys blanched. "Surely you don't think . . ."

Crawford scowled, lifting his walking stick and striking the tip against his secretary's chest. "You once told me you were a religious man." His eyes narrowed. "Pray, Mr. Humphreys," he whispered fiercely. "Pray that my daughter hasn't been taken for ransom. Or you, my friend, will pay dearly. Very dearly indeed."

* * *

Either Aloise Crawford hadn't remembered him, or she was the consummate actress.

Nearly an hour later, Slater crossed his heels and regarded the woman sprawled on the opposite seat of the coach. Try as he might, he couldn't escape the nagging reminder. This girl had been his betrothed, had visited his home at least a half-dozen times, witnessed his downfall. Despite all that, she refused to show any signs of knowing him.

Damn her. How could she have forgotten? He knew the years had changed him, made him harder, more bitter, but she must have some inkling of his identity. She couldn't have erased the night of her mother's death from her memory so completely.

He glared at Aloise, willing her to awaken. She'd roused from her stupor when he'd joined her in the coach and seen to her wound. Despite the light of the lanterns, she'd shrunk away from his touch, then caught a glimpse of her own blood and wilted in his arms. In time, she'd even drifted into sleep.

After their encounter on the beach, Slater wasn't positive that she *truly* slept. At any moment, he expected her to fly from her prone position, throw him into a stranglehold, and demand he let her loose. This woman had fire.

As well as damned sharp teeth.

She stirred, her brow knitting in pain, and Slater stoically resisted the impulse to draw her onto his lap and stroke her hair. Bloody hell, had he gone mad to think such a thing? This woman had betrayed him. She could have cleared Matthew Waterton years ago of all implications to Jeanne's murder, but she'd chosen to remain silent, thereby giving credence to her father's lies. She didn't deserve his pity, only his condemnation.

Straightening, Slater forced his mind to other more important matters—such as what he planned to do now. He had to keep her with him long enough to see if she'd truly forgotten him or merely played some perverse game. Either way, the situation was fraught with hidden dangers. Until he discovered the extent of her perfidy, Aloise must be kept away from her father. Yet, this was no docile lamb he could lead by the nose. He would be wise to remember that fact and plan accordingly. She would kick and scream unless he could find a means to keep her with him of her own free will.

Her own free will . . .

His eyes narrowed, falling on the bundle of belongings which had tumbled from beneath the waist of her gown. When he'd first set eyes on the swell of her stomach, he'd never dreamed that it held little more than a change of clothing. He'd thought that she must have married, or become some man's lover. It never entered his mind that such a shape was merely a clever ploy to unconsciously enlist people's more tender emotions. A ploy that had fooled even him.

Ignoring the memory of the tightly corseted torso and wispy underthings Slater had encountered when he had loosened her stays, he focused instead on the contents. Her cache of belongings was paltry to say the least. Not at all what he would have expected of Crawford's daughter. The clothing she'd brought with her was simple and unadorned. There were several books—a rather ribald novel and two travel journals—a satin bag filled with gold coins, and a locket.

He palmed the piece, opening the tiny hinges to reveal the painting inside. *Jeanne.* A knife seemed to turn in his chest. Jeanne had given both Slater and her daughter the miniature portraits the Christmas before she died.

Slater closed the piece with a determined snap. He'd suffered through too many emotional trials this evening. He didn't need to wallow in memories. His first glimpse of Jeanne's daughter had given him enough of a start, making him feel as if he'd come face-to-face with a ghost.

Thrusting the locket back into the bundle, he inadvertently bumped the haversack, causing something to spill free from the folds of her petticoat.

"Sweet heaven above," he whispered as he reached out to touch the elaborate necklace, fingered the stunning design of animals fashioned in gold and the glowing rubies studding the tiger's eyes, the peacock's tail, the ostrich's neck.

He glanced at Aloise, then back at the piece in his hand. Of course. Of course!

The coach drew to a halt, and shoving the rubies out of sight, Slater peered out of the window to see that they were at the crossroads. Curry urged his horse forward. "Which way?"

"Straight to my estates at Ashenleigh."

Curry regarded him in astonishment. "Ashenleigh? But that's only a few hours' journey from here. We've been able to avoid Crawford by taking the back roads. Surely you don't want to take a chance he might follow you!"

"Just get us there. As soon as possible. Meanwhile, have Clayton and Marco ride on to Crawford's estates at Briarwood and see if we can't develop a spy in his staff. I need to know when Crawford's bridal guests are scheduled to arrive and which roads they intend to take. Send Hans ahead to inform Miss Nibbs of our schedule. I want him to prepare fresh horses and choose a housemaid of the same size and coloring as Miss Crawford. See that she dresses in a similar style and that Louis and Rudy are ready to ride by first light."

"What exactly do you have in mind, Slater?"

"A bit of a jest," he stated after a slight pause, refusing to comment further, but he did not completely disguise his own pleasure.

"Crawford will find our trail eventually; we'd be better off changing course and heading safely out of the area."

"Ride to Ashenleigh."

"But—"

Slater waved away his friend's protests. "Aloise has lost a bit of blood. She needs a bed, a fire, and a good night's sleep."

Will stared at him in amazement. "She needs *what?*"

"You heard me." He knocked on the roof of the phaeton and it jerked into action.

Slater heard the scrabble of his friend's mount as he hurried to catch up. "Heard you, but didn't believe you."

"I am merely ensuring that she does not expire on us. She's no good to us dead."

Will snorted in disbelief.

"Ashenleigh, Will."

"Yes, sir!" Curry saluted nicely and shouted instructions to the driver, but as he allowed his horse to drop in line with the other men, Slater couldn't miss his parting shot. "Just see to it that you guard yourself well. She's got a wicked aim with that knee, she does. I'd be seeing to the family jewels."

The carriage rocked, rumbling into the rutted thoroughfare.

Family jewels. Curry's remark might have been uttered in fun, but it brought another facet of his objective firmly to mind. The Bengal Rubies. The collection that Crawford extended so tantalizingly to Aloise's prospective mates had belonged to Slater's father. They had been presented to him as a gift for translating an ancient Hebrew script that George III had obtained in his youth. The king had been so pleased to discover mention of his ancestors' role in the Crusades that he had ordered that the most well-known jewels in all England be reset and given to a humble schoolmaster in Cornwall. Rubies said to have been blessed by Richard the Lionhearted to reward those who were honest and true, and curse those who were impure. The gift had stunned all those the king had allowed to know of such *largesse* as well as Elias Waterton.

Slater fought back a sigh of regret. His father had been so proud of that honor, so humbled. From the moment he'd been given the pieces, he'd declared that they would never leave his family's possession. They would never be bartered, sold, or traded—no matter how dire the family's finances. They would be protected with all the loyalty and honor the Waterton clan possessed.

Elias would have been devastated had he known the way Crawford had discovered the existence of the Bengal Rubies and claimed them as forfeit for his son's supposed disgrace.

Slater's fingers tightened over the necklace. Once he'd finished exacting retributions for past wrongs, Oliver Crawford would rue the day he decided to arrange the death of an innocent woman and destroy the Waterton name. Crawford would be exposed for the devil he was. To see such an objective fulfilled, Slater would steal the two things Crawford valued most.

The daughter he planned to use to obtain a title and an heir.

And the infamous Bengal Rubies.

4

THE ROCKING OF THE SHIP HAD DEVELOPED AN ODD sort of intensity. No longer a gentle swaying, there was a distinct bounce, a jostle, a . . .

"I thought you'd never regain your wits, mistress."

The deep, murmured remark melted from the stillness, stroking Aloise's frayed nerves and urging her to awaken. She yawned and blinked, but rather than focusing on the rough linen sheets of her bunk, she encountered tufted velvet squabs.

"I don't believe I've seen another woman faint with precisely the same talent you've displayed. Your fall proved to be quite graceful and so perfectly timed."

A choked sound lodged in Aloise's throat as the memory of her encounter on the beach rushed over her with the strength of the tide. "No!" Jerking into a sitting position, she flattened herself against the corner, sure her father waited nearby, his cane raised, his eyes malevolent.

The shadows revealed no such horrors. A single man sat opposite. The bearded stranger. Obscured by the ebony secrets of the night, his form could not be clearly discerned, but Aloise felt his presence as surely as the pulse that knocked at her ribs.

"It took you so long to awaken, I'd begun to fear

you'd developed a brain fever of some sort . . . or cracked your head on a rock."

Aloise's breath came in sharp pants as he reached out, thinking he meant to strike her for some act of disobedience. He merely clasped her chin, forcing her to look at him, really look at him.

She didn't flinch, didn't falter. His eyes gleamed for a moment, willing a reaction she didn't understand, then his expression became enigmatic and he shifted his hold. Aloise was stunned into inactivity when the blunt-tipped fingers skimmed her temples, her cheek. The caress was unexpected and startlingly gentle.

"Don't."

The word burst from her lips, but he ignored it. After several long moments, he returned to his seat. "Never fear, maiden. I mean you no harm."

Aloise regarded him in patent disbelief. He was a man. As far as she was concerned, the gender had a talent for inflicting the most subtle kind of emotional and physical pain.

"I only wished to ascertain the extent of the damage," he continued.

"I don't want you to touch me. I don't like to be touched."

He watched her with black, black eyes. A distinct gleam of satisfaction entered their depths. "Then obviously, you've not been properly touched. Not yet, anyway."

Aloise gasped. The words hung in the air, full of an unspoken meaning and a delicious forbidden expectancy. "A gentleman would never say such a thing to a lady."

"Ahh, but I never claimed to be a gentleman. In fact, I have been known to take great delight in performing numerous deeds of wickedness."

The hair prickled at the back of her neck.

"Who are you?"

Once again, he watched her intently. Like a spider watched a fly embroil itself in the stickiness of a web.

"That depends on who you ask. Some claim I'm the devil himself."

In that second Aloise became aware of the woolen cloak draped about her lap and the curious flatness of her stomach. She felt the spot even as her gaze leapt to the bundle lying next to the man's thigh. The shawl she'd used as an outer covering for her belongings had been opened. The contents lay neatly within the center as if this man had done little more than untie the knot. However, Aloise knew he had searched each item quite thoroughly. She had no doubts he'd found her only extra chemise, the stockings, garters, and petticoats, the collapsible panniers, the gown, the books, the bag of gold, and the locket.

As if sensing her thoughts, he picked up the fragile necklace and opened the catch, revealing the painting inside. One brow lifted in silent query.

"My mother," she supplied somewhat reluctantly.

"You look a great deal like her."

She shrugged, refusing to let him see that such a remark secretly pleased her.

"You are journeying to see her? Was that why you were aboard the clipper I saw?"

Aloise could have lied, but something about the fierceness of his gaze forced her to speak the truth. "My mother died years ago."

"How?"

The word came to her from a long distance, demanding a response. A dull ache settled deep in her brain.

"Some sort of accident."

An odd breathless tension gathered in the limited space.

"Or so I've been told." The words slipped unbidden from her tongue and could not be withdrawn.

"You don't know?"

The query, said with just a touch of sardonic humor caused her to stammer, "I, well, yes. Of course. But she died when I was small."

"I see," he drawled.

Aloise clasped her arms and rubbed at the gooseflesh that pebbled her skin. As always, thoughts of her mother brought a brackishness to her tongue. An overwhelming sensation of panic. And the pain. The dull throbbing pain embedded in her temples.

"I have no memories of her at all."

The man was silent for some time, then offered. "You must have been very young."

She didn't answer. How could she? How could she explain to this man, this stranger, that she had lost a whole portion of her childhood in a void of forgetfulness that refused to budge. Then again, why would she *want* to explain such a thing to him?

The man grew thoughtful, quiet. After some time, he dropped the locket and retrieved one of the bound travelogues, glancing at the title printed on the water-stained spine.

"Africa," he said slowly. "An interesting choice of reading for one so young. One so beautiful."

Aloise tipped her chin a little higher, refusing to allow him the satisfaction of seeing how he'd completely unsettled her. To find a woman prostrate at one's feet demanded action—even in this day and age of letting people fend for themselves. Upon discovering she was not pregnant, but hiding a bundle beneath her gown, simple curiosity would demand an investigation. She was not surprised that such events had occurred, but she was disturbed. Disturbed by the way this man had obviously interpreted so much from her meager booty. That he had taken a peek at her belongings and had somehow been able to recognize parts of her soul she'd thought well hidden.

"Tell me . . . why the avid interest in such a savage land?"

"I thought I might go there someday."

"What do you expect to find? Adventure? Wild beasts?"

"Peace."

"You don't seem the peaceful sort to me. I would peg you as a woman in search of—"

"Solitude."

"—passion."

"Hardly."

"So young and yet so cynical."

"I prefer to think of myself as world-wise."

"Perhaps. But I would wager that you have much to learn." He set the travel account back in its place, glanced briefly at the other reading materials and added, "Things that cannot be found in books. Things that can only be taught by experience, as well as by the . . . experienced."

"Meaning you?" The words blurted free.

"I would never be so bold as to suggest such a thing to a woman whom I've only just met."

A strange swirl of exhilaration and wariness settled inside her. Obviously, this man had no manners. His comments were shocking in their familiarity, completely and utterly improper. Yet, Aloise couldn't find the words to discourage him. He twisted everything she said into some audacious double entendre.

Indeed, the entire situation was extraordinary. This man had whisked her away from her pursuers. He had ensconced her in his coach and removed her bundle from its intimate hiding place, touching her in places no man had dared. Far from apologizing for such liberties, he seemed pleased by the outcome.

A burst of reaction skittered through her at the very thought. In the faint gleam of moonshine that spilled over the window frame, she could see one of those hands resting against the aperture. The fingers were slender and well formed, blunt, and dusted ever so slightly with dark hair. Had they brushed against the linen of her underthings? Had they explored the line of her stays?

Lifting her gaze, she discovered that he still watched her.

"How long have we been traveling? An hour? Two?"

Her heart beat in her throat as she waited for his answer, knowing that the passage of time would give her the clue she needed as to the distance they'd traveled.

"Two hours have passed—"

She issued a silent sigh of relief.

"—since our encounter on the beach."

Her cheeks flamed at the memory. The kiss. How she'd responded. "Who are you?" she demanded slowly. "What have you done with me?"

Once again, his lips tipped in the slightest of smiles. She could barely see the movement, but she felt the effects to her very toes.

"Never fear, milady. Since your lapse into unconsciousness, I did naught but bind your wound, loosen your laces, and lighten your burden."

Her chin tilted rebelliously. "I am expected to thank you, I suppose."

"That is entirely your choice."

"Then you will forgive me if I do not."

He shrugged, not in the least bit discouraged. Instead, he turned his attention to the belongings beside him. The frayed pink silk riband from her chemise caught his gaze and he fingered it with the inestimable appreciation of a connoisseur.

Aloise's eyes widened at the sensual way he rubbed the delicate band, back and forth, back and forth, watching her to see her reaction. She knew she should say something to stop him—he was examining her *under*things, her forbiddens—but she refused to give him the satisfaction. She might have lost a wee bit of control by fainting at the sight of blood, but she was no shrinking violet. No indeed.

"You had a bit of a gash on your arm where the ball grazed you, but it did not prove necessary to stitch. It's quite safe to look."

She hesitated, not sure she should do such a foolish thing, but his statement had emerged much like a challenge. Chancing a single glance, she saw that the sleeve of her gown had been cut away and a stark white bandage had been neatly wrapped around the exposed circumference.

"I've been told I'm quite handy at doctoring such wounds. There shouldn't be much of a scar."

The thought that he'd worked on her open flesh caused her stomach to roll, but she fought back the sensation.

"I do believe you owe me an explanation in return for my ministrations."

"What would you possibly need to know?"

"Did I hear you correctly when you claimed to have *fallen* overboard?"

Her head jerked and all gruesome thoughts of her injury scattered to the wind. On the surface, the stranger's query appeared quite natural, but Aloise sensed a wealth of depth beneath the simple question, as if he knew more about her situation than he was prepared to reveal.

She eyed the careful arrangement of her belongings at his side, but there was nothing there that could have given her away. Nothing at all.

"I believe that's what I said," she carefully stated.

"Hmm. How convenient to have done so at a time when your things were already hidden on your person."

"Yes. Yes, it was."

"So why not wait for the sailors to retrieve you and continue on with your journey to . . ."

"London. I am on my way to London."

A long silence followed her answer, one punctuated by the rasp of the wheels over gravel and the squeak of the harnesses. The stranger continued his scrutiny, intently, thoughtfully, though she could see little more than a sliver of his profile.

"Tell me, mistress, from whom were you trying to escape?"

"Escape? As I told you; I fell."

"Your fall was most fortuitous considering the number of people who were intent upon retrieving you."

"Perhaps."

"They appeared quite worried."

"Did they?"

"In my estimation. In fact, I have been thinking that I should instruct my driver to return you to Tippington and your retinue."

When he would have tapped on the ceiling of the coach, she hurriedly snared his arm. "No!"

"No?"

His wrist was strong, finely boned.

"I . . . do not wish to return."

"May I ask why?"

Dodging his question, she released him and drew deeper into the shadows, hoping that they would conceal her own expression as well as they did his, but the angle of the moonlight seemed determined to thwart her efforts. "Have we left Tippington far behind?"

He nodded, but did not speak.

"I see." The rush of shapes speeding past her window was entirely unfamiliar to her—but then, she had not been to England for years.

"Where are we?"

"Many miles north."

There was a definite haste to their travel. A reckless abandon. "We seem to be moving at a great clip."

"I thought it best."

Aloise didn't even try to decipher that remark. Therein lay great danger.

"If you could stop the coach, I won't trouble you any further. I realize I must have interrupted your own schedule."

He didn't move.

Growing desperate and just a little frightened, she insisted, "You must let me go."

"Must I?"

"Yes."

"I'm afraid I can't do that."

"Why ever not?"

"If indeed you fell overboard, it would be very remiss of me to leave you unprotected in the wilds of Cornwall. You'll need a change of clothes, a warm fire, and a soft bed. Then I shall have to notify whatever family you have in the area. No doubt, they would have made arrangements to fetch you from the ship. I'm sure they're quite worried."

Aloise experienced a pang of foreboding. She did not relish having the man discover that she had no real home to speak of and her only family was the father who had tried over and over again to force her to his will.

"Don't you think that would be a wise thing to do?"

"I suppose it would be . . . if I had family."

"Everyone has family of one sort or another. If you once had a mother, you must surely have a father. I do not believe that one so vibrant and lovely as you was hatched from an egg." He continued to toy with the riband, brushing it between his finger and thumb with a sensual thoroughness. "On the other hand, if you are not who you claim to be . . ."

The phrase held a distinct word of warning, as if he wished her to confess that her predicament was not as innocent as she would like it to appear. He abandoned the chemise and pierced her with a gaze that drilled into her very core.

He knew something, of that she was sure. But what. *What?*

Some time passed before she dared to inquire, "What do you intend to do with me?"

He shifted slightly in his seat, his long legs spilling into the narrow aisle and crowding her unbearably. He radiated a heat she couldn't ignore. He was so *big,* so uncomfortably, unconditionally male.

"That depends entirely on who you are . . . and why pistol fire followed your rather inauspicious midnight swim."

No wonder he didn't believe her tale. If she'd fallen overboard as she'd claimed, the sailors would have no reason to shoot at her. She couldn't rely on her explanations of the stupidity of the crew. Not without explaining her entire situation.

"You heard the shots?"

"I did. As well as the commotion being made by your companions once they reached shore. They followed us for a time, you know. But through some careful maneuvering my coachman was able to lose them."

Staring at him consideringly, she wondered how best to proceed. She could tell him the truth—that she meant to escape her father and flee to London and a new life—but the explanation was weak to her own ears and would only result in her sounding like a petulant child. This man might side with her father and haul her back to Briarwood like a runaway filly.

But what were her alternatives? What could she possibly say to allay his suspicions? "My traveling acquaintances did not want me to leave," she finally stated, hoping the vague answer would satisfy him.

Her hopes were in vain.

"Why?"

"I . . ." She could not think so quickly. He leaned forward, bracing his elbows on his knees and coming into such close contact with Aloise that she felt sure he filled the whole coach with his presence.

When she did not answer, he provided his own explanation. "Mayhap they did not want you to go because you had taken something that did not belong to you."

She stared at him blankly. "I don't know what you mean."

"Don't you?"

He returned to his former position, providing her with much needed breathing space, but the sensation of relief lasted only a moment. Then he reached into her bundle and held up the shimmering ruby necklace she'd hidden there.

"Am I supposed to believe this is yours?"

5

HE THOUGHT HER A THIEF.

A *thief!*

Aloise blanched. No wonder he'd gone to such lengths to abduct her. He thought she'd stolen that necklace and by keeping her until the owner was found, he could claim a handsome reward.

True, she *had* taken the jewelry, but from her father. As far as Aloise was concerned, having the piece didn't constitute stealing, per se. It *did* belong to her. It was part of *her* dowry.

She realized she still had to convince this man of her ownership. Blast it all, dressed as she was in a simple gown and a distinct absence of ornamentation, she must look like a peasant who would have no access to pretty baubles.

Summoning her haughtiest attitude, she peered down her nose at him. "You are quite mistaken. Those *are* mine, I assure you."

"Really." The drawl of that single word was her judge and jury, proclaiming her guilty as tried. "Have you some proof of your claims?"

The wind of superiority puffed from her sails as quickly as it had come. Desperately, she fought to think of something she could say to allay his suspicions. "O-one of the stones on the catch is missing."

"A detail which could have been determined upon a brief investigation."

"If it's a reward you seek—"

"The only reward I require is to ensure that justice is served."

His words rang with such a strength of conviction, Aloise was stymied. What was she going to do? She could try darting from the coach, but she needed the necklace and the coins to start a new life.

"That sack and all its belongings are *mine.*" She lunged toward him, hoping to snatch the piece away, but his free arm snapped around her waist, trapping her against his chest. She became overtly conscious of the steely strength of his form, rigid muscles scattered with hair, strong arms, a corrugated stomach. Her senses were inundated with his scent as his embrace tightened, pulling her even more snugly to his body. One of his hands strayed to her thigh, tarried there, then climbed upward, ever upward to the swell of her hips.

She forgot to struggle. She forgot her intent. Her heart thudded so strongly in her chest, she was sure that he could feel it. His fingers spread wide, clasping her skirts, rubbing them against her legs in a tantalizing fashion. Just when she believed she would be able to bear no more, he released her. Aloise immediately scrambled back into her seat, but her pulse continued to pound in a most alarming way.

"Don't." It was the only word she could manage to force free.

She waited for some scathing remark from the man, some colorful turn of phrase, but to her astonishment, he did not speak. In fact, she had the strangest sensation that she was not the only one who had been affected by that chance encounter.

"I frighten you, don't I?"

She swallowed, not certain how she should respond.

He leaned forward, snaring her chin and forcing her to meet his gaze. A fiery brilliance lingered there, burning her with its strength. "You should be frightened, little one. It is a very healthy emotion considering your dilemma."

Aloise was not sure if he referred to the threat of thievery or her being alone and unarmed.

"Stop this coach!"

Unfortunately, her command had little visible effect, and in fact, only amused him further. Releasing his hold, he leaned back against the squabs.

"Once you've proven your ownership, I'll let you go. In fact, I'll gladly take you to your destination"—he shrugged—"save it be Africa. I don't relish such a long sea voyage as of yet." Lifting the necklace to the light spilling in from the coach lanterns, he challenged, "Come, maiden, prove what you will."

The words reverberated between them, and they both knew that Aloise had no way of doing such a thing. How could she convince him that the necklace was hers when she had nothing midst her belongings to substantiate such a claim?

He waited patiently for her reply and she resisted the urge to kick him in frustration. Instead, she returned his verbal volley with, "Can *you,* sir, prove that it isn't mine?"

Though he didn't immediately speak, she sensed an unexpected approval on his part, as if he were pleased with her show of defiance.

"Mayhap I will." He rapped on the roof of the coach. "Rudy, bypass the authorities for this evening. Continue to my estates."

A long pause followed then the driver answered somewhat uncertainly, "Yes, Cap'n."

The coach rocked and swayed and the tempo of the hooves' clatter increased. Aloise glanced outside but the dark obscurity of the countryside offered her no clues as to their direction.

The bearded stranger was the first to speak. "Since

you are unwilling to make any claim toward a home here on England's shores, I shall take you to mine."

"Then what?"

"Then we'll wait. Once we've arrived, I'll send a messenger back to Tippington. If, in fact, you have stolen these jewels, such news will be easily obtained and I'll return you to the authorities posthaste."

She had no fear of being apprehended by the law. Even if her father discovered she'd taken the rubies, he would not announce such a thing due to the ensuing scandal. But, if in the process of his investigation this man alerted her father to her whereabouts . . .

Blast and bother. It would only take a whiff of rumor for Oliver Crawford to pursue her like the hounds of hell.

"How long do you intend to wait for your news?"

"A week should suffice."

"If there are no reports of stolen jewels?"

"You and your bundle may continue on your way. In fact, I shall put my coach and driver at your disposal. In the meantime, you shall be my . . . guest. You may do what you will to convince me of the veracity of your claims. If indeed, you are the owner of these pretties, then a week in your presence should allow me a glimpse of the education of a lady. After all, breeding will out."

Aloise struggled to keep from frowning in annoyance. Drat it all. She should have paid more attention at Sacre Coeur. She'd spent so much time away from class the last few years she was at the school that her skills at needlework, card playing, and gossip had been sorely neglected. Instead, she'd spent her mornings in the library, filling her brain with such "useless" information as travel, philosophy, science, and mathematics.

Still, she felt sure she could play the simp well enough to dampen his suspicions for a day or two. It shouldn't take much longer than that to escape. She must have grown quite good at such endeavors if her father had been forced to hire so many bodyguards to keep her in tow.

"Have we a deal?"

"What alternate choices are you willing to give me?"

"I could take you immediately to the authorities."

"That would never do."

"I thought not."

"Then I suppose I shall have to accede to your wishes."

"So it would seem."

"What guarantees do I have that you are not the worse evil? For all I know, you could be intent on ravishment."

He chuckled. "You have my promise as a gentleman."

"You've already told me you claim no such affiliation."

"True." His voice dropped in timbre, becoming husky and slumberous. "In that case, you have only my word. I will not harm you. I cannot say the same about the authorities should you choose that route. The prisons in the area have a rather nasty reputation."

The coach rocked, turning into a narrow drive. Leaves dusted the top of the conveyance, providing a scuttle of warning, a murmur of intrigue.

"Please avail yourself of my hospitality."

The foliage parted to reveal a massive estate nestled on the rise of a hill. Several dozen candles glittered behind the windows like lightning bugs in a bottle.

"Hospitality?"

The phaeton slowed, making its approach.

"Like you, I have been uprooted from my true home. However, I am not so without means that I cannot offer you proper food and shelter. Even if you are somewhat reluctant to accept my charity, it is yours to use and you must not hesitate to ask if there is something you require."

The conveyance rolled to a stop and he opened the door, stepping onto the pea-gravel of the drive. Turning, he extended his hand to help her alight. When she didn't immediately comply, he added, "I assure you, the entire arrangement will be on the up-and-up. My housekeeper will serve as your chaperone if need be. After all, if you are as innocent as you claim, there would be no sense in saving you from one dire situation only to sully your reputation in the process."

"I appreciate your foresight," she muttered, unable to prevent the slight tinge of sarcasm. But she couldn't bring herself to move. He eyed her so intently, she wondered what thoughts he entertained.

"Surely you must understand my predicament. As a law-abiding citizen, I should keep you here with me until the truth can be ascertained. After all, I have been willing to give you the benefit of the doubt."

Molten velvet. The tone of his voice drizzled over her nerves, causing her to hesitate.

"Trust me, *cherie.*"

For some inexplicable reason, Aloise found herself accepting his proffered hand. His grip was just as she'd remembered. Firm. Reassuring. His palm large enough to engulf her own.

"Your fingers are cold."

"Yes." She barely managed to form her response.

"As well as the rest of you, I suppose?"

"Yes."

"Then we shall have to see about finding a way to warm you."

When she stepped to the ground, stumbling slightly, he scooped her into his arms. She would have gasped, but she couldn't gather enough air in her lungs for even that simple sound. A tingling effervescence pummeled her skin, and though she tried to convince herself it was the result of a lingering chill, she feared the explanation for her reaction was far from that simple.

A host of men swarmed around the carriage, changing the horses, then ushered another woman forward and enclosed her inside. Within seconds, they were gone, leaving a disturbing stillness in the yard. A slight breeze toyed with the leaves in the trees causing them to rattle mysteriously. The light of the approaching dawn seemed muted. Somber. As if the horizon had been dusted with a layer of soot.

The man who held her walked to the front steps of his home, and Aloise quickly absorbed as much of the house's exterior as she could—gleaming marble columns, a stately facade, leaded windows. The cool gusts of wind caused her to shiver slightly, huddling closer to the man's warmth, but before she could analyze her reaction, the front door opened to reveal an old woman holding a brace of candles.

Her lips were drawn tightly together. A puff of pewter-colored curls poked from beneath her mobcap, her entire body taking on a jaundiced color beneath the candle glow that bathed her. She appeared far from astonished to see some unknown lady being held aloft in her master's arms. Indeed, she appeared almost resigned.

"Miss Nibbs, we have a guest. Will you please take her to the Rose Room then prepare a bath?"

The woman made no sound, no gesture, no change of expression to show that she had heard. She merely disappeared inside, limping noticeably on gnarled limbs.

The stranger followed much more slowly, stepping into a foyer aglitter with scores of lighted tapers. Aloise peered about her in astonishment, noting the somber portraits, the black marble walls, the gilded trim. The oval entryway was bordered on one side by a scrolled staircase; a set of double doors led into a massive drawing room on the other end. A huge crystal chandelier hung over their heads, the branches alight with candles, while the inky parquet floor beneath their heels gleamed with their combined reflections.

The uneasiness she'd experienced outside intensified. A huge hand seemed to lock about her chest until it became difficult to breathe. The throbbing ache of her head that she had been courting for hours returned full force. She tried to shake the sensations away, but vague impressions swam to the forefront of her mind's eye, tantalizing her with the thought that she had seen this place . . . *somewhere.*

Aloise quickly pushed the thought aside. She hadn't been allowed to visit England very often in the last fifteen years. When she had returned, she'd invariably been taken to London to meet her father's new wives. She had little recollection of any other buildings, not even her father's estates in Briarwood where she had lived as a young girl.

"Mistress?"

Briarwood.

She barely heard the low query, barely saw the way the old woman turned at the bottom of the stairs to eye her carefully. As if expecting her to know some hidden knowledge.

A faint nausea settled in her stomach. The pain in her head grew sickening. Blinking, Aloise tried to keep her gaze firmly focused on the sights about her, but other images kept superimposing themselves on her mind. Glittering white walls. Slippery floors.

A storm.

Urgent screams.

"No." The word burst from her lips. Aloise stiffened as the horrible half-formed images crowded fast and strong. Throughout her childhood she had been tormented by awful dreams of a jarring ride, rocky bluffs, a windswept coastline. But the nightmares had always been somewhat the same, beginning with ornate frescoes. Marble floors. Crowded corridors. A house.

This house, she realized in horror. The colors might have changed, the accessories, but the structure itself could not be mistaken. She *knew* this place.

Dear sweet heaven, what was happening to her?

Pressing her fingers to her throbbing temples, she tried to wriggle free, tried to escape, run. But the stranger held her fast, forcing her to confront the truth. She had been here once. As a child. She had *lived* here.

Uttering a low, guttural moan of fury, she fought to be released, but her struggles were ineffectual against his iron-clad hold.

"Is something amiss?"

Amiss? The brief images that flashed through her head could only be the result of one thing. This man had brought her to her father's home. He'd brought her to Briarwood!

"Let me go, you bastard," she ground out. Fighting in earnest now, she managed to free her feet, but long before they touched the floor, the stranger's arms wrapped around her body, bringing her so close to his frame that she could not mistake his gender.

"Damn you!" she hissed. "How dare you drag me along like some toy on a string." She tore loose and ran into the drawing room, expecting to find her father ensconced in the chair in front of the fire, sipping brandy and scowling at her for her impertinence.

You should have been a boy. Those would be the first words he spoke, said with the proper amount of loathing and disappointment so that she would automatically feel the guilt for something completely beyond her control.

She heard the man move into the room and whirled to confront him.

"Is something the matter? You are more than welcome at Ashenleigh, I assure you."

She opened her mouth to retaliate, but one word stuck in her brain. Ashenleigh. *Ashenleigh?*

A piercing relief was swiftly replaced by a slow wave of horror. "Ashenleigh?" she breathed.

"Yes, have you heard of it?"

He was watching her. Like a hawk watched a mouse. Taunting her, testing her.

"Who has *not* heard of Ashenleigh?" Even in her isolation on the Continent, Aloise had read articles in the *Tatler* that had outlined the titillating gossip of an unknown, unnamed foreigner who—without ever visiting the site—had purchased the property bordering her father's estates, then had sent a host of solicitors and stewards to erect a manor house identical to Briarwood in every respect save one. Instead of a clean shimmering white, Ashenleigh was said to have been furnished entirely in black. Cool, mysterious black.

Who was this man? *Who?* Why had she had the misfortune of falling into his clutches? What did he intend to do with her?

"I hadn't realized my house had garnered such attention as to have developed a reputation with strangers."

Stunned, she had to force herself to speak. "Apparently there are those who find it beautiful enough to tell tales."

The man took two steps, three, crowding her, his features becoming brooding, dark, almost cruel. "You flatter me. But I cannot claim the whole of the credit for its design. I based it on the house that rests in the opposite valley. Have you heard of it as well?"

"Yes." She barely managed to scrape the word from her mouth.

This time, Aloise couldn't answer. She couldn't force a single syllable free. Instead, the name she wished to banish from her soul reverberated in her head like a death knell. *Briarwood.*

She was only miles away from her father's home.

6

HER FATHER WOULD FIND HER HERE. ALOISE KNEW HE would. A stinging desperation gripped her heart. It was only a matter of time. She had to get away! Now! This night!

"You look very weary."

The stranger's low comment took her unaware. She had been so steeped in worry that she had forgotten how closely he observed her.

Afraid that he might read a portion of her intent, she quickly schooled her features. But she couldn't still the quickened tempo of her heart.

"The journey and your injury have taken their toll. Therefore, I think it would be best if you retired now. We'll talk more at a future time."

Aloise's hands clenched into tight fists and her desperation was tempered by a surge of fury. There would be no talk. This man was partially to blame for her predicament. She didn't know how much of her true identity he knew, or if the entire situation was simply a grand coincidence, but she didn't plan to stay long enough to find out. As soon as this stranger turned his back, she would have to abandon her things and go.

"Good night, mistress."

When she would have left him, he cupped her cheeks, holding her immobile and forcing her to look at him. His gaze sought something within her, delving so deeply into her soul she feared he would know each thought she entertained. But after several minutes, he leaned toward her and pressed his mouth to her forehead, softly, sweetly, with such tenderness that her throat inexplicably tightened and she blinked in surprise.

"Miss Nibbs will take you to your room."

It took more effort than it was worth to turn and follow Miss Nibbs up the winding circular staircase. Behind her, she felt the light of the candles begin to lessen and realized her host was dousing the tapers one by one, obscuring his own shape in gloomy shadows. When she chanced a glance, somehow needing to imprint the sight of him one last time in her memory, he bowed, ever so slightly.

"You are most welcome at Ashenleigh, mistress." The words melted out of the darkness at the foot of the stairs. With that single phrase, he made her overtly conscious of each move she made, the way her clothes clung limply to her body, her hair straggled down her back. His gaze caressed her like a bare finger, trailing from the hollow of her throat, between her breasts, down her abdomen, the touch so real, so tangible, she felt a heat beginning to seep into her cheeks.

She was not a beautiful woman. She knew that.

But with a single glance, he made her feel like a princess royal.

Tears crowded in her throat, hot and strong. Tears of anger and frustration . . . and perhaps even a trace of regret. Turning resolutely away, she focused instead on her future. He might have kept her belongings thus keeping her funds limited, but as soon as she left this place, her new life would begin. She would become the woman she wanted to be. She would join the missionaries, travel to far-off lands, and turn the world on its ear.

Alone, a little voice mocked and she pressed her lips together to keep them from trembling. She had been alone all her life. She could survive such a fate.

When Aloise dawdled in her progress, Miss Nibbs huffed beneath her breath in a way that could only be interpreted as impatience. Motioning for Aloise to quicken her pace, she turned down the hallway, slipping deeper and deeper into the cool shadows to be found there. If not for the faint light of her candles, they both would have been swallowed completely by the black, black corridor. The glow from the tapers danced and shimmered, reflected by myriad shiny surfaces, until the ebony and gold carpet runner beneath her feet appeared to sparkle with fairy dust. If Aloise had not known better, she might have believed that she had stepped into some magical land and this was the castle of a king.

The thought brought her up short. No, the bearded stranger who had abducted her and kept her here against her will was no king. He was a man. A man who had twisted her wishes to suit his own.

The old woman came to a stop beside a gilt-trimmed door halfway down the hall. Cherubs flew in frozen relief above the lintel, looking grim and a little bit naughty. "This will be yours."

Aloise started at the gravel-toned statement. She had assumed that the elderly lady had not the faculty of speech since she hadn't uttered so much as a word to her master or anyone else.

Seeing she had surprised Aloise, the old woman's lips quivered slightly. Apparently, Aloise was destined to amuse everyone she saw.

Without warning, Miss Nibbs cupped her chin, forcing Aloise to look down at her. "I knew he would find you," she murmured. "How pretty you are."

Aloise frowned in confusion, but Miss Nibbs had already swung the door wide and stepped inside. "Your chambers," she said.

She opened her mouth to demand an explanation of the woman's odd comments, but the old woman shook her head as if sensing her question. "You will know what I mean soon enough. It is not my place to say more."

Taking her hand, Miss Nibbs drew her inside. A whisper-soft tinkling greeted Aloise's ears. Instantly, she sought the source of the sound. A sparkling wind chime of cut crystal had been hung in front of an open window. The tune it played was slightly mournful, ringing with odd discords as if the prisms had been tuned in a minor key.

The elderly lady waddled toward a privacy screen, pulling it slightly aside for Aloise to see that a tub had already been prepared for her. She took a cotton bathing sheet from a shelf in the armoire and draped it over the chair near the fireplace. Then, she brushed by Aloise and exited the room. "You've all you need. He's already seen to that," she offered as she closed the door behind her and locked it with an audible click.

Stepping nearer to the rollicking flames, Aloise was struck anew by the sensation that this place was familiar to her. That she had seen this room once before. As a child she fought to capture the fleeting memory. But the colors were wrong.

The chamber was black, just as the rest of the house had been. Ebony lacquered walls and marble floors shone with a decadent patina that screamed of wealth, elegance, and intrigue. The somberness ended at that point, softened somewhat by the mauve flowers and mint green leaves patterned into the Oriental rug. Pale pink draperies of a shimmering brocade trimmed in maroon were looped back to reveal sheer lace panels of pristine white. The delicate baroque furniture had been painted a corresponding rose with elegant gilt accents.

Pink. Her favorite color.

Aloise gingerly settled on the chair in front of the fire. The hair at the back of her neck prickled slightly, and she looked over her shoulder as if someone were watching, then scolded herself for such folly. She was alone. Completely and utterly alone.

Forcing all gloomy thoughts aside, Aloise jumped to her feet and crossed to the window. Peering down into the darkness, she saw that the ground was nearly thirty feet below. Too far for her to jump without breaking her neck.

Drat it all! There had to be a way to escape. She refused to be imprisoned here. She refused to be bested by a stranger.

Whirling, Aloise planted her hands on her hips, surveying the room from all angles. There were delicate ladies' chairs, settees, and swooning couches, a vanity laden with cosmetics in crystal decanters, armoires aplenty, and numerous mirrors. In the center of it all, lay the bed. A massive four-poster affair mounded with feather pillows and bolsters, heaped with lace-edged linens and satin duvets.

Linens.

Of course!

Running forward, she flipped the bedding away and stripped the sheets, wincing when her arm twinged in protest. Tying the ends together, she formed a makeshift rope, all the while congratulating herself on her ingenuity.

However, when it came time to execute her escape, she discovered one slight disadvantage. The railing of the veranda had been fashioned from solid slabs of marble, leaving no place for her to secure the rope. Most of the furniture in the chamber was far too light and delicate to offer a firm anchor, which left her with no other choice than to tie the sheets to her bedpost.

Frowning, she whipped the linen ladder around one wooden leg, then unraveled the cord she had formed and threw it over the edge. Just as she had feared, it reached no farther than midway.

Blast! The comforters were too bulky to tie together, and she had nothing else to use.

Think. Think, Aloise! she scolded herself. Then a simple solution occurred to her. Quickly stripping off her clothing, she tied her dress and two petticoats to the rope. A space of about ten feet remained, but she felt quite sure she could make such a jump.

Throwing the cloth ladder over the balcony again, she took a deep breath of the early, mist-thickened air. Dawn had encroached even farther into the sky, lightening it to a delicate golden glow. She would have to leave now, before the sun could gain any more inroads into the sky.

Offering a silent prayer for fools and adventurous maidens in distress, she crawled over the balcony, gripped the sheets, and began her descent.

The entire situation proved much more difficult than she had imagined. Her arm throbbed where she'd been injured and she closed her mind to the warmth she felt seeping through the bandages. Hurrying, she damned the way the weight of her body caused the sheets to shift as if the knots were coming free. The hem of her chemise kept tangling around her legs, but she hadn't the strength or the will to crawl back. Only a few yards remained. Then she could drop to the ground and be on her way.

Her feet left the safety of the rope, signaling that she had gone nearly to the limit of her ladder. Breathing a silent sigh of relief, she moved down as far as she could, then glanced into the courtyard below to gauge how best to land.

Rowrr.

The noise melted out of the foliage, sounding frightening and completely unfamiliar. Still suspended in midair, Aloise looked about her, seeing that she had lowered herself into a formal garden of sorts. Try as she might, she couldn't see the source of the guttural cry.

Rowrr.

The growling came again, louder this time, followed by the rustling of leaves. Aloise's eyes widened in distress. Sweet heaven above, were there beasts in the garden? Boars? She should have thought of such a thing. She should have realized that her host would not have left her near an unlocked window without thinking she might use it.

The bushes murmured another insistent warning and Aloise looked toward the sound just as a fierce amber and black head appeared, a long, lean body, powerful legs, a swishing tail. Great stars above! The man had a tiger in his garden. A tiger!

Gasping, Aloise tried to ascend the rope, but her wounded arm buckled in exhaustion and she only managed to cause her body to swing back and forth on the end of the tied-together linens until she dangled above that animal like some huge pendulum or a tempting, wriggling treat.

Realizing she was only exasperating matters, Aloise stopped her struggles. Her hands were beginning to slip. The rope shuddered as if the bed had started to shimmy free from its moorings.

Desperate now, Aloise called, "Here, kitty, kitty." Her greeting was little more than a croak. "Nice kitty. Kit—"

Her fingers slipped and she screamed as she felt herself falling, falling. But just when she thought the ground would slam against her tender backside, two arms snapped around her waist, breaking the impetus of her plummet.

The silence that followed was awful. Squeezing her eyes shut, Aloise didn't need to see who had come to her aid.

"Going somewhere, mistress?"

7

I THOUGHT I'D GET A LITTLE AIR," ALOISE MUTTERED flippantly, but when she looked at her captor, it became clear that he was not amused.

"How very unwise of you." In the encroaching light of morning, his licorice-black eyes glittered most alarmingly. So much so, that Aloise wondered if she might have been better off tangling with the tiger. "Do you often parade about your hosts' gardens in your stays and chemise?"

She refused to be cowed, even when the tone of his voice hardened. "Having never been invited anywhere, I couldn't say."

"Hmm." After that thoughtful sound, he carried her across the courtyard, toward a pair of French doors that had been thrown open to the dewy air.

"You may set me down, I assure you."

"No. I don't think so."

She glanced over his shoulder, wondering if she should try to wriggle free and run, but the tiger continued to watch her with bright, gleaming eyes, its tongue occasionally sweeping out to lick its jowls as if regretting the loss of a tasty morsel.

The man didn't speak, making her wonder if she

were about to be inflicted with some sort of horrible punishment. Her father had always seen to it that she was castigated for any show of willfullness. Why should this man prove any different?

Hoping to diffuse the volatile situation, Aloise deftly changed the course of the conversation. "What an unusual pet you have."

"Sonja is not a pet. One wrong move, and she will have you for breakfast."

Aloise tried to tell herself that the man was merely jesting, but after careful scrutiny of his rock-hard jaw and the intent stare of the tiger, she was forced to heed his warning. At least for the moment.

"How did you come by such an unusual . . . garden ornament? Most people would have settled for a birdbath rather than a predatory animal."

"Sonja was given to me while I was abroad."

Despite herself, Aloise felt a pique of interest. "Abroad?" she repeated, unable to prevent the note of reverence that entered her voice.

"Yes, *chérie.*" He looked down at her then, darkly, his eyes filled with meaning. "*I* have been to Africa."

She would have immediately pummeled him with questions, but something about the slight twitching of a muscle in his jaw prevented her. Without preamble, he marched up the stairs, opened the door to the Rose Room, and dumped her on the untidy bed.

Sighing at the condition of her bandage, he stalked across the room to tear off a portion of her bath sheet and use it to bind the wound. Aloise averted her eyes from the sight of the fresh streaks of blood, but such an action caused an even more alarming sensation since she became aware of each touch, each brush of movement, each warm caress.

"Rest," the stranger ordered, jerking her from her thoughts. Then, he turned and abruptly exited into the hall. Before locking her in he stated, "I would not venture out for any more air." One black brow lifted in clear warning. "Sonja is not the only creature who likes to prowl through my garden looking for something to feast upon."

With that, he shut the door, leaving her with nothing more than her tangled linens, the mournful notes of the chimes, and the disgruntled grumbling of the tiger to keep her company.

However, minutes later as she stripped off her stays—hiding the one ruby she'd managed to keep—and wrapped herself in a pink satin duvet, she couldn't deny the gooseflesh that peppered her skin. As if she weren't quite as alone as she would like to think.

"You've got that overly intense brooding look again, Slater. It rarely bodes well for the object of your concern."

Slater didn't bother to turn as Will Curry moved into the sitting room behind him. He continued to stare out the window pane into the encroaching dawn, trying to ignore the fact that a mere wall away, Aloise Crawford had divested herself of everything but her chemise and had fallen asleep.

When he'd seen her clambering down to the garden he'd been too angry to take much note of his guest's attire. But after leaving her, he'd returned to this room and peered through the eyeholes of the ornate plaster mask built into the wall. One which corresponded to a similar ornament on the other side.

In all the years of wondering what had happened to Aloise Crawford, he had never dreamed that she could prove to be so lovely. Somehow, it had salved his conscience to convince himself that she'd taken after her father, becoming a mousey-haired, meek-tongued woman with Crawford's beaked nose and all the passion of a roasted potato. He'd sworn she would prove to be cold to the bone.

He'd been wrong. So very wrong.

He couldn't deny how much she looked like her mother—and acted. Good hell, she had a temper. He rubbed the spot where she'd bitten him—*bitten* him! In the past thirty-six years of his life he had endured hunger and deprivation. He'd been shot, knifed, beaten, and whipped. But no one had ever bitten him. No one had ever managed to take him off guard in that manner, damn her hide.

". . . say, old boy, aren't you listening?"

"Hmm?" Jerking back to Curry's insistent demand, he finally turned to confront his friend.

Just as he'd suspected, Curry's puckish features were clouded with a frown of displeasure. Other than being a bit rumpled and dusty, he appeared none the worse for wear after their riotous journey, but Slater guessed that his temper was not so unaffected.

"At long last, I have your attention. Or at least a portion of it." Will snapped the door closed. "Would you like to tell me just what the hell you plan to do now?"

"The thought of a hot bath crossed my mind."

"Damn it, Slater, that's not what I meant, and you know it."

"Then what *did* you mean, Curry?" Slater's tone grew steely, warning Will that even as his friend, there were bounds to his familiarity.

His efforts were wasted. Curry flopped onto the settee, hooking one leg over the arm, not in the least dissuaded from pursuing his course. "You know very well that I'm asking what you're going to do with Mistress Aloise Crawford now that you've got her imprisoned in the Rose Room—and what in heaven's name do you intend by having Louis and Rudy and a chambermaid gallivanting all over the countryside in your coach?"

Slater moved to the sideboard to pour himself a snifter of brandy. "I'm merely keeping her out of her father's clutches for a time."

"Why? Why not take her to the authorities, have her relate what she saw fifteen years ago, and be done with the whole affair?"

"She claims she doesn't remember her mother. At all."

"Do you believe her?"

He briefly thought of the way she'd struck her head that night so long ago. "I haven't decided. But I won't let her leave in any event."

"How do you plan to ensure she stays here? Imprison her in the Rose Room?"

"In part." He waited an instant, knowing that Curry would have a great deal to say about his unorthodox procedure. "I have also accused her of thievery. She must remain with me until her claims otherwise can be proved true."

"That should endear you to her."

Slater shrugged in apparent unconcern.

"I suppose you'll spend the intervening time pricking her conscience for the true extent of her memory."

"That I will. In the meantime, Louis and Rudy will lead Crawford on a merry chase, keeping him occupied until I'm prepared to let him know where to find his daughter."

Curry opened his mouth, hesitated, then threw his hands into the air. "Fine. Do what you wish. You will anyway." Curry's scrutiny centered keenly on Slater. "She's very beautiful, don't you think?"

Slater didn't move, didn't blink. "Depends on your point of view, I suppose."

"Lush figure, dark coloring, a spirit of fire, how many ways do you need to study her?"

Slater compared the woman who'd fought with him on the beach with the one who had tried in vain to charm a tiger the same way one would charm a recalcitrant kitten. His expression lightened slightly. "She is a model of contrasts."

"That fact intrigues you."

The room pulsed in silence, becoming so quiet that Slater thought he might have heard the tinkling of the wind chime in the other room. "Possibly it does."

Curry rose. "In that case, I shall anticipate the next few days with great pleasure. Meanwhile, I intend to go in search of my own hot bath. You may continue to brood at your own leisure."

"I never brood."

"Mmm. So you keep telling me."

Will exited the sitting room, leaving a restless quiet in his place. Slater remained still for one minute, two. Then, as if drawn by a velvet cord, he padded into the hall to his private office.

Miss Nibbs had been this way as well. He could tell by the scores of tapers that had been lit in the corridor. Since losing her original position in the Waterton household fifteen years ago, and being forced to take sanctuary in a friend's cellar to avoid Crawford's wrath, Miss Nibbs had grown to despise the dark. Slater, on the other hand, had become a creature of the night.

Extinguishing the candles and leaving a wake of inky shadows, he stepped into his own private sanctuary. An overflow of his father's books and maps had been stacked here after the library had been filled. The precious reading materials were the only things Miss Nibbs had been able to salvage from the cottage after Crawford had ransacked the place. She'd kept them in boxes and trunks, somehow knowing that he would come back. Knowing he would have his revenge. When his solicitor had managed to locate and approach her about working in Ashenleigh, she had brought the things to their rightful home. Her gift to the boy she had never forgotten.

Taking the last candle, Slater left it aglow, entering the room that harbored the oh-too-familiar musty scents of old books and paper. The smells were even more intense since his father's collection had only been moved into the house mere days earlier. Miss Nibbs had been quite busy since receiving word that her master would soon return.

For long moments, Slater stood still in the doorway. Moving slowly, he crossed the room to a set of heavy velvet draperies. Hooking them behind the brass rosettes imbedded in the gilt ornamentation of the alcove he stared up at the sweet face that regarded him so quietly, so seriously.

The artist had captured Jeanne's exquisite features to near perfection. Although Slater had been able to provide the man with nothing more than the tiny miniature in Slater's possession, the painting had taken on a life of its own. A warmth.

"I'm sorry, Jeanne. So sorry," he whispered, knowing that their was no way he could atone for his mistake of years' past. But at least he could try to expose the truth. Right the future.

"Well, Jeanne . . . I have finally found her. Aloise is here with me. And she is beautiful. Much like you."

Maybe Slater was imagining things, maybe he read more into the artwork than anyone else would find there, but in the dewy warmth of dawn beginning to stretch its fingers through the far window, he thought he saw a slight smile lingering deep in her eyes. The very idea caused a shaft of sadness to spear his heart.

This woman should have lived to see this day.

She should have lived to see the woman her daughter had become.

"Get up."

Aloise woke to the abrupt command, blinking over the top of the single duvet that had managed to stay on the bed. She barely had time to gather her wits about her when Miss Nibbs marched into the room, *harrumphing* in displeasure.

"What have you done?" she demanded cryptically, gesturing to the coverlets spilling onto the floor and the sheets still knotted and wound around the leg of the four-poster.

Aloise had not bothered to repair her room. Her surroundings must look odd indeed, but she refused to explain herself to this imperious crone. Therefore, she blinked, fixed the woman with a hard stare and retorted, "I'm a light sleeper," thinking that it was truly none of this woman's business what went on in Aloise's bedchamber, regardless of the condition of her linens.

The old woman was clearly not impressed with her explanation. She frowned in Aloise's direction, her gaze raking the length of her disheveled figure. "You did not try to escape, I hope."

"I did."

The woman opened her mouth in shock at such audacity then added, "Evidently he caught you, since you are still here."

Aloise refused to respond to such a pointed reminder of her failure.

The woman folded her arms beneath her ponderous breasts. "I can see that you didn't follow the master's instructions and bathe."

"No. I did not."

"He will be highly displeased."

"Then the master may do the bathing if he wishes. *I*, however, was not in the mood."

The woman's chin trembled in irritation. "How is your mood this morning?"

In all truth, Aloise would have loved a bath. Saltwater and travel dust caked her skin and made her feel decidedly sticky.

The woman grunted again. "Don't bother to answer. What *you* want is of little consequence. The master will be obeyed."

Aloise opened her mouth to offer a pithy remark, but Miss Nibbs gave her no opportunity.

"If you are to wash properly, I will have to send servants to empty the tub."

"Fine."

"Then fill it again."

"Fine."

Miss Nibbs swept from the room, and glad for the respite—if only for a minute or two—Aloise buried her head beneath a pillow. However, it was not the servants that Miss Nibbs had gone to summon she realized in dismay when even the down-filled bolsters could not drown out the thump of boot heels on the marble staircase. Aloise knew in an instant that Miss Nibbs had sought the owner of the house to chide Aloise for her negligence.

Aloise's legs churned in her haste to rise from the bed, unintentionally hiking her chemise high about her thighs just at he walked through the door. She scrambled to push the fabric back into place, an uncomfortable blush staining her cheeks at having been caught with so much bare skin exposed.

Her host stopped just a few yards past the threshold and Aloise was struck to the core by her first glimpse of him in broad daylight.

Dear Lord, had she really thought she could seduce this man? She gazed up and up at his inordinate height, noting his forbidding coloring and the gleam of eyes that were accustomed to being angry.

"I trust you slept well."

"No. I did not."

Miss Nibbs gasped at her rudeness, but Aloise was not about to take back the words. She had not asked to be brought here; she had not asked to stay. This man had kept her by force, bent her to his will.

His lips twitched ever so slightly at her impertinence, but did not tip far enough to curve into a smile. He flicked a glance at her disheveled underthings, then the knotted linens still trailing toward the window.

"Miss Nibbs, I'm afraid our guest had a bit of a mishap after retiring which forced her to . . . abandon her clothes for a time. Therefore, you will need to see to laundering them. I believe you will find a dress and two petticoats dangling outside her window. Clayton will help you get them down."

The old crone grumbled to herself, but went to do as she'd been bidden, leaving Aloise alone with her host. Alone and quite unprepared for the crackling energy that settled into the room around them.

As much as she had grown to dislike Miss Nibbs's patronizing tone and her fawning attention to this man's wishes, Aloise nearly called her back. She did not want to be left with this stranger. He was much too large. Much too intense.

He must have sensed a bit of her unease, because he moved farther into the room as if to catch her should she try to bolt. "I've sent one of my men to Tippington to make inquiries."

"I did not steal the necklace."

He sighed as if wearied with the same argument they'd held earlier. "Well, I believe that today I will give you the opportunity to prove to me that you are the lady you claim to be."

He walked around her in a large circle, eyeing her as if she were a mare on the block. "First, though, I see that you are in dire need of an appropriate wardrobe."

She stiffened her shoulders and glared at him. "There is nothing wrong with my clothing."

"Save that it is knotted and soiled and hanging outside your bedroom window," he said turning his back and walking to the door.

Furious at being so easily dismissed, she added, "Then I'll wait until it has been cleaned."

Grasping the knob, he stepped into the hall. "No. You won't. Because you see, *chérie,* my men and I have been away from England for a very long time. We are not yet accustomed to the stunning beauties to be found on this little island, and the costume you are wearing—however charming—manages to be quite transparent when you stand in front of the window. Such as you are doing now."

The smile he offered her was positively wolfish. Her cheeks burned and her hands automatically rose to cover herself, but they both knew such a gesture had occurred much too late.

"I will send the servants up with more hot water—and you *will* bathe, my dear. Then I expect you to join me in the breakfast room in one hour."

With that, he closed the door, leaving her trembling and decidedly nervous. She knew without a doubt that this man had studied her body through the all-but-transparent fabric of her shift. If the heated gleam of his eyes was any indication . . . he hadn't been completely unaffected by what he'd seen.

The thought was inexplicably, incomprehensibly disturbing.

8

LESS THAN SIXTY MINUTES LATER, ALOISE HEARD A KEY turning in the lock of her door. She had bathed in near-glacial-temperature water—no doubt thanks to Miss Nibbs—combed her hair, and swathed herself in the pink satin duvet. Even so, she felt completely unprepared for another verbal skirmish with her host.

It was not her host, however, who waited on the other side of the doorway. A lean gentleman with blue, blue eyes and an engaging grin bowed to her. "Good afternoon."

"Is it really afternoon?"

"I'm afraid so." He offered her his arm. "Are you ready for a slight repast? I'm to escort you downstairs."

"I would rather you escorted me from the property."

He sighed most affectedly. "Alas, I can't do that. But I assure you that the meal you are about to partake of will be quite filling. The boys and I have already eaten."

He waited, his elbow still crooked in her direction. Since she had no other choice, Aloise hiked the bed linens more securely about her waist and allowed him to take her into the hall.

"Who are 'the boys'?" she asked as they made their way toward the stairs.

"You'll meet them soon enough. I don't think I'd be telling tales to say that Slater has managed to attract a very diverse band of friends to share his exploits."

Slater. Was that the bearded stranger's first name or his last?

"Have you and 'the boys' been with him long?"

Her escort eyed her keenly, but divulged no real information. "I suppose."

Once at the bottom of the staircase, he led her down the marble hall to the rear of the house. Even now, in the middle of the day, the black of the walls absorbed the bright sunlight streaming through the multipaned windows, enveloping the corridor in mystery.

Her companion stopped and reached for the brass door handle, but Aloise touched his wrist.

"Please . . ." she begged in earnest appeal. "Won't you help me? Won't you take me away from here?"

The gentleman shook his head from side to side. He looked sympathetic, but she could see that she hadn't swayed him from his innate loyalty to the stranger.

Growing slightly desperate, she gripped his sleeve. "Don't you see? I've been abducted—brought here through force and conspiracy."

"Yes."

His blatant admission startled her.

"Then why would you want to condone what has been done to me?"

"Because I won't turn my back on a friend."

"Even when he breaks the law? Even when he damns me to a living hell?"

He touched her cheek, softly, briefly. "Has he done those things, little one? Or has he liberated you from an even more demeaning situation."

His eyes glowed with a hidden knowledge. One that made her shiver slightly. But before she could question him, he swung open the door into a small dining room. "*Voilà, mon ami!* She is here at last."

"Thank you, Curry. That will be all."

At the far side, near a bank of guillotine windows, a figure turned. The bearded stranger. Slater.

Aloise felt Curry's hand on her back, pushing her forward, but he needn't have bothered. There was something about him, something about the way the sunlight streamed over his back and around his head, forming an eerie sort of halo, that drew her to him.

"I see that you followed my instructions and bathed the travel from your skin."

She looked behind her, thinking to draw strength from the presence of a witness, but the man called Curry had disappeared.

The sound of Slater's boots against the marble floor caused her to start. Clutching the duvet to her neck, she tried to discern what he might be thinking, but he remained inscrutable, closing the distance between them until he stood a mere hair's breadth away. His body crowded her, inestimably large, inestimably fit.

Reaching out, he adjusted the drape of the coverlet over one shoulder, brushing his knuckles ever so slightly against her bare skin. She trembled at the contact, not able to prevent the instinctive reaction.

He must have noted the sensation because he finally took a step backward, his lips curving in the slightest of satisfied smiles.

"You look very fetching."

Disturbed by the warmth that had settled like thick honey between them, Aloise shot him a scathing glance. "That old bat you call a housekeeper stole my chemise."

The stranger seemed far from perturbed by her accusations. "How very wise of her."

Aloise stiffened in indignation. "What exactly do you mean to convey with that comment?"

"Merely that your taste in . . . attire leaves much to be desired. Especially since you are intent upon proving to me that you are a woman of quality."

Returning to the table, he pulled out one of the

chairs in silent invitation. Realizing that she had no other real choice, Aloise sank onto the cushions and waited for him to take his own seat. After helping her to settle, he did not immediately move. Instead, he paused to finger a lock of her hair. When she regarded him curiously, he finally stepped away.

"I hope you're hungry. Hans cooked enough for an army."

"I suppose I could force myself to eat a bite or two." Actually, the tempting aromas were causing her mouth to water and her stomach to rumble, but she would expire of starvation prior to admitting her need to this man.

"Good. I'm glad to hear it. We have a busy day ahead of us." He removed the lid to a silver chafing dish revealing fried kippers, eggs, and sliced potatoes.

"Busy day?" she asked somewhat absently, overcome by her sudden hunger.

"As I mentioned upstairs, we need to see about finding some proper clothes for you."

"I have clothing of my own—including a change of dresses in the haversack you confiscated."

"Most of which was soiled and hardly fashionable."

"Still, I demand that you return it to me at once!"

"All in good time, *chérie.* All in good time." After selecting a bun, two scones, and a spoonful of stewed apricots, he placed the plate in front of her. Then he chose a halved pomegranate for himself. Rather than taking his own chair, he draped one thigh over the corner of the table, making himself quite comfortable mere inches from her elbow.

After chewing a few seeds, he reached out again to skim his knuckle over a wave of her hair. When she shifted away, he hooked a finger beneath her chin, forcing her to look at him, forcing her to admit that—for now—she was completely at his mercy.

He did not chide her, but returned to the original thrust of his conversation. "I assure you that I'm more than happy to accommodate your wardrobe needs. Something in blue, I believe. Or perhaps yellow."

Aloise opened her mouth to speak.

"You needn't thank me."

When she tried to assure him that she'd intended nothing of the sort, he took the opportunity to drop several pomegranate seeds inside. At the unfamiliar taste, her brows creased and her mouth pursed in distress.

"But first you must eat."

She barely heard him as she sprang from her seat and rushed to spit the seeds into the fireplace. Reluctantly, she returned—only because she had to do so in order to take a hefty draft of water from her glass—but she made quite sure she chose a goblet from the opposite side of the table.

One black brow lifted. "I take it you've never tasted a pomegranate."

She rubbed at her mouth with the back of her hand. "It's awful."

"Mayhap, much like many of the pleasures of life, it is an acquired taste."

She glared at him for his too-familiar tone, but he merely grinned and continued. "I've heard that the pomegranate is symbolic of life and the resurrection. I prefer to think of it as a symbol of a woman and her . . . fertility. After all, who but a woman can give life?"

A fire stoked in the pit of her belly. Perhaps because of his words. Perhaps because of his talk of children. Or perhaps, just perhaps, because his heated regard had settled low on her stomach.

"What do you think?"

Damn his bloody soul, this man was toying with her. Taunting, tempting, scheming. Her father had probably hired him to lead her willy-nilly to this place, batter her hopes, and force her to comply with his wishes. *Damn* him!

Without even thinking, Aloise grasped the first dish she encountered and hurled it at him.

"You loathsome hedgehog of a man!"

The plate landed high of its mark, shattering against the wall. Before he could defend himself, Aloise had corrected her aim and thrown the saucer. He barely managed to duck in time for it to sail over the table and explode on the floor.

"You bastard!" She grasped the water goblet and it flew through the air, spilling its contents over her target and glancing off his shoulder.

"Aloise!"

"Damn you! What a petty, evil, *scurrilous* thing to do!"

She saw the fury darken his mien, but she did not anticipate how quickly he could move. He stormed across the room and pinned her against the wall. It was at that moment, she was struck by a thunderous thought.

He'd called her by *name*.

Aloise didn't even bother to think, but rammed her knee into his groin for the second time in as many days. This time, her aim proved a little more true, because the stranger growled in anger and doubled over.

But when she would have dodged away, there was a scrabbling noise in the hall, like toenails skidding over polished marble. Sonja bounded into the room, teeth bared, the hair at her nape bristled in anger. Roaring in displeasure, the tiger hesitated in the threshold, surveying the scene, then turned gleaming eyes in Aloise's direction.

Sweet angels in heaven, it meant to eat her alive! Grasping the covers wrapped around her feet, Aloise jumped onto a chair, and from there into the middle of the table, sending cutlery and dishes crashing to the floor.

"Shoo . . . shoo!"

She waved her arms, but the huge cat continued to

pad forward. Its mouth had drawn back in an awful grimace. The fur of its body stood on end making the animal appear all the more menacing.

"Do something!" She whirled in Slater's direction, but the man had sunk to the floor, sitting with his legs bent, his elbows braced on his knees.

"Why should I?" he asked after taking a few minutes to gather enough air to speak. His fury descended like a palpable shroud.

She scuttled backward along the length of the table, but the tiger continued to trail her. "Can't you see? It means to devour me."

"Maybe I should let it."

Abandoning her watch on the tiger, she glared at the man on the floor. She supposed she hadn't ingratiated herself through her actions for any sorts of favors, but surely he didn't mean to feed her to this beast!

"Please."

The word was uttered most grudgingly, but there was no doubting its intended sincerity.

The man struggled to his feet, stood hunched there for a moment, then lifted his head to say, "Sonja, *calma.*"

The tiger stopped, glanced at her master, at Aloise, then relaxed, muscle by muscle, hair by hair. A sound emerged from its throat that sounded like something midway between a yowl and a purr, then she turned her attention to the kippers and porridge strewn about the floor and began to lap them up with great glee.

Slater then turned his attention to Aloise.

"Get down."

There was no denying the threat buried deep in the simple command.

Aloise shot a look at the dining cat who stood just inches away on one side of the table, then noted the fury darkening her host's brow as he stood on the other. Neither direction looked entirely safe. "I don't think—"

"Get *down.*"

Aloise glared at the man, resenting his influence over her. But he had placed her in such a position that she couldn't argue with him. At least not for the moment.

Drawing her silken cocoon as tightly around her body as was possible, she stepped onto the seat of a chair and from there onto the floor.

Slater walked toward her, slowly, purposefully, and she took an involuntary step backward, sandwiching herself between the table and the lean strength of his thighs.

He reached out to clasp her jaw, forcing her to look up at him, to acknowledge the brittle fury of his gaze. "You will not attempt to injure me again."

She didn't speak.

"If you do, I will feed you to Sonja and be done with you."

Despite the farfetched idea, the words he spoke rang with a vibrant intensity. So much so, that she didn't doubt he would do as he had promised.

"Do we understand one another?"

She would have given her soul to have been able to utter a flippant remark. But she couldn't. Not with those black eyes boring into her.

"Very well." He backed away. "I will send a servant with a broom and you will clean this mess. Do not disobey me."

Turning on his heel, he marched into the hall. The tiger, after one regretful glance in Aloise's direction bounded after him. The door slammed shut and a key turned in the lock.

Filled with a nameless panic, Aloise hurried to the first guillotine window, then the next, and the next. Locked. All locked. In such a fashion she could not find the catch to release the sash.

Whirling away, she stared at the breakfast room. The black walls closed in on her, suffocating her. What was she going to do? The stranger anticipated her every move, making escape seem more impossible with each passing hour.

What was she going to do?

He would return. She had no doubts of that. He knew things about her—much more than just her name. But what? *What?* Was he in league with her father? Was he the next matrimonial prospect? Or was he merely what he claimed to be: a man driven to see that justice was served. Heaven only knew her father had a temper that could inspire an enemy or two. In any event, she knew that when he stepped into the room, she would have to be on her guard. Otherwise, he would look at her with those licorice eyes, and incite in her a feeling that she had been trying to deny since she'd encountered this man on the beach.

Want. A want for things she could never have.

A sob clutched at her chest, but she fought it back. Allowing her knees to give way, she lowered herself to the floor and began to clean.

A few minutes later, she looked up, drawn by some unknown force.

Slater stood in the doorway, watching her intently. She had not heard him enter, and wondered if he had merely decided to usher the servant he'd summoned into the room. But he was alone. When he continued to gaze at her, an unexpected softening touching his lips, she paused in her endeavors.

"Have you decided against summoning someone to help me?" she asked.

He didn't seem to hear. "Come with me, Aloise."

"But—" She gestured to the mess.

"Leave it."

His tone was almost gentle. Almost.

A curious tightness gathered in her throat as she stood in the midst of the littered crockery and the ruined meal. Unwanted tears gathered fast and strong as she joined him in the portal and she blinked the moisture away. She would not be weak. She *would not!*

He held out his hand, palm up, in silent invitation. Unable to prevent the action, she acquiesced, allowing him to lace their fingers intimately together.

For several seconds, he didn't move, didn't speak. As the silence gathered around them thick and strong, Aloise realized she had already displayed an awful vulnerability. She had surrendered herself to this man's will, however momentarily. In the space of an instant, she had allowed his strength to overcome her anxieties, soothe her.

And damn him to hell and back, she could not find the will to regret offering him that tiny portion of power.

"Well, man. What have you got to say?"

Crawford eyed his secretary in barely concealed anger. Soon after dawn, he had abandoned his own chase of the phaeton that he believed held his daughter and had returned to Briarwood, assigning a host of guards to bring the girl back by midday. He could only hope that Mr. Humphreys had arrived with such news.

"Where is she?"

Mr. Humphreys's lips pressed together. "She isn't here," he finally admitted.

"Where . . . is . . . she?"

"We . . . don't know, sir."

Crawford slammed his walking stick on the side of the leather chair where he'd been seated, enjoying his brandy, and contemplating how he could best punish his daughter for her disobedience.

"B-but we do have a lead on her whereabouts, I believe," Mr. Humphreys hastened to assure him. "After inquiring at the village, we were able to determine that the coach which took her has been seen in the area." He glanced at the sheaf of papers in his hands. "It belongs to a newcomer in the area."

"Newcomer?"

"I have not yet determined his name, but he is the owner of the house in the opposite valley. Ashenleigh."

Hearing the name of the neighboring estate, Crawford felt the fury bubble inside him. The instincts that had warned something was amiss with this entire charade fairly pummeled him now. *Damnit!* Who was this McKendrick? First, he had dared to build a mirror image of Briarwood and now he seemed to have had a hand in helping his daughter escape.

"Bring my coach around."

"Yes, sir." Mr. Humphreys scrambled to do what he had been told, but hesitated in the doorway. "What do you intend to do?"

"Find my daughter," Crawford growled. Then he would make her rue the day she had ever decided to enlist the help of a stranger to thwart her father.

"Come with me, Aloise."

Slater saw the way Aloise relented, the way her body relaxed, ever so slightly.

He didn't know why he'd been drawn back to the breakfast room. After Aloise had managed to fell him, he'd meant to leave her there for an hour or so to rethink her hasty actions. But he hadn't been able to stay away. Her dejection, her frustration, her panic pulled at his soul as sharply as if she'd actually cried out. When he'd opened the door to see her on the floor, her face a mask of untold misery, he hadn't been able to leave her that way. After all, he was the man responsible for her plight. Now. As well as all she had suffered through the years. Looking into those huge brown eyes, he realized that she was no more capable of lying than Jeanne had been.

This woman truly didn't remember what had happened that night so long ago. She couldn't possibly remember.

Holding Aloise's fingers a little more tightly, he

drew her down the hall behind him. But they had only taken a few steps when she balked and refused to go any farther.

He lifted one brow in silent inquiry, seeing the proud tilt to her chin, the flush to her cheeks. Her frustration had not completely vanished. She might have given him her hand, but he knew by the sparkle in her eyes that she would soon be gathering her courage for another escape attempt. He would have to be on his guard every minute of the day. Even so, Slater could not deny that he found himself feeling delighted at the challenge rather than peeved. He couldn't remember a time when a woman had so intrigued him.

When Aloise did not speak, he tugged at her hand. "Do you intend to stand here in the hall?"

She didn't even seem to hear his question. "How do you know my name?"

Ah, so that was the problem. "Miss Nibbs informed me that the name was sewn in your chemise. I did not think you would stoop so low as to steal another woman's unmentionables."

She frowned at his glib explanation, clearly suspicious of him, but unable to claim he'd lied since her name had indeed been stitched—quite untidily—in pink thread on the neckline of her gown. No doubt the evidence of some exercise in embroidery she'd experienced some time in the past.

When she did not force the matter, Slater took her the length of the corridor, halting at a pair of double doors located in the eastern corner of the estate.

"Where are you taking me?"

"Since you did not prove to be as hungry as I had thought you would . . ." he drawled, knowing her stomach must be rumbling mightily at the moment but needing to reassert his power over her, ". . . I thought we should tend to other more basic needs."

Releasing her hand, he threw open one of the doors and ushered her inside. The narrow music room was in chaos. Women swarmed about bolts of fabric and piles of lace. Gowns, in various stages of completion, had been thrown over every available surface: tables, settees, even the pianoforte.

Stepping into the room, Slater picked out a tiny Frenchwoman who was clearly in charge and inquired, "Madame LeBeau, have you something ready for my guest?"

9

AT SLATER'S QUERY, EVERY WOMAN IN THE ROOM BEcame silent and turned. A palpable wave of admiration flowed toward the man, so much so that Aloise wanted to stamp her foot in disgust. These ladies could not have become more subservient had they knelt and bowed before him.

"Slater!" A tiny, birdlike creature with a carefully arranged powdered wig rushed to take his face between her hands, kissing him on either cheek. "You 'ave come to see my work?"

"Of course. I've also brought you the woman who will be wearing your creations."

Madame LeBeau quickly surveyed Aloise, not seeming in the least surprised to see her wearing nothing more than a pink satin comforter. Her lips curved in a genuine smile and she clapped her hands together. "What a charming leetle one you have found. She eez small, just as you said, so delicate, so beautiful."

Without waiting for a response from Slater or Aloise, she whirled toward her seamstresses. *"Vite, vite!* Bring zee gown we 'ave just finished. Come, mademoiselle."

Aloise was ushered behind a privacy screen tucked

against the far side of the room. There, she was stripped of her comforter and bid to stand still as a host of women swarmed over her like bees, helping her to don silken hose and garters, a delicate lawn chemise, brocade stays, and cotton petticoats. One pair of women tended to her hair, while another buffed her nails, dabbed perfume behind her ears and in the hollow of her elbows. Then she was swathed in a yellow silk underskirt embroidered with birds and a tightly tailored jacket with a beaded stomacher.

Madame LeBeau stood back to eye the finished product and beamed in delight. *"Trés magnifique!"*

Before Aloise had the breath to offer comment, the privacy screen had been pulled away, and she found herself face-to-face with her host.

How he had managed to cross the room so quietly, she did not know. She became instantly aware of his heated regard as he surveyed her new costume from the tips of her satin slippers, to the rich embroidered hems of her skirts, the artful arrangement of her panniers, the tightly cinched circumference of her waist, and the pearly mounds of her breasts pushing against the low, square neckline. When at long last, his gaze settled on the upsweep of her hair, the delicate lace cap, the tilted straw hat, her eyes, her lips, Aloise was beginning to feel decidedly breathless—a condition that had nothing to do with the pressure of her stays.

"To look at you thus, one could honestly believe you to *be* a lady, Aloise."

Aloise opened her mouth to offer a pithy remark, but the clear admiration he displayed forestalled her and she found herself offering a meek, "I'm pleased that it meets with your approval."

Once again, he took her hand, lacing their fingers together, then turned his attention to the seamstress. *"Merci,* Madame LeBeau. I trust the rest of her things will be ready as soon as possible."

"But of course."

Without another word, he drew Aloise into the corridor. She scarcely noted where they were going. Instead, she became bewitched by the sensation of being clothed in luxury: the whispering of her hems, the caress of lace, the rustle of petticoats.

Slater cast a glance in her direction, one which delved into her soul for every thought. Could he see how much she'd been affected by this gesture? Could he guess that this was the first time that she could remember being allowed to use anything half so lovely, so rich?

"Thank you, Slater." The words spilled from her lips without volition, taking him by surprise and he stopped in midstride.

"You are more than welcome."

The two of them grew still.

"The gown is beautiful."

"As are you."

His reply caused a warmth to blossom deep in the pit of her stomach. When he reached out to cup her cheek in his palm, she could not prevent the way she nudged a little closer to the heat to be found there.

"Whatever happens, Aloise, the dress is yours."

She blinked at the tears that sprang unbidden to her eyes. Foolish womanly tears that she damned but could not prevent. Needing to assert a little of her own will to dampen the rush of softer emotions, she stated, "The gift is far from necessary. I *do* have clothing of my own. Clothing which is far less inviting, but serviceable nonetheless."

He laid a finger against her lips. "Some things are done—not because they are necessary—but because they feed a portion of the soul. Your soul, Aloise, was meant to be housed in beauty."

His statement caught her unaware, piercing her very heart and filling it with a yearning such as she had never encountered. A longing. A need. A need for more sweet words such as these. For validation of the worth of her dreams.

"Slater!"

Any comment she might have made was cut short as Curry skidded to a stop at the end of the corridor and motioned for Slater to approach.

Immediately, her host's face grew masked.

"Excuse me, Aloise. I won't be but a minute."

He conferred briefly with the blue-eyed gentleman and Aloise was able to grasp only a few words. Evidently the coach she had ridden in from Tippington had been seen and someone had given chase.

She saw the way Slater took immediate control, firing a set of muted orders. Then he strode toward her, taking her elbow, and pulling her forcibly to one of the outer doors.

"What—"

"I thought we'd take a ride."

Holding her hat to keep it from flying off her head, Aloise had no choice but to follow.

The air outside was invigorating, fresh, smelling faintly of rain and cut grass. But Aloise was not given the opportunity to enjoy her unexpected release. Slater hustled her to the mews where a pair of horses were being drawn from the stables.

"I trust you can keep your seat, mistress," Slater warned as he clasped her about the waist and lifted her on the sidesaddle.

She grappled with the unfamiliar position, not about to tell this man that she had never really ridden. She knew that a lady of station was taught to ride as soon as she was taught to walk, but such things had been deemed "inappropriate" by the tight-kneed headmistress at Sacre Coeur. Therefore, Aloise had never been given the opportunity to learn the intricacies of the equestrian arts. This was one test she was destined to fail.

However, she feared that Slater would not have paused for such an explanation anyhow. Swinging on his own mount, he took her reins and his in a masterful grip, and urged both animals into action.

Nearly jarred free from her perch, Aloise gripped the pommel and clènched her teeth, praying that she would not die in her attempts to prove her better birth. But once out of the clearing surrounding the house, Slater slowed the animals and turned.

Attempting to right herself, Aloise damned the trembling of her body and looked about her, hoping to find some sort of landmark to help her gain her bearings. By insisting on this outing, her host had presented her with the perfect opportunity to escape. She was away from his house and his guards. If only she could find a way to dodge his clutches. She may not be a practiced horsewoman, but she thought she could maintain her seat long enough to ride a few miles and give herself a bit of a head start.

Slater who had been watching the road below, glanced behind him, then grinned.

"You look as if you've seen a spirit, mistress."

"Judging by the precipitous nature of our ride, one could say the same about you."

"Merely avoiding unwanted guests."

He studied the avenue below again, and Aloise had the briefest glimpse of a pair of coaches barreling toward Ashenleigh before he clucked to his stallion and urged the horses deeper into the trees.

"I am capable of handling my own reins, thank you."

"I doubt it." He looked at her then with obvious amusement. "One would assume by your stance that you have not had much acquaintance with the back of a mare. An interesting fact since a lady of breeding is usually taught to ride at an early age."

She tilted her chin in upmost dignity, but it did not have the desired effect of wiping the humor from his eyes. Especially when Aloise made the mistake of trying to reposition her hat. The horse, startled by the shift in balance, sidestepped. Gasping, Aloise scrambled to readjust her precarious position, lunged too far, and tumbled to the ground.

A low rumbling chuckle caused her to look up from her less than dignified position. "You did that on purpose!"

He held his hands out in a gesture of innocence. "I had nothing to do with your mishap, I assure you."

She glared at him, wondering what he would do if she scrambled to her feet and ran into the trees.

Probably follow her with his horse and snatch her up midstride, she realized in disgust. But there had to be a way to rid herself of this man. She was out of his house—nearly free! She couldn't let such an opportunity pass.

Untangling herself from her hems, she struggled somewhat ignominiously to stand.

"Are you hurt?"

Slater's show of concern caused Aloise to pause, then brighten. Of course. Of course! If she feigned an injury, he would have to dismount and she could surely frighten his own horse away.

Staggering slightly, she braced herself against a tree. Gasping, she muttered between clenched teeth, "I do believe I've twisted an ankle."

Slater frowned, apparently not quite believing her show of vulnerability. Nevertheless, he swung to the ground, leaving the reins of both horses to trail unfettered upon the ground. She need only grasp her own reins and shoo the other horse away. "Let me see what you've done. Hold still."

She did as she was told, waiting as carefully as a swallow while he knelt and grasped her hems.

"Here, take these."

She barely had the wherewithal to take the gloves he offered her. At the moment, her mind had been diverted by those hands, strong, fine-boned, naked hands, as they lifted her skirts free and tenderly stroked her calf, her shin, her ankle.

Sweet stars above! Who would have thought such a

rash of tingling could undermine a person's soul at such a simple touch? Never had she dreamed that the caress of a man's fingers could leave her dazed and unable to think.

"I don't believe you've wrenched it too badly. Perhaps just a slight pull of the muscle."

He rose then and her skirts settled back into place, but Aloise could not calm her heart so easily. It had taken upon itself an odd sort of rhythm, a quickened beat. She needed to move now. She needed to frighten his horse.

"Aloise?"

"Yes?" She could barely form the word. He stood so near to her. So big. So dark.

"You look pale."

"I do?"

He rested one of his hands on the rough bark of the tree behind her.

"Yet, a little flushed as well."

"Oh." The sound slipped from her lips, half wonder, half plea. The foliage around her melted away, leaving the soft splendor of shadows and might-have-beens. She tried to straighten, tried to summon a bit of independence. "I told you once. I don't like to be touched."

He merely grinned. "Liar." His knuckle skimmed the curve of her lower lip. "You are a woman of untapped passion. Touching will become merely the least of your pleasures."

A rash of gooseflesh followed his words and Aloise sternly reminded herself that she could not allow him to spin her a pretty cage. She didn't belong here. She needed to go, but she couldn't prevent a twinge of regret. Mayhap if she had met this man in another time, another place, she would have been tempted to stay. Mayhap, she would have employed all of her fledgling charms to garner his attention. To have danced in his arms. Kissed.

But they *had* kissed. Once.

Her eyes settled on the firm curves of his lips. Lips that she had so briefly tasted.

She tried to shake herself free from the rush of wildness that spilled into her veins. The fall she'd taken must not have been as harmless as she had first supposed. Aloise felt quite certain that she had momentarily taken leave of her senses. She should be rushing toward the horses, she should be felling this man with her knee. Instead, she stood still, breathless, as Slater looked at her, his eyes becoming dark and slumberous.

His head dipped. His lips brushed against hers. Warmly, insistently, they tasted her, molded her. His arms moved around her back, pulling her tightly to him. She moaned low in her throat, needing his warmth.

Dear heaven, was this what passion felt like? The mouth that moved against hers knew its purpose, its goal. The tongue that swept into her mouth knew how to pleasure her and cause her to tremble.

When he drew back, Aloise visibly shook. She gripped at his coat for balance, sure that if she released him, she would sink to the ground.

"Tell me, Aloise, how many times have you been kissed?"

Her chin adopted a proud angle. "Hundreds of times. Thousands."

"Aloise . . ." he warned.

She remained stubbornly silent.

Slater tucked a finger beneath her chin. "Tell me." His voice was low, insistent.

She tried to avoid his gaze, tried to prevent the sinking sensation in the pit of her stomach. Tried and failed. "Obviously not often enough to become very good at it."

Her answer surprised him. Pleased him. A warm smile teased his features and he pressed his mouth to her forehead, her cheek, her jaw.

"Ah, my dear, Aloise. You *are* very good at it. Very good indeed."

"Then why have you stopped?"

The moment the words slipped free, Aloise could have withered and died of embarrassment. How telling. How infantile. How wanton.

Slater merely smiled. "Because, my dear, that kiss is merely a prelude of things to come."

Slater saw the quick frown chase across her features and he knew that his comment had startled her. Tamping down a smile, he took her hand and drew her irretrievably toward her horse, lifting her on the saddle. After her fall, she clung even more tightly to the pommel, casting regretful glances at his own mount. Just as he'd suspected, she hadn't limped, hadn't suffered so much as a twinge of pain. Therefore, she must have been intent on escape. Little had she known that each thought she'd made had been written on her face as plain as day.

It was time to see if he could read her musings so easily in other matters.

Taking the reins to both horses, he retraced the path they had taken earlier, then turned south along the sea bluff until he saw the cottage where he'd been born. Hesitating, he endured the pangs of regret, of nostalgia, the overwhelming waves of bitterness and guilt.

Feeling Aloise's gaze, he quickly schooled his features and urged the horses on. "We'll rest here for a minute."

She eyed him curiously since they had only just resumed their ride, but he paid her little mind. He was intent upon the house and all of the changes that had occurred during his absence.

Part of the roof had collapsed in a none-too-distant storm. The walkway was thick with weeds and moss, but the surrounding foliage was dark and thick and lush with wild roses.

Directing the animals to the rear of the building, he dismounted then helped Aloise to do likewise.

"Where are we?"

Her voice was soft. Tremulous.

"This was once the cottage of a pair of schoolmasters. Elias Waterton. And his son."

Her features grew pale, ghastly pale, and Slater nearly regretted his impulse to bring her here. But he had no time to change the course of events. Aloise shook free of his grasp and walked toward the dilapidated building.

Slater watched her carefully, looking for the most subtle sign of guile, but she seemed truly confused by what she saw—as if the place were familiar to her, but not quite remembered. Her hands lifted to press against her temples and she made a soft *moue* of distress, but she did not pause. Rather, she bent and stepped beneath the shattered beams into what had once been the keeping room.

When Slater followed, he discovered that the cottage had served as shelter for the things of the forest during his absence. Birds' nests were wedged beneath the rafters and a score of faded tracks testified that it had been inhabited by the local wildlife. The furnishings had long since been taken, leaving only the tamped floor and the damaged walls.

"Where are we?" Aloise's query was barely audible. She whirled to face him, her eyes wide and haunted. "Where have you brought me?"

Forcing himself to ignore the quavering tone, Slater demanded, "Do you know this place?"

"No."

Her eyes said she lied.

"Do you?" he demanded again.

"No, I . . . I don't . . . think so."

He clasped her shoulders and she winced at his close proximity to her wound. But he had to know. He had to know if she remembered this place. Him. She had visited this house as a child. She'd sat on this very floor poring through his father's books. She'd climbed on Slater's knee, demanding he teach her the rudiments of reading. She'd been a child, but she should remember him. She should *remember* him.

Her eyes squeezed shut and her body shook. "I feel . . . so . . . so . . ."

"What, Aloise? What do you feel?"

"Sick." The response was barely given when she dodged away from him and stumbled to the door. The heavy planks, swollen by years of bad weather, refused to budge. Fully conscious now, she gazed desperately about her, finally focused upon the missing wall where she'd entered and ran for the bushes. She'd hunched over an untidy mound of privet that had once served as a border, her empty stomach managing little more than dry heaves.

Slater felt an immediate rush of shame. *He* had done this to her. He had vowed to help her, to protect her, and yet, in forcing her to remember the past, he had caused her even more pain.

Moving outside, he supported her by the shoulders until the retching noises ceased. Then, swinging her in his arms, he lifted her on his own horse, tied the reins of her mount to his saddle, and settled behind her.

"Where are you taking me?" she asked as he urged the stallion into a brisk walk.

Touching the clamminess of her brow he murmured, "Home. We are going home, Aloise."

"Who . . . are you?" she demanded weakly. "Why are you doing this to me?"

He didn't answer. He couldn't.

"Those jewels are mine, despite the fact that I have failed your tests today."

She still believed he meant to judge her actions, he realized. So he hadn't given himself away as much as he would have thought. But in allowing her a glimpse of his past, he would now have to continue the charade of believing her a thief. He would have to continue with those contests of ladylike virtues so that she did not guess his true intent had been to make her remember.

When he did not speak, she clutched his sleeve. "I *am* a lady."

"Tomorrow, you may try again to prove such a thing."

Slater kept the pace of their horses at a brisk walk knowing by the quick glances Aloise cast into the trees that—despite her condition—she was still intent upon finding some way to dodge him.

The woman was incredible. Her will was extraordinary. Her beauty indescribable. The yellow suit only added to her loveliness, her fragility. Like a jewel encased in a gold setting, she had taken on an added luster.

Had she known the original purpose of their outing, she might not have been so free with her emotions. Their impromptu ride had been spurred on by Curry's report that Oliver Crawford's men had tired of following the decoy coach Slater had sent to intercept Aloise's father. After questioning some of the nearby villagers, they had reported to Crawford that the conveyance belonged to Slater McKendrick, his new neighbor. Riding pell-mell to Cornwall, he had come to demand a reckoning.

Knowing that it was far too soon for Aloise to see her father or vice versa, Slater had led her into the woods, leaving Curry to reassure the man that no one had seen his daughter or really cared what might have happened to her. He had been told to punctuate such views with the story that the coach Crawford had been following had been stolen from Ashenleigh's mews by a randy hostler and a disgruntled maid.

Slater could only hope the man would believe such lies. After he'd so foolishly tried to jog her memory, Aloise needed to be returned to the comfort of a fire and a warm bed. Although Slater looked forward to the day when he would confront his nemesis, the time had not yet come. Slater still had to delve into Aloise's consciousness and see how much of the past he could force her to recall—but gently, this time. Gently. He might wish to shield her from such unpleasantness, but Aloise was the only other witness who could insist that the truth surrounding Jeanne's death be told.

Topping the rise, Slater noted the "all's clear" signal of a satin wrapper thrown over one of the rear terrace railings. A gathering storm had caused an early darkness to settle, bringing with it a definite nip to the air. Neither of them had been prepared for the brisk sea breeze, and glancing back at his charge, Slater could see that her nose had pinkened and her arms wound about her body to fend off the cold.

"Only a little farther, Aloise."

She nodded to show she had heard, but did not look up. Slater felt a twinge of guilt, but he quickly reassured himself that this had been the only way to keep her safely away from Crawford. He would see to it she was offered a warm meal, a hot bath, a spot of rum, and then she would be as right as rain.

As they neared the manor, one of the hostlers bounded toward them to take care of the horses. Slater swung to the ground. When he moved to help her dismount, she acquiesced in a very uncharacteristic manner, stumbling slightly against him. It was then that he realized her skin was like ice.

Damn. He'd forgotten that he was much more accustomed to the out-of-doors than this woman could ever be.

Swinging her into his arms, he carried her across the yard and up the front steps. Miss Nibbs, seeing him from the side window, quickly opened the door.

"Send a hot bath to the Rose Room."

"She bathed this morning."

"Do it," he snapped, then regretted his impatience since it reminded him of another night, another woman. "Please, Miss Nibbs."

The old lady grumbled at the waste of water, but after a quick glance of concern, obeyed of her own free will. Taking Aloise into the drawing room, Slater set her on one of the settees, then poured a measure of rum and returned to her side. She had risen to her feet and stood staring uncertainly at her surroundings.

"Here, drink this." He nudged the glass in her direction.

Lifting the libation, she sniffed at it suspiciously. "What is it?"

"Rum."

Her nose wrinkled. "I despise rum."

"Drink it, you look as if you could use a little bracing."

She considered the idea, then nodded. The pungent liquor was nearly to her lips when she inquired, "I don't suppose you've anything else available. Wine? Champagne?" When he shook his head, she asked hopefully, "Chocolate? I do so love a good cup—sweet, thick, velvety smooth. Rich."

"No. I'm afraid you caught me unprepared. My cellars have not yet been fully stocked."

She sighed in genuine regret. "What a pity."

"It's a good brew, I assure you. Drink."

"Very well." Gingerly resting the rim to her mouth, she took a tiny sip. Shuddered.

"All of it."

"Oh, really, I think I've had quite enough."

"If you don't drink it to the dregs, I'll wait until you've been rendered unconscious from a chill, then pour it down your throat."

His tone had been perfectly civil, but she glared at him anyway. However, his threat brought about the proper result since she did as she was told, then shivered again. Wrapping his arms around her shoulders, Slater drew her close to his chest, trying to ignore the way his body had begun to respond in an altogether unsuitable way. But the flushed quality of her skin and the sheen of her hair brought a swirl of emotions: confusion, longing, nostalgia.

"What, sir, do you intend to do with me now?"

When she moved to rest her head on his shoulder, gripping his shirt for balance, her legs shifted suspiciously. Slater immediately swerved away.

Taken by surprise at the abrupt movement, she touched her brow. "What in the world—"

"Merely protecting myself, *cherie.* You've a nasty aim with that knee of yours."

"Hmm. Practice." Her odd retort caused her to burst into a peal of giggles. Just as suddenly, she became perfectly serious. "Have you any more rum?"

The woman was already well on her way to being truly snockered. The rum must have hit her empty stomach and gone straight to her head. Or she was playacting? Even after the shocks of the afternoon, Slater wouldn't put anything past her.

He reconsidered having given her another draft, but since he needed her biddable and tame, another drink might not prove to be such a bad idea.

"Come. Sit over here by the fire first."

Slater helped her to sink into one of the settees. When he would have backed away, she clung to him ever so slightly. Not as a simpering female would, or in a coy bid for attention, but as if she truly feared what might happen to her should he go.

"You won't leave me?"

The query was nakedly forlorn, without pretense, without guile.

"No."

"No one else has ever stayed. Not for good."

Her comment caused him to hesitate, but when he would have said something, she let go of his support and reclined against the back of the couch, tucking her fists beneath her ear and drawing her knees up to her stomach.

She appeared so small in that position. So small and fragile and weak. Slater could break her with one unkind word, one unguarded glance. Oddly enough, he found that was the last thing he wanted to do.

She looked so much like Jeanne.

But this was Aloise. Her daughter.

His onetime betrothed.

"What about the rum? Have you more?"

"Yes."

"I should like some, please—if it's not too much trouble."

He hunkered beside the chair. Unable to resist, he touched her, crooking his finger and skimming a knuckle across the curve of her cheek. "Mayhap you should have something to eat first."

She nudged against him. "I'm not 'tall hungry." Her tongue swiped at her lips, darting in and out so suddenly that Slater experienced a sudden and most inappropriate sensual pang. To deny the fierce sensual attraction he felt, he must deny the air he breathed. She aroused a part of him he'd thought had been destroyed. A tiny corner of his soul that had once believed in chivalry.

"Rum. I should like . . . sommme rummm."

Ever vigilant to a possible escape, Slater splashed a small measure in her glass, and returned. "Come. Here are your spirits."

He helped her to clutch the vessel. In doing so her breast rubbed against him. Valiantly, he tried to deny that forbidden pressure and the answering fire being stoked in his belly.

Humming a ditty to herself—something that sounded distinctly like a bawdy limerick he had once heard—she drained the contents, then smacked her lips.

"It's still quite awful, you know. Quite, *quite,* awful. But I do believe I'm beginning to develop a taste for it." She smiled at him, a silly drunken smile.

"Tell me, do you like rum?" The phrase held all the satin-bound overtures of a proposition.

"Nearly as much as brandy."

"Per . . . sonally. I like chocolate." Her fingertips walked up his chest, lingering ever so slightly in the crisp hair to be found there.

"I believe you mentioned that fact."

"I have never been to one of those chocolate houses. But I should think they are wonderful places." That dainty hand curled around his neck, delving into the waves of his hair. "According to Alexander Pope, chocolate is the elixir of the gods . . . or some such idea in the same vein. I am inclined to agree."

She pulled, irresistibly, irretrievably, until his mouth hovered above hers. Wary, but intrigued, Slater allowed Aloise to have her way. In doing so, he pinned her skirts to the chair so that she could not try to fell him again with her knee. However, that appeared to be the last thought from her mind.

"Tell me, how do you like your chocolate?"

"Bitter and black."

"I thought as much."

Her lips closed over his and there was a tentativeness to the caress, a tasting. Her lashes flickered shut and she appeared to savor the newness of their embrace.

Slater grew still in surprise. Dear sweet heaven, she never ceased to amaze him. He'd always been able to peg his women in the past, to decipher their motives and even manipulate their moods. But this woman left him guessing. Shy and vulnerable one minute, feisty and ill mannered the next, she was a riddle to a man accustomed to keeping his own emotions well hidden.

His arms slid around her back, measuring the slight build of her torso and the tiny circumference of her waist. Bending lower, he opened his mouth and pressed his tongue to her lips, bidding her to open to him. She balked at first, then reluctantly obeyed.

She was sweet. Too sweet. Her mouth was a honeyed cavern. Her teeth small and even.

Despite her boldness, Slater sensed that the act of mingling tongue with tongue was new to her, so he taught her slowly. Advancing, retreating. A quick study, she soon followed suit. Within minutes, he moaned deep in his throat, holding her so fiercely, their hearts could have been one.

When he backed away, she took a calming breath. "Just as I said. I like it sweet, thick, velvety smooth. Rich."

He chuckled, pleased by her inadvertent audacity. The ladies he'd entertained over the years had either been ready for a tumble or as frozen as ice. This woman courted a disturbing mix of innocence and feminine wiles.

"'Tis only the first course."

"Mmm." She murmured another word that sounded distinctly like "rum" then stroked his forearm with her knuckles, up and down. Up and down.

"Mistress?"

She strayed to his ribs, explored each indentation with the curious wonder of a stranger allowed to explore an unfamiliar realm.

When she would have delved lower than was proper, he caught her shoulders. Before he could say a word, her lashes flickered and she stared at him beneath lazy lashes. "You think I'm a child, but I know what to do with men," she murmured, her speech slightly slurred. "You see, I've been a student for many years . . . many . . . many . . . years." She smiled in a way that was infinitely beguiling. "He thought he could stop me. He thought he could . . . lock me up . . . in that house. But I learned all I needed to know from books."

Swinging her legs to the floor, she stood, wrapping her arms around his hips and drawing him closer, closer.

"Not merely the novels . . . you un'nerstand, but art books . . . sculpture . . . plays. Then . . . on nights as black as Croesus . . . I peeked through the keyhole . . . watching the guards . . . with their women . . ."

He felt a rush of horror at her words. What had happened to her all these years? Where had Crawford kept her? What had she endured?

She gripped the taut muscles of his buttocks. Disturbed by her drunken bravado, Slater tried to prevent her advances. "Aloise, I don't think—"

"Then neither will I," she whispered, releasing him, but only for a moment. She grasped the lapels of his waistcoat and drew him down for a hungry kiss. Passion warred side by side with youthful exuberance.

Slater felt himself responding wholeheartedly. He could not have stopped the increased tightening of his body had the room been set on fire. But Slater was not so far gone that he did not taste the hint of desperation in her caress. The fear.

When she drew back, her eyes glittered with a forbidden mixture of emotions. Restlessness. Passion. Distress. With her hat coming loose from its pinnings and her coiffure dissolving into loose silken tendrils, she appeared both the temptress and the abandoned waif.

Why had he ever thought that her father could mold her into something she was never meant to be? This girl could no more adopt his cruelty and indifference than fly. She was a thing of light and nature, free, loving, passionate. Rather than dampening her spirit, the trials she must have suffered beneath Crawford's care had merely intensified her willingness to give. To love.

He cupped her cheeks between his palms, staring deep into her eyes. Eyes as dark and eloquent as a forest glade. Eyes that could never hide their true feelings. Eyes so like Jeanne's—yet different, younger, filled with hope.

"Please, Slater . . . let me go free."

The words tumbled from her lips, husky with the emotions she fought to conceal.

His thumb rubbed against the curve of her lower lip. A wave of possessiveness inundated him. This woman was his. *His.* They had once been bound together by contract and tradition. Crawford might have destroyed the papers, but Aloise was Slater's to claim. To keep.

She must have thought by his silence that he considered her plea, because grasping his wrists, she uttered again, "Please."

"You long for peace."

"Yes."

"In the world beyond these walls."

"Yes!"

"There is no peace to be found there. Merely a life of hardships: hunger, poverty."

"I . . . *will* be free."

"To what end?"

She fought to consider his question despite her inebriation, her eyes filling with a buried pain. "I don't . . . know."

"I could change all that for you, Aloise."

Her brow creased in confusion.

"You're correct in assuming that life can be filled with adventure. But there's no adventure to be found in scrambling hand to mouth for survival."

"If you give me my things . . . I can . . . sell the necklace. It . . . will offer me a means to live."

"For how long? A month? A year? Then what will you do?"

She held a hand to her forehead as if his questions proved too difficult.

"I'm strong . . . I'll make . . . my way."

"What if I were willing to extend other alternatives your way?"

She regarded him suspiciously and Slater knew he would have to tread with great care. "Why should I consider any offers . . . you might make. You think . . . I'm a thief."

"Maybe I'm beginning to believe in your protestations of virtue." When she didn't speak, he added, "I know what it's like to be without a home, Aloise. I know what it's like to need the comfort of friends."

Her eyes grew bright and he pressed his advantage. "If you would be so inclined, I believe I could find a place for you in my household."

A place as his wife. He didn't utter the words aloud, but deep in his soul he knew he was making the right decision.

She shook her head, then clearly regretted the action. "No."

"Why not? You must admit to the comforts found at Ashenleigh."

"Miss Nibbs would object . . . to the arrangement."

"She has no say in such matters."

"I have . . . plans of my own."

"Plans which could be delayed."

"But—"

"Stay, Aloise." He stepped closer, leaning down so that his breath caressed her cheeks, her lips. "Stay here for a while. Of your own free will."

She trembled ever so slightly, but he felt the betraying movement.

Her eyes squeezed closed. "You have a way of seducing a person's thoughts to match your own."

The whisper was filled with untold regret, a drunken melancholy. But, she was relenting; he knew she was. Leaning closer, closer, so that his lips nearly brushed her own, he urged, "Come, love, let' me seduce you. Then you will never want to go."

10

THE GIRL'S BATH IS READY."

Miss Nibbs' gruff comment shattered the intimacy of the moment.

Slater took a step back and Aloise took a quick breath of relief. The rum had definitely affected her senses. Otherwise, she would not find herself thinking that there was something about this man. Something familiar. Something intense and worldly, that put her instantly on her guard. As if he had the power to steal her soul away.

"Go upstairs with Miss Nibbs, Aloise. Warm yourself in front of the fire, bathe your chilled bones in heated water, then, come supper, I will have my answer."

With that, he turned on his heel and strode from the room, leaving her standing in confusion and amazement.

Miss Nibbs eyed her closely. "I can only speculate as to the question he's asked which requires a response." Toddling forward, she held Aloise's chin, staring deep into her eyes. "Do not hurt him. He has been hurt enough."

With that cryptic comment, she took Aloise's arm and helped her upstairs.

Once in her room, with the lock latched quite noisily behind her, Aloise stumbled to the fire, then sank on the rose-patterned rug. She really didn't feel well—whether it was due to the liquor or the day's events, she didn't know. Even so, she had developed an odd truce of sorts with her host. But to stay here, to become a member of his staff?

Her shoulders stiffened. No. Her mind might swirl from the drink, but she had her head about her enough to know that wasn't at all what she wanted. She had things to do. Plans of her own to follow. She didn't want to become his housemaid, dusting and washing and cleaning for the rest of her days. And yet . . .

Lifting her eyes, she surveyed the black walls, the ceiling painted like a spring sky studded with laughing cherubs. After living in such a place, it would prove difficult to move on. It might even prove difficult to leave . . . him.

"Well, sir? What do you wish to do now? According to McKendrick's assistant, Aloise has not been seen. Even our men have told us that the woman in the phaeton we saw was not she."

Crawford barely acknowledged his secretary's murmured comment.

"McKendrick has my daughter. Somewhere. Somehow."

"But, sir—"

"She is nearby. I know it. I feel it."

"But why would those men lie to us? We've never had any dealings with them before."

Crawford took a moment before speaking, not about to reveal to his own man that he sensed some devious intent beneath his daughter's disappearance. Since it came so close to his own attempts to see her married, once and for all, he was beginning to wonder if McKendrick had heard rumors of Crawford's plans. Crawford had tried to keep the actual auctioning process silent, but it was commonly known that he was looking for a mate for his daughter. Did this man, this upstart, intend to force Crawford to acknowledge him as a possible candidate by abducting the girl and arranging a scandal?

Impossible. For all Crawford knew of the stranger, he had no title, no connections of worth. He was an entirely inappropriate candidate.

But that would not discourage a man intent on claiming the rubies.

Turning from the window of his coach Crawford pierced his secretary with a steely gaze. "I want you to investigate this . . . McKendrick. I need to know everything about him: his family, his lineage, the source of his money."

"Yes, sir."

"Then I want you to post a guard on the ridge overlooking his estates. At the first sign of my daughter, I want the man to report directly to me."

Mr. Humphreys nodded. "Very well."

"Oh, and Humphreys—" Crawford called in a silky voice to the bewigged gentleman leaving the room. "*This time* . . . do not fail me."

The old man blanched at the none-too-subtle threat. "Yes, sir. As you say, sir."

The door closed and Crawford stared out into the encroaching light. "I will find you, Daughter," he whispered to the shadows, to himself. "Make no mistake of that."

"I'm pleased that you found at least a measure of the peace you seek within the confines of my home."

Aloise jerked, drawing her knees to her chest and flattening her hands over her breasts at the sultry remark. Blinking, she focused on the man who had entered the room and drawn a chair next to the tub, all without the slightest sound to alert her of his presence.

Slater's lips lifted in amusement at her instinctive

reaction. "I didn't mean to startle you. Miss Nibbs said she'd left you here over an hour earlier. When we heard no sounds issuing from the chamber, I believe she feared some sort of accident."

Aloise tugged at the linens draped over the side of the tub and shielded herself with them, doubting very much that Miss Nibbs had taken even a moment to worry about her health. The soaked fabric offered only a modicum of modesty.

Stretching his legs out, Slater sprawled in his chair, content to stay for the duration. Obviously, he felt little compunction about interrupting so private a moment. In fact, he seemed inordinately pleased.

"I believe the rum has left your system. You appear a little more clearheaded."

Her lips tightened in annoyance. "Did it ever occur to you that you should knock on entering a woman's room?"

"I did knock." He abandoned his negligent pose and Aloise heaved a silent sigh of relief when he appeared ready to leave. But to her consternation, he propped his elbows on his knees, continuing to study her with his black eyes. "You did not answer."

"You should have sent Miss Nibbs to investigate."

"Miss Nibbs was needed elsewhere."

When Aloise didn't speak, a tense expectancy filtered into the room. The air became hushed and still.

"You've kept your bandage dry. How very wise. Now we won't have to see to it again tonight."

She remained mulishly silent.

"Did you enjoy your bath?"

The direct question demanded a direct answer. "Yes. Thank you."

"I'm pleased."

"Why?"

"I wouldn't want it said that I was a less than proper host."

Aloise regarded him in amazement. Less than proper? The man had crept into her *boudoir* and now watched her bathe! What did he consider to be *im*proper?

The mere thought of such possibilities caused her to shiver. There was an infinitely overpowering quality about this man. Indeed, she would go so far as to say innately erotic. He was the sort Sacre Coeur had warned its charges to avoid. The sort mothers feared their daughters would encounter, and fathers sent away at sword point.

All of which only deepened his unconscious appeal.

"Are you cold?"

He dipped his little finger into the water next to her thigh.

She jumped.

He only smiled. That predatory, pantherish smile.

"Mayhap, you should consider abandoning your ablutions. You might catch a chill." He looked up, following the wet linen draped to her stomach, her ribs, and stopped on the fullness of her breasts. The nipples had hardened into tight buds—not only from the cold, but from his regard. She could only pray that the arm she'd crossed over her chest hid such a sight from his view.

He drew an idle circle in the water, then touched the outside of her ankle. Aloise forgot the tepid temperature as he trailed a scorching path to her knee, then hesitated there.

She didn't have time to draw breath to berate his familiarity. He stood, holding out the bath sheet that had been warming by the fire. When Aloise made no effort to rise he added, "Come, my dear. Your skin is closely approximating the texture of a prune. Unless you tend to court pneumonia, I suggest you abandon your bath."

"Leave the sheet and go."

"If you insist." He draped the towel over the chair. "There's a robe in the armoire behind you as well as a night rail, feel free to use them."

She did not thank him—though the words jammed

behind her teeth so drilled was she in the proper social niceties. She refused to thank a man for abducting her, imprisoning her in his home, tormenting her body and soul, then walking unannounced into her chamber while she was in a state of undress.

He must have sensed her quandary because his black eyes took upon themselves that warm glow she was beginning to associate with his wicked sense of humor. One which came unfailingly at her expense. "I will leave you to rise at your leisure."

His boots made no sound across the thick carpet as he withdrew. The man was incredibly quiet, in word, in movement, and in deed. But she was beginning to realize that the silences masked a deeper layer of energy.

Aloise waited what she felt was a reasonable amount of time for him to leave the room, then stood from the tub, quickly drying herself and reaching into the armoire for the items Slater had offered.

"Oh."

The telling sound escaped before she had a chance to retrieve it. She trembled as she touched the garments suspended on silver hooks. After the gown she'd been given this morning, a keen feminine hunger filled her breast. Pride dictated that she should stay wrapped in the sheet and refuse any further aid, but she could not resist the temptation to try on the pieces. Just try them on.

Taking the night rail from its mooring, she sighed at the cool caress of raw silk. The ivory fabric was so fragile, so translucent, that when she drew it over her head, it spilled over her shoulders and down her body like a fairy's mantle, clinging seductively to the damp spots she had failed to dry completely.

There was no mirror in this corner of her chamber, but she could imagine how it looked, and even in her mind the shift was exquisite. Aloise fingered the net lace at the cuffs and the hairpin insertion placed at intervals on the front yoke. She had never owned anything half so bewitching. Her father did not believe his daughter should court vanity by wearing rich clothing unless such trappings were used to lure a wealthy husband.

She grew still, staring into the dark interior of the armoire in indecision. On the far side, she saw that sets of masculine attire had also been hung on the hooks. His. Because of their length and the breadth of the shoulders, she was sure the things belonged to him.

Dear heaven, had she stumbled into some house of decadent entertainment? Was this the room of his fancy-piece? Was *that* the position he meant for her to assume?

Aloise felt the blood rush from her face. What had she done? What manner of man had she allowed to assume control over her life?

She quickly sought out the buttons of the night rail, trembling with indignation and a subtler panic. She should take the garment off. If Slater were to see her dressed thus, he would take such overtures as encouragement—something to be avoided at all costs.

But then . . . she hesitated, struck by an even more horrible thought. The situation might prove far worse should he return to find her dressed in nothing but a towel.

Reaching for the accompanying cover-up, she saw at a glance that the *robe de chambre* followed the latest fashion with a square-necked bodice, tight sleeves, and flowing skirt. Slipping it over her shoulders, she fastened the hooks at the front, and stepped from behind the screen.

"Very pretty."

Aloise stopped in midstride, staring at the man who had not left as she had supposed, but sat ensconced on the bed, resting his back against the gleaming headboard.

A shimmy of alarm raced down to her toes. The man meant to bend her to his will. He meant to ravish her, here and now, in this black room, on that elegant bed.

Slater made a *tsk*ing sound in his throat. "You think far too much, my dear."

"I don't know what you mean." The words were barely audible.

He slid from the bed and closed the distance between them. Once again, she was struck by the silence of his passage. There was a predatory ease to the way the muscles of his thighs moved beneath the wool of his breeches.

"I frighten you."

He'd already made that comment, but this time she denied such an emotion. "No."

"Then what I make you *feel* frightens you."

When she opened her mouth to refute such a telling statement, he dammed her words with a single finger pressed against her lips. "Never fear, I have no immediate designs on your body—delectable as it may be." He skimmed her with a glance from head to toe, making her overtly conscious of her borrowed finery. "I simply wanted to ensure that you had all you needed for the night. That's why I waited on the bed."

She jerked free, taking a step away—not from fear, she reassured herself. No, she did not fear him, no matter what he said. Nor did she fear any emotions he might inspire. She was simply not a fool. To entertain such liberties as he proposed, she would be considered very foolish. To entertain the prospect of his veiled proposition, she would have to be well on her way to madness.

"There are chairs you could have sat on. There was no need to plant yourself on my bed."

His eyes narrowed at her bitter tone. "So the little lost kitten has unsheathed her claws, hmm?"

When she would have spun away from him, he grasped her elbow, forcing her to collide with him, chest to chest, hip to hip. He snared her chin, studying her face with an enigmatic expression, one that held a touch of wonder and a trace of anger. Then, just as quickly, his features were shuttered from all evident emotion.

"Had I chosen any one of the chairs, I still would have been able to see behind the screen. Something which I'm sure would have wounded your sensibilities," he added.

He tugged her to the fireplace where a table and two chairs had been placed in the buttery glow. A tray laden with tea, tiny sandwiches, and an assortment of shortbreads awaited her. When she made no move to sit, he circled behind her, curling his hands over her shoulders.

Aloise trembled, wondering if a draft had somehow permeated the room. The heat of his skin seeped through the weave of her clothing, causing her to center on that one point of contact. She sensed the strength of his frame behind her, radiating an energy like none she'd ever encountered. One her own body craved to absorb.

Despite all this man had done to her, she had the strangest urge to lean back until each plane and angle of his body was pressed against her own. Just as they'd been earlier, downstairs. Where he'd offered a position in his household.

Jerking away from his grasp, she sat in her chair with excessive force, glaring at the man who had tried to scold *her* for not living up to the station of her birth.

Slater seemed far from affected by her mood. "I know you haven't eaten much this day."

"Thanks to you."

He ignored that remark. "Therefore, I ordered your teatime meal to be brought up here so that you could eat at your leisure. What with the gathering storm, it should be quite cozy here by the fire." He took the seat opposite and motioned for her to begin.

"You aren't having anything?"

"I will find something to . . . nibble on later. But I thank you for your concern. Please. Eat."

She hesitated and he said, "I will have a cup of tea if it will make you feel more comfortable. If you'll pour . . ."

So he had decided upon another of his tests, had he? This time, Aloise felt a swell of pride. If there was one thing Sacre Coeur taught its young ladies, it was how to entertain.

In a flourish of pomp and grace, she took a cup and saucer, balancing them without the slightest quiver of china. After filling the cup halfway she inquired, "Milk?"

"No."

"Lemon?"

"Thank you, no."

"Sugar?"

"One."

Deftly handling the delicate silver tongs, she selected one cube of sugar and dropped it into the fragrant brew then handed him his cup, her chin tilted in victory.

"So . . ." he drawled. "You are familiar with the art of pouring tea."

"Intimately."

"Then you must either be a lady . . ."

She grinned in triumph.

". . . or a well-trained servant."

When she opened her mouth to offer a scathing remark, he lifted a finger in warning, his eyes brimming in laughter. "As I recall, a true woman of breeding does not argue with the master of the house."

Her lips snapped shut in displeasure.

After a moment of warring wills—one which Aloise feared she would lose—Slater reached for one of the rounds of shortbread and broke off a piece. "You must pour yourself a cup and eat something as well, otherwise Hans will be most upset. He's Bavarian, you know, and quite known for his temper. I rescued him from beneath the sword point of an angry baron who thought he'd been cuckolded; but despite his weakness for married ladies, Hans has managed to learn to make tea like a true Brit. Come, my dear." His fingers grazed against her. "Try it once. You *will* enjoy it, I assure you."

Aloise opened her mouth, intent on some scathing remark and he took the opportunity to insert the morsel.

"Chew."

It was delicious, that fact she could not deny. She had not eaten in what felt like ages and the delicate nutty flavor tasted like manna from heaven.

He looked pleased by the way she suddenly dug into the fare, eating with the relish of a prisoner set down to dine with lords. As she consumed her meal, he settled comfortably into his chair. Resting his elbows on the armrests, he steepled his fingers and studied her over the tips.

For some time, there were no words between them. If not for the chink of cutlery and the snap of the fire, the room would have remained silent. But Aloise was far from unaware of her companion. He was forever analyzing her—and though he did not appear to dislike what he found, Aloise sensed a hidden resistance as well.

She had nearly finished all the shortbread and was sipping at the last bit of her tea when he surprised her by speaking again.

"You remember nothing at all?"

The words were low, dark, slightly dangerous.

She looked up at him in confusion. The shadows grew suddenly darker, the firelight less cheery.

"Your childhood," he prompted when she did not speak. "You told me once that you did not remember your childhood."

She had told him no such tale—only that she had no memories of her mother. Aloise carefully set her cup on its saucer, feeling an unaccountable shiver wriggle its way up her spine.

"What a pity," he drawled when she refused to

respond. "Everyone should have happier times to fall back on when adulthood rears its head. Don't you think?"

"Why are you so interested in my past?"

He shrugged. "Merely making idle conversation. Passing time."

Aloise would have labeled his manner far from idle, but when he did not speak again, she continued with her meal. Therefore, his next statement proved as startling as those which had come before.

"You're quite stunning, you know."

She paused in midswallow, taken unaware by his sudden remark. Wiping her hands on the napkin provided, she wondered if she would have to make a dash for the fire poker in order to defend herself.

He must have sensed her intent because he made a waving gesture. "As I said earlier, I have no designs on you, tonight, I assure you."

Tonight.

Tonight?

Setting her napkin on the table with great care, she rose to her feet, pushing her shoulders into a line of brittle dignity. "Then that makes us even, sir, since—being a lady of breeding—I would not wish to be touched by a scruffy-faced, ill-mannered, overbearing know-it-all like yourself."

Rather than infuriating him, her words only amused him further. "Of that you are certain?"

"More certain than the sun rising in the east each morn."

"Then I suppose we are in accord." Once again, his eyes gleamed in the light shed from the candles. "You are not at all what I expected."

Aloise had been about to march to the opposite end of the room, but subsided at his remark. "Expected?"

He didn't answer her right away, but regarded her over his hands, making her feel that he could strip each layer away and see to the very core of her soul.

"What do you mean 'expected'?"

His gaze intensified, nearly burning her with its power. She was struck by a wealth of meaning obscured behind his inscrutable expression and an intent she was powerless to interpret.

"Merely that when I encountered you on the beach, I hadn't thought so vibrant a woman could be hidden beneath the saltwater and grime."

Aloise felt there was much more he left unuttered, but when he did not continue, she realized he'd told her all he intended to say.

A sound of irritation pushed from her throat and she strode the full length of the room then realized how easily he could interpret her nervous actions, thereby knowing how much he'd disturbed her. Grasping the bath sheet, she returned to her chair as if her only intent had been to retrieve a towel to dry her hair.

Turning toward the rollicking flames, she tried to block Slater from her line of sight, busying herself with the still-damp tresses. But such peace was not to be so easily obtained.

"Tell me about yourself."

She refused to meet his perusal, refused to allow him to pull untold secrets from her soul in the uncanny way he had in the past. A dull throb began deep in her head. One which she had felt earlier. At the cottage. This man knew something. Something he wasn't telling her. But what? *What?*

"Why would you want to know anything about me?"

"If, as you say, you've nothing to hide, why wouldn't you want to tell me about yourself, about your education, your training, your family."

She looked at him then, wondering what he might think if she told him of a father who had never forgiven her for being a girl. Of a forgotten childhood. Of years in a stern private school. Of days filled with tedium and drudgery with only the occasional marriage attempt to break them up.

No. She couldn't tell him that. She wouldn't. It would reveal far too much about the nature of her upbringing. The loneliness she'd endured.

"Prove to me you're a lady," he taunted softly.

"Would you be willing to respond in kind?" The words popped, unbidden, from her mouth, but she didn't try to retract them. The thought proved too irresistible by far. Although she had determined that the other members of the household called him Slater, she had no tangible information about this mysterious man.

"I might supply you with a detail or two about my life, if you are as forthcoming with yours."

He grinned, "Very well. What would you like to know?"

"Your full name."

"As you have already deduced, my friends call me Slater. Slater McKendrick."

The towel nearly fell from her grasp. "The explorer?"

He nodded and Aloise felt an unwilling thrill of discovery. She knew of this fellow. She had devoured his treatise in the library at Sacre Coeur. His travels were legendary in France, his exploits renowned. Yet, from all indications, the man himself continued to be shrouded in mystery. It was said that he had surrounded himself with a host of men wanted for various crimes of passion and that only a blessed few in all Europe had actually met him. Aloise had somehow stumbled into their charmed circle.

She blinked at him in sheer delight.

"Is something wrong?"

"No, I—"

Slater rose and crossed to the vanity. Taking a silver-backed brush he returned, stepping behind her and drawing her hair over her shoulders. Slowly, softly, gently, he began to work the tangles free, moving from the tips, ever upward to her skull.

Her lashes flickered closed. The towel she held was forgotten as she surrendered to the heady sensations that stormed through her system. This man had traversed the earth. He had discovered strange beasts like Sonja and charted unknown lands. Now those same hands smoothed over her shoulders, drew across the damp tresses there, and caused an unknown heat to course through her veins. Such actions inspired an unaccountable excitement. So much so, she was almost willing to forget his altogether irritating personality.

When Aloise had plunged into the frothy sea, she longed for mystery and excitement. Who would have guessed that she would have found such things within seconds of being washed ashore?

Without thought of possible repercussions, she reached to touch him, to ensure that he was not a figment of her imagination. His ministrations stilled beneath her inquisitive caress and she was able to discern the ridges of his knuckles, the strength of his wrist.

"You have a habit of playing with fire, *chérie.*" The comment fairly melted from the shadows. The shadows she was beginning to associate with this man.

"Do I?"

Aloise knew she had been warned, that she should back away. But on that point of contact, she found that the heat she had discovered earlier that day began to drizzle through her. All without the benefit of rum.

Mindful of her wound, he lifted her out of the chair and turned her to face him. "Why?"

Aloise didn't know exactly what information he required. She only knew that he had taken her in his arms, holding her weight against his own. Then his head bent, and his lips closed over hers.

She barely had the presence of mind to clutch his shirt to maintain her balance. There was no real need for such a precaution. He kept her close. So close, their thighs laced and the fabric of her night clothes bunched between her legs.

He overpowered her. In thought, in deed, in intensity. His mouth moved to her cheek, her chin, roaming her face and neck and teaching her delights she had never imagined. Sucking, nipping, wooing. When he pulled aside the fabric of her gowns and exposed her shoulder, she could not refuse. Did not want to refuse. He kissed her there, and lower, skimming the curve of her breast. Passion raged through her extremities, forcing her to delve deep in her soul for control. She would not allow this man to rule her. She would not trade her father's reign for this man's.

"Slater?"

His head lifted. His expression grew still, masked.

"I won't become your mistress."

Despite the thundering of her pulse and the trembling of her limbs, she infused her voice and her stance with as much iron-willed determination as she could muster.

"You won't?"

"No."

His lips twitched and once again, she was struck by the fact that she had secretly amused him. "Then perhaps you should wait until such a thing has been asked of you. For you see, Aloise, I have no desire, none whatsoever, to see you ensconced in Ashenleigh as my paramour."

With that parting remark, he smiled enigmatically and backed away, stepping over the hairbrush which had dropped to the floor.

"Sweet dreams, Aloise." His voice was husky. Deep. "Feel free to sleep as late as you wish tomorrow morning. After all—whether you prove to be a lady or not—you *are* my guest. Once you are well rested, we will resume your tests."

The teasing reminder echoed in Aloise's brain as he left the room. She could not shake the feeling that something far more subtle than a battle of wills had occurred between them. Something warmer, richer.

Something that she did not entirely understand.

11

MADEMOISELLE?"

Aloise snuffled deeper into her pillow, sure that she had dreamed the gentle call. Miss Nibbs would not awaken her in such a manner. For the past five days, the old woman had summoned her from her bed each morning with a shrug of resignation and a snort of disapproval, then escorted her downstairs to yet another of Slater McKendrick's tests of gentility. So far, she had been asked to fence and sketch, play the piano, sing, and sew.

Unfortunately, she had not proven very adept in such matters. While fencing with Slater's men, she had managed to slice open one gentleman's chin and another's vest all before they'd even begun their match. Her sketches had proven to be barely recognizable smears of charcoal, her musical abilities painful to the ears, and her needlework a horror beyond belief. If not for the fact that she had been able to hold her own in other such tests—a game of backgammon, flower arranging, gardening, and correspondence—she feared that Slater would have long since branded her a commoner.

Therefore, the soothing voice summoning her to rise must be a dream.

"Mademoiselle?"

The bed dipped at her side and Aloise moaned a little. Then, the most astonishing thing alerted her senses. Chocolate. The sweet rich scent of chocolate.

"I 'ave brought you a treat, Meez Aloise. Zomething to soften zee coming of morning. It eez from my own private cache."

Aloise blinked, discovering the tiny French seamstress perched on her bed. She had only seen her twice since that first time, both occasions for fittings. Such events had been formal affairs, but this morning, Madame LeBeau had abandoned her wig in favor of styling her own tresses, and Aloise was struck by the youth of the woman, the exotic quality of her black hair and black eyes.

"*Bon!* You are awake."

Madame LeBeau handed her the delicate teacup. "Drink please. We 'ave work to do."

Aloise peered over the mounding duvets. "Work?"

Madame LeBeau opened the door to admit her army of assistants. Aloise was drawn from her nest of comforters, powdered, perfumed, and coiffed for the day. As the women swarmed about her like busy bees, Aloise found she could summon little more energy than that required to enjoy the experience of being pampered and savoring her chocolate.

"Very well. What do you think of zee gown?"

Madame LeBeau snapped her fingers and a pair of women held a full-length glass for Aloise's inspection. This time, she had been dressed in gray silk—a rather restrained style considering the elaborate costumes she'd been given for most of the week.

The fabric hung full and stiff from her panniers, ending a respectable three inches from the floor. Above, the bodice tightly hugged her torso, the square neckline artfully covered by a swathe of lace that wound about her neck, then had been inserted into the tabs of her stomacher and left to dangle below like a peasant's apron.

"I think zat gray eez very beautiful on you, Aloise."

At the tiny woman's strange comment, Aloise lifted a brow in silent inquiry.

"I 'ad many pretty zings for you to wear, but Slater asked zat you be put in zomething . . . plain."

"Plain?"

"Of course, I 'ad no such zing." Her chin tilted proudly. "I do not design . . . 'plain.' "

Aloise became quite still, eyeing herself in the mirror. She prayed it would not be considered vain for her to take a slight glimmer of hope at Madame LeBeau's words, to think that she might, just might, have affected the great Slater McKendrick so much that he now longed to dampen a portion of his emotions. Through each of her tests, he had kept a certain distance between them, but time and time again she'd found herself being watched in a very disturbing manner. She had been alarmed, then secretly pleased by the growing light of hunger kindling in his gaze.

"Do you know him well, Madame LeBeau?"

"Georgette, please. Madame LeBeau eez so formal, and I am not a formal woman."

Aloise smiled in genuine delight. "Very well. Georgette."

"I know him but a leetle. What woman could ever know such a man?" She offered a Gallic shrug. "My brother, Louis—"

"Louis?"

"—eez one of Slater's friends. Slater leeterally saved my foolish brother from zee gallows. Zat eez why, when Slater sent word to me in London saying he was in dire need of a seamstress, I told zee duchess zat I 'ad to go. I came to Ashenleigh zat very night—bringing a good portion of zee woman's clothing, I might add." She beamed. "But you are a far more beautiful setting for my creations zan zat old . . . how you say? . . . cow?"

Aloise couldn't prevent the chuckle that escaped

from her lips, but she quickly sobered. "Your brother was sent to the gallows?"

Georgette nodded. "You will find zat each of Slater's men 'as a story to tell. Louis was accused unlawfully of treason, Marco of bribery. Zee czarina damned Rudy for kidnapping a child, and Hans . . ."

"Has a penchant for married women."

"Exactement."

"What about Curry?"

Georgette leaned close, obviously delighted to share in the gossip. "Eet eez said zat he stabbed his brother in zee heat of passion."

"Did he?"

She frowned. "I think not. In zee years I 'ave 'eard Louie speak of zem all, I 'ave come to believe zat Monsieur McKendrick's men 'ave all been unjustly accused." She chuckled. "All, zat eez, except Hans. And one must forgive one so young, don't you agree?"

"How did Slater discover such interesting companions?"

Georgette patted her on her knee. "Zee man has a talent for finding zee wounded, zee distressed. Is zat not why you are here, *ma petite?"*

Aloise straightened in surprise, but Georgette did not allow her time to speak. Issuing a burst of orders in French, Georgette waved her assistants away. They quickly gathered their things and left the room.

"Come, Aloise. Now we will find Slater to see how 'plain' he thinks you can be."

The woman took her hand and drew her from the room as if the two of them had been old friends for some time. Once at the head of the stairs, she paused, putting a finger to her lips.

Slater stood in the foyer below, glancing through the letters that had been left on a silver tray. Nudging Aloise with a hand at her shoulder, Georgette indicated that she should descend the staircase and surprise him. Aloise wasn't so sure that such a thing was a good idea. After all, the man's back was turned. She should take the opportunity to dart outside, try to escape. The past few days had been too wearing on her emotions. She'd discovered that she'd enjoyed banter with this man, pitting her will against his own. But even as the thought flashed through her head, she took a step, another, and another, slowly, deliberately.

What was happening to her? Only days had passed, yet she found herself being seduced to surrender to his ploys. To succumb to the gilded temptation of luxurious clothes, decadent rooms, and hot baths. As well as this man.

Slater McKendrick.

As if she had said his name aloud, he turned. The force of his scrutiny became as tangible as a naked hand. He eyed her from the shiny tips of her black boots to the delicate lace cap balanced on the back of her head—and there was no doubt that he found her appearance less than "plain."

The foyer seemed to suddenly shrink, become an intimate place, one filled with anticipation and wicked indulgences. From somewhere behind and overhead, Aloise heard Georgette's soft laughter. "She eez very ugly in zat dress, eez she not, *mon ami?*" Then she disappeared somewhere down the upper hall.

Silence stretched between them like a taut silver thread. One beaded with anticipation, hesitancy, and just a touch of fear.

"Good morning, Aloise."

"Slater."

The necessary niceties did little to alleviate the tension. In fact, they only underscored the rather strained quality of their breathing.

"You are well rested, I trust?"

"Yes. Thank you."

"Good." He dropped the correspondence he'd been holding onto the salver and brushed past her, taking her arm and tugging her behind him. "Then you are ready to prove once and for all that you are a lady."

When he would have pulled her along behind him, she balked.

"I have completed enough of your silly tasks to prove I could be the queen herself!"

He paused, turned. "Have you? Have you indeed? Then this task, this last and final test, should not prove too difficult, should it?"

At the mention of one *last* test, she allowed herself to reluctantly consider the idea.

"What did you have in mind?"

"Merely a chance to see the . . . depth of your education."

"Education?"

"I told you days ago that I had a position for you should you care to take it."

Dear sweet heaven, had he changed his mind and decided she *should* become his mistress? Was that the education to which he referred? A sensual education that could only be determined by proving she was a virgin?

"Let me go!" She tried in vain to stop their progress, finally grasping a marble pillar and holding on for dear life.

He sighed. "If you will release the post, you will see I mean you no harm."

"But—"

He stopped her protest by lifting her face and swooping to steal a kiss. One that was at once masterful and involving, sapping her of her defiance even as it filled her with another more potent thrum of desire.

"At least I've found one way to quiet your complaints," he murmured when he finally lifted his head. Peeling her free from the support, he drew her the rest of the way down the hall and threw open a set of double doors.

Aloise, expecting some den of iniquity with a huge black bed, gazed about her in confusion at the vaulted room filled with crates and boxes and trunks.

Slater eyed her strangely, darkly, as if he knew some

secret brand of information that she had yet to fathom. "I trust, as a lady, you've been properly schooled in the art of running a household."

His shift in conversation took a moment for her to grasp, but her shoulders straightened in utmost dignity. "I spent thirteen years at a women's academy in France."

His eyes glittered strangely at the knowledge. "Good. Then I'm sure you've been introduced to the art of reading?"

"Yes."

"Writing?"

"Yes!"

"Overseeing servants, meal preparation—"

"Yes, yes!"

"—As well as the proper methods of inventory."

His words took her completely by surprise.

Slater strode forward to pull aside the draperies that had shrouded the windows, allowing her to see the extent of the job he wished her to perform. The ballroom fairly burst with items that had been stacked and stored in the chilly marble cavern.

"As you can see, I've amassed a huge collection over the years."

Looking at him, she suddenly knew what he intended. He wanted her to see the extent of his travels, the volume of his wealth. He wanted her to submit to him, to surrender to his will, to become part of his following just as his men had done.

"I won't become your slave."

"I haven't asked you to do so."

"Oh, really?" She gestured to the hundreds of crates. "You want me to make a list of all the treasures you've amassed over the years, and you think such an act will prove me a lady?"

"It could."

She marched toward the door. "Damned if I'll do your bidding."

His hand slammed against the wood. "You will do

as I say, Aloise." The voice was hard, implacable. "You will look in each box, examine each treasure, and catalogue each item. As you do so, you will think, long and hard. You will ask yourself: *Is this what I want to give up? A life of adventure, a life of passion?* All for what? A little bit of pride?" When she refused to answer, he forced her to look at him. "My offer of a position in my household still stands. This is the way to prove you're smart enough to take it." With that he let her go. "I'll check on you come noon."

"But—" Aloise backed away, eyeing him in astonishment. "I haven't agreed to work for you! I told you I didn't want—"

"To be my mistress. And if I recall correctly, I told you at the time that such a . . . position was not my intent. The offer I intend to extend involves a much higher level of dependability."

His brows lifted, and he moved to her, so slowly, so purposefully, she was reminded of the way Sonja prowled through the garden.

"Therefore, I will leave you with a choice. You may perform this simple test, prove to me once and for all that you have been given the education which would have been awarded to a woman who could own such a pretty bauble as I found in your belongings. Or you may return to your room where you will spend the rest of the week behind locked doors."

Drat, he'd cornered her—and he knew it. If she refused his offer, there would be no possible way for her to escape. At least if she gave in to him now, she had a chance, however slim it might be.

"You have ink and paper?" she asked through gritted teeth.

"But of course. On that desk over there." Offering her a slight bow and a knowing grin, he backed from the room, audibly locking the door.

"Blast it all," Aloise muttered under her breath, rushing to each of the windows in turn. But even before she had checked the first one, she knew they would be locked. Short of breaking the glass and alerting Sonja and her host to her activities, she was trapped.

Completely and utterly trapped.

"What, pray tell, are you doing?"

Slater looked up from where he'd been listening outside the ballroom door. He'd heard Aloise rush to the windows, then heard what sounded suspiciously like a curse.

"Merely keeping our guest busy."

"As well as away from you, it would appear."

Scowling, Slater offered, "I don't know what you mean."

Curry grinned. "She's very beautiful."

"I believe we've had this conversation," Slater interrupted wearily.

"Yes, but things seem to be developing at a great clip this past week. I've never seen you surrender so much time to the company of a mere woman."

"Just part of the ruse."

"Is it?" Curry straightened from where he'd been leaning against the wall. "Admit it. You like Aloise. She interests you. When you look at her, you don't see her with the eyes of a jaded explorer presented with yet one more stunning female." He tapped Slater on the chest with his finger. "You look at her as if she were a rare discovery. A jewel beyond price. *That,* my friend, worries you no end. Because, you see, you no longer think that she betrayed you all those years ago, that she refused to expose the truth. Instead, you are beginning to believe that *you* may have betrayed *her.*"

Slater felt a pang of guilt at his friend's words, one he'd experienced more often than he would care to admit in the last few days. As Curry disappeared down the hall, whistling tunelessly to himself, Slater felt unaccountably uncomfortable.

Because his old friend was right.

He had betrayed Aloise.

He continued to betray her by refusing to tell her the truth.

Unconscious of his own actions, he made his way to his study. Once there, he knew what he sought, what had called to him. Sinking into one of the chairs, he stared up at Jeanne's portrait, trying to ignore the swirling emotions that churned in his stomach. But try as he might, he could no longer deny that Aloise affected him. Not just physically.

But emotionally as well.

How many reactions to a woman could a man endure? Slater wondered idly, remembering the searing anger he'd first displayed toward Aloise. Then the frustration at her supposed memory loss; the irritation of her escape attempts; the unwilling sense of pity. And now the possessiveness. A deep, overriding possessiveness.

Never had he felt this way about any woman. Nor had he ever thought he would feel such things for Aloise. Bloody hell! He'd known her when she was but a child. He'd witnessed runny noses and skinned knees. He'd seen her dressed in flannel and playing with dolls.

But such images had long since been superseded by Aloise the adult.

The woman.

His betrothed.

Over the past few days, he'd seen so many interesting sides of her personality. Her determination, her gentleness, her anger, her laughter. Each emotion had tugged at his heartstrings until he found himself utterly . . .

Besotted. There was no other word to describe it. He wanted to be near her, he wanted to indulge her. He wanted to make her laugh and see her run through the halls with her petticoats flashing. He loved to enter the house and hear her off-key melodies. He anticipated joining her for dinner each evening, watching her struggle to appear unaffected by the half-dozen forks and numerous goblets.

She enchanted him completely.

How could such a thing have happened? He didn't want to love her. He didn't want the responsibility. He didn't want to open himself up to the possible pain. That was why, after planning on spending the afternoon with Aloise and wooing her with his tales of adventure, he had grown angry instead and left her alone.

Great bloody hell. What had he done? Had he unconsciously allowed her to wriggle deeper into his affections than he had ever dreamed possible?

His gaze skipped to the portrait. That smiling, all-knowing portrait. "Did you guess that such a thing would happen?" Slater demanded.

Jeanne didn't answer—not that he was so far gone that he thought she would—nevertheless, he couldn't help feeling that if she'd been here, Jeanne would have been pleased by this sudden twist of events.

His hands curled into fists against the leather armrests and he fought the unfamiliar sensation of being out of control. Of having his heart lean toward things his head told him to forget.

"Was this what you wanted all along, Jeanne? Hmm? When we both conspired against Crawford to wed your daughter to a common schoolmaster, was this your goal?" His head dropped against the chair and he regarded her with half-closed eyes. "Did you mean for me to become her champion?" His throat grew tight as emotions he fought to resist burgeoned inside him. Pain. Regret. Fear.

"Did you mean for her to become my obsession?"

After so much time in Slater McKendrick's company, Aloise did not see him for two days. Her meals were brought to her by a servant and each evening she was ushered from the ballroom to the Rose Room where she was offered a hot bath and a warm meal. Except for Sonja, who occasionally scratched at her door and yowled in greeting, Aloise might have thought herself virtually forgotten by anyone other than the staff.

She knew such was not the case. Although her host had given every appearance of abandoning her, she felt his presence in the house as surely as the storm clouds that gathered in the afternoon sky. She'd grown highly attuned to the chambermaids' whispers about their mysterious master, the way they feared his temper and valued his praise. She learned to listen for each of his men: Rudy's bearlike grumbling; Marco's complaints; Clayton's ruminations; Curry's laughter; Hans's jokes; Louis's propositions. She longed for Georgette to talk to her again, to tell her more about Slater, but the woman appeared occupied in other areas of the house. The Frenchwoman had evidently told her as much as she was willing—or able—to do.

With the passage of time, she longed for some sort of human companionship, but she soon had no more time to dwell on such things. As of this evening, seven days had passed since she'd come to Ashenleigh.

Seven days.

Upon entering the last item on her inventory list, Aloise breathed a soft sigh of relief. Tonight, Slater would check her list and proclaim her education sound. Then he would have to let her go. He would have to honor his promise to give her passage to whatever place she chose—save it be Africa. Her lips twitched in remembrance of his words, and staring at the items she had unpacked during the past few days, she had ample evidence that this man had indeed traveled to such exotic lands.

When her anger at being so imperiously pressed into service had subsided, Aloise had actually come to enjoy her time in the ballroom. Each box, each crate, had revealed untold treasures: vases from the Orient, bottles of Arabian perfume, ivory tusks, exotic seeds, ornate pieces of armor. From the beginning, her imagination had been sparked and her appetite for adventure honed. This man had seen the world! What tales he could relate to her.

If she dared to ask.

If she dared to stay.

Slapping the ledger onto the desk, she firmly thrust such an idea from her head. She had her own adventures to find, her own life to live, her—

The door opened and Slater McKendrick entered, tall, bearded, lean. Once again, she was struck by the way this man seemed forever cloaked in shadows, mystery. He had only to step inside and close the door behind him for the vaulted ballroom to become suddenly too small, too close, too intimate.

"Good evening, Aloise."

The words stroked her senses and she tried to steel herself against the sensation. Unfortunately, she hadn't seen the man for some time. Too much time. She hadn't realized the way she'd waited for him. Her body trembled with a strange energy. Her mouth grew dry, her hands damp.

Dodging his scrutiny, she grasped the ledger and held it out to him.

"I've finished," she stated bluntly, glad that her voice revealed none of the shaking of her limbs.

He set the small trunk he had been holding on the floor and took the book, thumbing through the pages.

Aloise felt a momentary twinge of alarm. In a fit of pique, she had begun the entries in Italian, then had continued thus through the entire exercise, not wanting this man to know the moment when her anger had faded into acceptance, then into wonder.

Slater didn't even blink at the obvious attempt at rebellion. "Very good. How wise of you to use another language in order to keep the information private. Apparently, your education was much more sound than I had suspected."

Of course the man knew Italian. She should have

considered such a fact. Unfortunately, she'd been so angry that first day she hadn't thought beyond much than needling his irritation.

"I fear, however, that you're not quite finished."

She stiffened in pride. "I assure you, I've checked and rechecked each box—"

"This trunk was inadvertently left in another room. Miss Nibbs obtained it for me years ago. The contents will also need to be inventoried."

She sighed and stomped toward it. He stopped her with a hand on her shoulder.

The contact was unexpected and thoroughly startling. A heat burst from that point of contact, causing her to straighten, back away.

"You still fear me."

This time, she didn't refute the statement he'd made twice before. She *did* fear him. This man made her feel things she didn't want to feel. He made her dream of impossibilities. He made her wish for pleasures that would always be denied her.

Slater tucked his finger beneath her chin. "Don't be afraid, cherie."

"You leave me no choice." The words were husky, yet firm. "You keep me here against my will, you try me and test me and believe me a thief, all under the guise of seeing justice served. But what of the wrongs made against me?"

He cupped her cheek. "Someday you will understand what I have done."

His cryptic comment only served to make her more angry.

"My seven days have been served. I wish to go now."

A shutter fell over his eyes, making them even more dark, even more inscrutable. "No."

Aloise stared at him in disbelief. "But you promised! Surely, you don't doubt that I'm a lady—after all the blasted tests I've performed."

"My messenger has not returned from Tippington."

"I don't care if the man is swimming the bloody Channel! You told me that if no word to the contrary had arrived, I could leave after one week. You promised me safe passage in your coach and the return of my jewels. I will have what you offered and have it now!"

"No."

She gasped in effrontery. "How dare you? How *dare* you lie to me? How *dare* you lead me on, then keep me here, against my will, after I have done everything you bade me to do!" Growling, she slammed her doubled fists against his chest. "Damn you to hell and back! You promised! Have you no shame? No honor?"

A blatant frustration rushed over his features so quickly she could scarcely credit what had happened. He pushed her against the wall, holding her wrists immobile above her head.

"Don't speak to me of honor, mistress. I've learned the value of such a word far more than you will ever do. I've fought to uphold my name, a name sullied in the midst of greed. I've been forced from my home and stripped of my birthright—but I've beaten the odds. For honor's sake. For pity's sake. For friendship's sake."

When she would have opened her mouth to question such odd remarks, he shook her slightly, damming the words in her mouth. "You would do well to remain silent about things you know nothing about. There are forces at work here, forces that you don't understand—and may never understand. Because of your gentler sex, I've protected you from emotional turmoil as best I could these past few days. But *do not push me, mistress!* Or you will soon know the extent of your father's perfidy, in terms so blunt that even *you* will cringe from what I know, what I've gathered."

The words echoed in the room, pulsed, swelling much like the storm clouds bunching against the distant line of trees. Then, as quickly as he'd grasped her, Aloise was released. Taking a deep, calming breath, Slater made a low noise of frustration, then stormed from the room, leaving an awful silence as well as a horrible realization.

This man knew who she was.

This man knew her father.

Dear sweet heaven above. He'd never believed her to be a thief. He'd never truly tested her ladylike qualities. He'd merely meant to imprison her, taunt her, torment her, thereby satisfying some debt he felt her father owed him—for she had no doubts that his cryptic comments had something to do with Oliver Crawford. She had felt enough of her father's wrath to know he had a nature prone to making powerful enemies as well as powerful allies.

Pressing her hands to her mouth she forced back a sob that bubbled in her throat. A tear fell from her cheek and plunged to the silk of her bodice.

Who was this man? What did he want of her?

And what had her father done to cause McKendrick's eyes to burn with such a fierce and anguished fury?

12

THE NIGHTMARE HAD COME AGAIN.

Slater stepped into Aloise's bedchamber, having been drawn there by faint cries, a whimpering. Crossing to the bed, he enclosed her in his arms, wondering what she would say if she were to awaken and find him here.

Twice in the past week he had come to her chamber to soothe her. He knew she suffered from a recurring nightmare of ghoulish proportions, one which caused her to tremble to the very heart of her being. He'd noted that such dreams came when the night was stormy and thunder rumbled.

His hand passed over her cheek and she began to grow quiet, grow still. "Shh, Aloise. Shh." His voice calmed her and she snuggled closer, inadvertently stoking a fire of need, a fire of want.

The first night he'd found her like this, Slater had tried waking her, knowing from her guttural cries and half-uttered sentences that she was reliving a portion of her mother's death in her sleep. But he'd since discovered that any attempt to bring her to consciousness during the height of such memories brought with it a terrible price. Invariably, such a rude awakening caused Aloise to forget the brunt of her dreams and suffer from blinding headaches the following day. The discomfort of her condition was so strong that she did not even sense his presence, only the overwhelming pain. It was better to soothe her back into sleep. To let her dream of happier things.

To let her forget.

The loss of her memories of that night had once irritated him, but now Slater found himself thankful that she hadn't been able to recall those events. As a child, they had been her only brand of protection against her father's wrath. Slater only wished that such blissfulness could continue a little longer, but events were accelerating to such a point that he feared Aloise would soon be *forced* to remember what she had seen so long ago. Not by Slater, but by her own mind.

She slept now, peacefully, like an angel. Returning her to the cocoon of her bed, Slater stood. He regretted what was about to take place, he regretted what he had to do, but the time had come for a confrontation with Crawford. For the past few days, he and his men had intensified their scrutiny of the man's affairs. They had kept careful track of the hoards of penniless aristocracy beginning to make their way toward Briarwood and a marriage that Slater was determined would never occur.

All that remained was to arrange for Aloise's protection.

Backing from the room, Slater prayed she would not grow to hate him for what he was about to do. He prayed that somehow, someway, she would understand.

Something awakened her, the distant thump of footfalls.

Aloise lay motionless in her bed, her heart pounding for some unknown reason, her head throbbing. Wincing, she stood, intent upon retrieving a cool cloth to press against her brow.

The dream had come again. She never remembered it clearly. She only knew that each time it rushed through her head, she awakened with a sense of dread, the same sick feelings of panic the sight of blood invariably brought. As well as the pain. The overwhelming pain.

Sighing, she tried to force such thoughts from her head, splashing her face with water, then returning to the fireplace where she poked at the burning embers. Dawn had not yet arrived, yet she felt loathe to return to bed.

She straightened, yawned, then grew still. Wary. To her complete astonishment, her chamber door lay slightly ajar.

No. It couldn't be.

But as she tiptoed closer, she discovered she was right. It was open. Not just unlocked—*open.* The thought caused her to stand for several minutes in indecision, wondering what she should do. For the first time in a week, a viable method of escape had been presented to her. But after Slater's refusal to let her go, she couldn't help thinking that the whole situation must be a trap. He didn't strike her as a careless man. The door must have been left that way deliberately.

But what if it hadn't?

For some time, Aloise sat in the darkness, staring at the panels as if they held an answer to her dilemma, then, spurred into action, she dressed in the yellow gown. The one that Slater had said was hers. Whatever happened.

Still . . . she hesitated.

It wasn't that she was afraid of her future. No, she wasn't afraid. She was merely . . . resigned. If she succeeded in leaving this place, she would be completely defenseless and all but penniless. Her only possessions would be the yellow dress, the single ruby tucked under her stays, and the memories of what had occurred in this house. With this man.

Blast it all! Why did she pause? Why didn't she simply skulk into the night and continue on her journey as she'd originally planned? She could be free of Ashenleigh and its master!

Free.

So why did the idea leave a hollowness in her heart? Why did she feel saddened, not enervated? What kind of spell had this man cast to make her linger? Make her believe?

Believe in what?

More.

That she could have more out of life than she had first thought. That she needn't surrender to expediency. That she could indulge herself in things she'd wanted so very long, so very much, desires she'd buried beneath her books and her studies, while refusing to acknowledge that a part of her needed. Wanted. Yearned.

For companionship.

For love.

For warm linens on frosty winter mornings.

A wetness plunged down her cheek and Aloise dashed it away. What nonsense. What sheer and utter nonsense! She must be growing morbid in her advancing age—or perhaps the moon was full.

Grasping her hat and a reticule she'd filled with toiletries, an extra pair of hose, and a half-dozen hairpins, she opened the door. Opened it and stared into the gloom of the hall.

She allowed no last glance of the room behind her with its black walls and rose-patterned rug. Moving determinedly, she crept downstairs to the inky shadows of the foyer.

If the moon were indeed at its fullest, there was no sign of it. The heavy clouds and threat of rain had choked what little light managed to struggle through the windows. She was left in darkness. A quality she would forever associate with this house. This man.

Impatient at her own behavior, Aloise reached to fling open the door and rush outside. The portal was locked—from the inside—with its key conveniently missing.

An anger surged through Aloise. Was this another of Slater's games? Did he mean to torment her with the opportunity to escape, then dangle the ability to do so just out of her reach? No! She wouldn't give him the satisfaction. She would quit this place. One way or another.

Systematically, she began moving through the house, checking those doors she knew existed. Each was locked, quite securely. Which left her with the choice of giving up her attempt, or searching the house room by room until she found a door or window left unlatched. But such a foraging expedition could result in bursting in on one of Slater's men or the servants.

Think, Aloise. Think!

Gathering her skirts, she hurried down the hall to the ballroom, shutting herself inside. Desperate measures called for desperate means. The rumble of thunder was growing nearer, more intense. She would wait until it grew particularly loud, then break one of the windows, hoping the noise of the storm would disguise the shattering glass.

The plan sounded weak—even to her. But as far as she could determine, there were no other real alternatives. None she was willing to entertain.

Feeling her way through the dark, she crossed to the desk where she knew a candle and flint had been left. With some effort, she was able to ignite the wick and form a tiny puddle of light.

Within seconds she became still. Wary.

The room had changed.

A cool finger of foreboding slid up her spine and she held the taper high, sure that she was mistaken, or that she had burst into the wrong room. But the somber portraits and gleaming marble supports were the same as those that had surrounded her for days. It was the furnishings that had altered.

The candle did not cast much of a glow, but it illuminated enough of the room for Aloise to see that the ballroom had been returned to its formal glory. The chandeliers overhead had been freshly polished and adorned with new beeswax candles. The protective dustcovers had been removed from the gilt furniture that edged the monstrous expanse of the dance floor. And the walls . . . the walls had been relieved of their heavy tapestries to reveal hand-painted frescoes of frolicking nymphs, grinning cherubs, flowers and sunshine and spring.

Everything else had been taken away—the crates, the treasures, the boxes. Everything, that was, except a single trunk. The last trunk Slater had brought for her to inventory.

Inexplicably, a hand seemed to close over her chest, tightening, tightening, so that Aloise could barely breathe. She found herself being drawn toward it with a morbid sense of curiosity she did not understand. Kneeling, she opened the lid.

As she stared down at the dusty toys, the blocks, the sewing basket, the picture books, a babble of voices filled her brain.

Come, Aloise.

The words fairly melted out of the darkness, and Aloise sobbed, realized that it was not a ghost who spoke to her, but a memory. A *memory.*

As quickly as it had formed in her brain, the familiar sounds disappeared, leaving her desolate. Lifting her head, Aloise stared into the darkness around her. Why? Why couldn't she remember? What was wrong with her? What horrible thing had she done that her mind had built an impenetrable wall around her childhood?

Setting the candle on the floor, she hesitantly reached into the trunks, fingering the dusty items which had been kept there. These objects held some special message. But what? *What?*

Just when she was about to concede defeat, the mellow warmth of her candle touched a shape that lay wrapped in a silk shawl. The shape seemed to call to her with the tender familiarity of an angel's song so that she reached out and drew back the covering.

A doll.

Come, Aloise. Show everyone your gift, then you and I will sing a lullaby for your baby so that everyone can see what a lovely bride you'll be. What a beautiful mother.

The voice whispered in the room around her. Touching a corner of Aloise's soul, plucking her heartstrings as surely as the melody reverberating in her head.

Sleep, my wee one, sleep . . .

A face swam in front of her mind's eye. One filled with sweetness and a mother's unbounded love.

Lo, Lilly, lo Lilly, lo Lilly, loo lee.

Her birthday party. There had been a dozen young children and their parents, hoards of visitors, sweets and music and people making a fuss.

Let everyone see what a lovely bride you'll be. What a beautiful mother.

"That night, she sang as I have never heard before or since."

Gasping, Aloise whirled to find Slater standing behind her. Dropping the doll, she sprang to her feet, bumping against the trunk and causing the lid to slam closed.

Slater automatically reached out to steady her, clasping her elbow.

"You knew her?" she asked in amazement.

"Yes."

"How?"

"I was there that night. It was your birthday. Remember?"

She nodded.

"You had just turned five."

She did not ask how he'd so easily divined her thoughts. She didn't want to know. This man was already able to delve too easily into her soul, to pluck out responses she felt should remain hidden.

"What do you want from me?" she whispered.

"I want to see you happy."

She yanked free. "If that were true, you would let me leave this place."

He regarded her with an expression that bordered on pity. "You can't leave any more than I can. I've finally come to the conclusion that destiny has brought us to this point. It will see the game through to the end whether we like it or not."

Aloise wrapped her arms around her body. "I don't know what you mean."

Slater eyed her with something akin to pity. Aloise must have roused him from slumber because his hair was tousled. His shirt hung loose and rumpled about his chest, leaving a good deal of the hair-spattered expanse to her view.

"Think, Aloise. What else do you remember?"

The air became suddenly close, too thick to breathe. When he took her shoulders, she tried to wriggle free.

"No. Let me go. I don't know what you mean."

"Think, Aloise."

But he was far too close to make thinking of any kind possible. He crowded her, overpowered her, robbed her of the capability to make her own decisions. A panic filled her breast. A dank foreboding that this man knew things about her, things she didn't want to uncover. Even his eyes said as much, willing her surrender to his artful persuasion.

A pain darted through her head, more powerful than any she had experienced. Nausea tainted her stomach. A horrible fear clutched at her limbs.

She had to get away! Now. Before it was too late.

Pushing him away, she dodged free. Rather than heading for the door as he had obviously expected, she rushed to the window. Ignoring his surprise, she grasped one of the ornate chairs and threw it through the leaded panes of the guillotine window. Then she was running into the night, into the blackness.

"Aloise!"

He gave chase, just as she knew he would. But she refused to pause, refused to glance over her shoulder. She would not allow him to take her back to that place, those fearful sensations of panic.

A chill wind pushed against her, bringing the thick scent of rain, but she didn't ease her pace. She had only one chance at liberation. Over the hill, she'd seen the beginnings of an overgrown maze. If she could make her way there and hide in the foliage until Slater tired of the chase, she could dodge to freedom before first light.

"Aloise!"

The call came louder, nearer, but the storm was on her side, dousing the betraying light of the moon and hiding her in shadow. Inky, black shadows.

Her side began to ache, but she ignored the pain just as she ignored the branches and bushes that seemed determined to grasp at her clothing and her hair. The maze loomed ahead of her, the metal folly dilapidated and scarred, the privet bushes wild and untamed. Someone had evidently begun repairs because a slight path had been made toward its center. Aloise drove to the heart, swiftly losing her way midst the twists and turns. Slater would not be able to follow. He would never find her here.

Seeing a natural alcove formed by a blighted bush, she dodged into the damp hole, ducking her head and wrapping her arms around her body, hoping that he would give up his search, that he would leave her. That he would understand her need to be free of this place—of him.

She could not go back.

She *would* not go back.

A clap of thunder splintered the night, sounding

much closer, much more threatening than it had mere minutes ago. To Aloise's intense dismay, raindrops began to spatter the dust around her, bringing their musky smell.

Her eyes squeezed shut. No. *No!* She didn't like the rain. She'd never liked it. Something about the suffocating presence of the heavy clouds and the strong winds had always frightened her since childhood. Those fears had not lessened with age. On the contrary, they had intensified, as if there were something horrible waiting for her in the buffeting weather. Some horrible monster she could not remember.

The blinding pain in her head intensified, shuddering through her body, causing her to tremble. No. No! She didn't want to remember any more. Not if the memory of something as harmless as a birthday party brought with it such pain.

"Aloise?"

The cry was distant, distorted by the rustling of the privet hedge. Huddling in a tight ball, Aloise tried to deny what she'd thought she'd heard. Not Slater, but a woman. A woman had called to her.

"Aloise, come. We've got to hide."

She whimpered as dank thoughts and a swirl of macabre images swam about her. Nightmarish visions of a storm, rocky bluffs, and blood . . . so much blood. Her stomach lurched. Her eyes sprang open.

"Aloise!"

This time, she looked up, looked up to see Slater standing above her. The rain had plastered his hair against his head and dampened the fabric of his shirt. In the guttering light of a torch, he appeared somehow even more large, more intense, more frightening than he ever had before.

She sprang to her feet and tried to dodge past him, but he caught her, held her, his arm like a steel band about her waist. Then it seemed to her that it was not he who held her, but another man, a gruffer, craggy-faced servant who muttered a host of epithets in her ears.

"Aloise!" Slater shook her and the image shattered as quickly as it had come.

"You've found her?" Curry darted toward the light, then stopped when he caught sight of Aloise.

She knew they were staring at her in great concern. She knew that her dress was mud-stained and ruined . . . her beautiful dress. She must look a sight with her hair straggling about her face. But she found she didn't have the energy to explain or protest. Her legs were suddenly trembling, her body growing numb.

Dear heaven, what was happening? She was shattering inside, piece by piece. Any minute, she feared that she would dissolve into dust.

Slater growled something to his companion, handing him his torch, then scooped her against his body just as she would have fainted.

Clutching his shoulders, she buried her face in his neck, shivering uncontrollably, and knowing that she should be stronger, less needy. But at that moment, she realized that Slater had been right. Destiny had brought them to this point. Her memories were still too vague, too horrible to acknowledge, but she knew there would be no escaping. Some force had brought her to this place, to this point in time. The moment had come to face her demons . . .

As well as her past.

From the top of the hill, a single man took note of the figures limned in torchlight. Grinning at the thought of being allowed to abandon his post in favor of dry clothes and a crackling fire, he made his way to Briarwood.

13

MISS NIBBS, SEND A HOT BATH UP TO THE ROSE Room."

Miss Nibbs took one look at Slater, then at the woman he held in his arms. "Oh, my. Whatever—"

"Just do it!"

"Yes, sir." She scrambled to do as she was told.

"Curry, have Marco and Louis board up the broken window. Then I want a guard placed there until we can get it repaired. Crawford's had a man snooping about the last few days, I don't want him investigating the accident any more than he should."

Curry saluted, rushing to do as he'd been told, leaving Slater alone with Aloise. As he hurried up the stairs to her room, she trembled in his arms. Her skin had grown positively pasty.

"Why, Aloise?" he whispered under his breath. To his infinite surprise, she answered him.

"I had to get away." Her eyes flickered, stabbing him with their velvety darkness. "But you have made that impossible, haven't you?"

Slater felt a stab of conscience. He supposed this situation *was* his fault. Had he known about Aloise's lack of memory ahead of time, he would have altered his plans substantially. But events had been set into motion. Events that now spilled in front of him like a runaway ball that gained speed with each passing minute. Much as he might like to shield Aloise from future unpleasantness, the time had long since passed to demand retribution of her father.

Shouldering open the door to her room, he set her on the floor. Despite her hushed protests, he snapped open the buttons to her bodice, then proceeded to help her with the rest of her fastenings. When he would have stripped her to the skin, she stopped him, moving behind the privacy screen to finish undressing. Moments later, she appeared in the night rail and robe.

Her hands nervously pleated her skirt, but she dropped them as if she were afraid of how much of her nervousness she'd revealed. Finally, her chin tilted and she demanded, "What do you intend to do with me?"

Such courage. Such fire. The fact caused Slater to soften his stance. He was not usually a man of diplomacy, but tonight he would try his level best.

"What have you remembered?"

Her brow creased. "Just the party. My mother was there. She sang."

"What else do you recall?"

"A storm. Panic."

Slater felt a tightening of his own body at her words. He had not been blessed with forgetfulness as she had. He'd lived with the events of that night for years.

"That was later. In the spring." He damned the huskiness he couldn't control.

"My mother was there. Two men. She fought with them."

Shaking her head, she refused to say any more, but Slater pressed on. "Do you remember anything else? Anyone else?"

"No."

"What about your father?"

"My father? What has he to do with this?"

"Do you remember his being there, Aloise?"

"No, I—"

Her eyes suddenly widened and she stared at him in dismay. "Who are you? Why are you doing this to me?" Her hands balled into fists. "Is this some sort of grand game? To torture me with things I can't remember? Or—"

The blood suddenly drained from her face. "*He* sent you. Didn't he? *Didn't* he? I should have known. You're nothing but his pawn." Marching toward him, she began to pound him on the chest. "How much is he paying you? What has my father promised to give you for your efforts? Me? *Me?* Damnit, are you my next matrimonial prospect?"

Aloise saw the fury darken his mien at her accusations, but she didn't care. A betrayal such as she'd never known spilled into her veins. This man had used her. *Used* her.

"Damn you!" She began to pummel him with blows.

The door opened and Miss Nibbs peered inside. "I have her bathwater."

"Not now, Miss Nibbs," Slater growled.

"But—"

"Get out!"

The door slammed closed, and Slater lifted her, then dropped her on the bed, pinning her there with his body, her arms stretched above her head.

She wriggled and fought, trying to gain some kind of advantage, but he held her easily, causing her merely to exhaust herself with her struggles.

"Stop it. Stop!" He shook her slightly and she grew still. "I'm not in league with your father."

The fury she felt launched anew. "You lied to me! You tricked me! You knew the whole time who I was. Didn't you?"

"Yes."

She groaned in anger. "I believed you. All the while you spouted that nonsense about taking me to the authorities and accusing me of being a thief, you meant to keep me here all along."

"Yes."

She bucked at him, trying to throw him off, but he remained full-length on her, his body pressing her into the feather bed. His hips ground intimately against her own, their thighs tangled together. Startled, Aloise grew quiet when she realized her struggles were beginning to have an effect on Slater.

"Why?" she demanded. "Why have you done this to me?"

He regarded her speculatively for such a long time, she grew uncomfortable. He knew something, something awful that he debated telling her.

Very slowly, he rose from the bed. "You've been away from home a long time, Aloise."

She rose to a sitting position, hugging the dressing gown to her body.

"Away?" The word burst free with an overt shade of bitterness. "How can one be away from something that never existed? I have no home in England. I have no home."

"Do you regret that fact?"

She shrugged, watching the man who watched her, and wondering what information he sought.

"How can one regret something that has never been experienced?"

"I'm not asking a hypothetical question, Aloise. Did *you* regret the absence of a home?"

She warily inched toward the edge of the bed. When he made no move to stop her, she rose and took a few steps away, needing a bit more space.

"I suppose."

"Did you regret the nature of your childhood?"

Aloise briefly envisioned Madame Giradoux, her

guardian-instructor at Sacre Coeur, a stern, pious, cheerless woman who felt that life revolved around the proper conjugation of irregular French verbs. Living so close to the country, Aloise had longed to explore the neighboring fields. Horrified by such an idea, Madame Giradoux had been the first to begin locking Aloise in her room. Still, Aloise hesitated in giving Slater McKendrick the entire truth.

"In some ways."

"What about the school you spoke of? Did you enjoy yourself there?"

He already knew so much, too much. Must she tell him more?

"What do you want from me?" she whispered. But he did not hear her—or if he did, he chose to ignore her query.

He took a step and the room quivered in anticipation, as if he were about to reveal some secret of the universe.

"Your mother? Did you miss her?"

"My mother?"

"Did you miss her softening influence? The way she would have sung to you at night? The stories she would have told?"

His expression grew nearly frightening. He reached to take her arms and she dodged away.

"What right have you to speak of my mother in such a fashion?"

"I knew her. She was my friend. That is why I was invited to attend the festivities surrounding your fifth birthday."

She was stunned. Other than Mr. Humphreys—who would not betray her father's wishes—no one had been able to tell her anything about Jeanne Crawford.

"You could not have known her. She died—"

"Fifteen years ago, last April."

"How do you—"

"What did he tell you, Aloise? How did your father explain her sudden death?"

"She died in an accident."

"Hardly."

Her brow creased. "I don't understand."

The room grew silent. Still.

"She was murdered, Aloise."

"Murdered?" she could barely say the word. Shaking her head, she tried to back away, but he snagged her elbow, pulling her irretrievably closer.

"You're mistaken. She died at Briarwood. A fall."

"She was killed, Aloise. Not five miles from where you stand now."

"No. My father would have told me such a thing."

"Your father? Your father hired the man who murdered her."

She began to tremble, not because of the horrible things he said, but because they might, just might, be true.

"No. You're trying to trick me again. You're telling me lies because you want me to do something I shouldn't."

"Think, Aloise. How long after your father's death did he remarry?"

"A few . . ."

"Months? Her name was Mary. Mary Little. Did you meet her, Aloise?"

She nodded. "I was sick at the time. So very sick. I remember because my father forced the women at Sacre Coeur to dose me with a horrible tonic. Even so, I was summoned from France to attend the wedding in London."

"What about later? On the birth of their children?"

"There were no children. They were married for five years, but there were no children."

"What happened to Mary?"

"She died."

"How?"

"Of the fever."

"When was the next time you were allowed home to England?"

"Upon my father's third marriage."

"You were what—twelve?"

"Thirteen."

"What was her name?"

"Lilith. Lilith Clark."

"How long were they married?"

"Three years. Lilith died." Her eyes grew wide and haunted. "Of consumption."

"How many more women came after that?"

"Two." She was shaking now, quite visibly. "They also died."

"Of other more mysterious ailments." He inched closer. "Did you know you had a sister?"

Her brow creased in confusion. "I have no sister."

"She died at birth. The same month your mother was killed."

"No."

"Did you know that soon after her conception, there were rumors that your father became ill. Very, very ill. His body grew so hot it had to be wrapped in wet sheets. Do you know what that does to a man, Aloise?"

She shook her head, trying to deny his intent.

"It kills something inside him, Aloise. It kills his seed."

"No!" She slapped her palms over her ears. "I don't want to hear any more!"

He took her wrists, forcing her to hear what he had to say. "Did your father love you? Did he care for you? Did he bounce you on his knee?"

Aloise choked on a sob she refused to utter, feeling a keen stab of pain. McKendrick was being purposely cruel now. If he knew so much about her, he must surely know the rest.

"Or did he willfully keep you as far away from him

as humanly possible, hoping that one day his fears would prove wrong and he would sire a son?"

Her face flamed. This man had seen straight to the core of the matter. He had dissected her heart and found that black kernel of yearning deep inside. She'd wanted her father's love, she'd *craved* it with all her might. When it had been denied, she had tried not to hate him. She'd tried to honor him as the Bible commanded, but she'd known all along he'd wanted a boy. A *boy*.

"When he finally admitted such a thing would never happen, did he bring you home?"

"No." The word pushed from her throat unbidden.

"What did he do, Aloise?"

She closed her lashes.

"He would never have a son to inherit his dynasty, but he became obsessed with the need for an heir. A male heir."

"A grandson."

"How many men did he bring to you to wed?"

She turned away, unable to bear more. But still, she answered, "Two. Sir Greenby—"

"Cavalry officer, retired, and confidante of the king."

"—Lord Kuthright—"

"Of the Kensington shipping Kuthrights, first cousin to His Majesty."

"No." Despite her denial, she could not block out the sound of his coming forward, wrapping his arms around her waist.

"Each man would have brought him power, a title, and a grandson, then could just as easily have been eliminated so that Oliver Crawford could mold his heir. Greenby had a history of heart trouble. He could have died in his sleep without comment. Kuthright's exploits with married women were notorious enough to arrange a duel if need be. Your father must have been displeased when his plans did not come to fruition and the men were disposed of long before they'd served their purposes."

She whimpered softly, feeling the cold settle to her very bones.

"There was one other, Aloise. A man to whom you were betrothed when you were but a child."

She remained mute, shaken.

"How did your father explain the severing of such an alliance?"

"Matthew died." A sob lodged in her throat.

The man who held her relaxed, bending to brush her ear with his lips.

"He is not dead."

She wrenched free, rushing to the door. It was locked. "No. No!" Dashing a hand at the damning moisture gathering at her eyes, she whirled to confront him. "Why do you insist on tormenting me with such lies? Do you want to grind more salt into my wounds? Do you want to pummel me with the fact that my father never loved me? That he rejected me?"

Her fist shook at him. "You know so much, but tell me, do you know the rest? That since the day of my birth I have been punished? Not for *who* I am, but *what.* A girl. A worthless female." She stalked toward him. "Even my name was a punishment. My father so wanted a boy that he wouldn't even consider choosing a girl's name. On my birth, he didn't bother to find another more appropriate. So, on the records of the church, I am Aloitious. Aloitious Pedegrew Crawford. *Aloitious!"*

She swiped at the tears that fell down her cheeks.

"Why are you doing this to me?"

He didn't immediately answer, apparently measuring her emotions against his own indecipherable intent.

"Tell me, Aloise, how much do you love your father?"

She couldn't answer. The truth was much too

horrible. She had avoided it far too long to want to face it now.

"Do you adore him?"

When she didn't answer, he approached, cautiously, warily. "Do you respect him?"

Aloise lifted a hand, forcibly damming the words that threatened to spill through.

"Do you even know him?"

When she would have backed away, Slater caught her, holding her still.

"Did he ever do aught of kindness for you? Did he ever tell you he loved you?"

"No. *No!*"

"Tell me, Aloise." His grip was warm and kind and gentle. "Tell me. You were sent to Sacre Coeur at such a young age. Were you happy?"

She shook her head.

"Tell me."

"I tried to run away."

"What happened?"

Her lashes shut and the tears eased free. "At first, my father was merely angry at the attempts."

"And then?"

She clutched at the fabric of his shirt. "He hired guards. They took me back to the academy then stayed to watch me."

"Did you try to leave again?"

She nodded, resting her forehead on his chest. "Once or twice. Each time, I was punished and brought back."

"Where did he take you then?"

She shuddered, remembering the dark, the dank smells, the scuttle of mice.

"Where, Aloise?"

She recalled the burly guards outside her door. Now and again, the guards grew bored and would try to join her in her chamber. They would back her against the wall, grope at her breasts. She would allow them to kiss her. Once. Twice. Just enough to allay their suspicions, then kick them and dart for freedom. Each time, her father's men found her. Punished her.

"Where did he hide you?"

She didn't want to think. She didn't want to remember. She reared back, but he would not release her. "What do you want?"

The room pulsed in a long, aching silence. Then he finally uttered a single word. "Justice."

"Don't you mean revenge?"

"The words are but two sides to the same coin."

"What has my father ever done to warrant your enmity?"

"Taken what was mine."

"Yours?"

He did not comment further.

"What do you want of me?"

"Your help."

"I can't help you. My father doesn't care about me. I have nothing to offer your cause."

"But you do." He stepped closer, so close that she could not mistake that there had been a subtle shifting in attitude. Somehow, she sensed they were no longer speaking so much about her father, as about her. "You have much to offer."

His touch slid from her wrist to her elbow, carefully avoided her injury, then cupped her shoulders. "I'm not as blind as Oliver Crawford, *chérie.* I see what treasures you offer. Great beauty, wit, intelligence."

"My father doesn't hold such things dear."

"I do."

"How will that bring about justice? My father cares little for anything but his name, his money, and those damned Bengal Rubies."

"He wants a grandson."

The words shuddered in the room and Aloise grew still, the tears drying on her cheeks. Surely, he couldn't mean . . . he didn't want . . .

But as she looked deep in his eyes, she thought she understood his objective.

"You are the one person who can thwart him, Aloise."

She slowly retreated.

"Even now, your father has invited a half-dozen men to Briarwood. All of them can give him the title and the heir he seeks. In exchange, he will part with the one thing he has to bargain."

"The rubies."

He nodded.

"No. My father might have done many things in the past that I disagreed with, but he would never barter me. He merely means to see me married."

"He intends to let a half-dozen men barter for your hand."

Prospects. Mr. Humphreys's last words to her had been of matrimonial *prospects.*

She felt a wave of embarrassment, a surge of disgust. She'd known there had been no love lost to her on Oliver Crawford's part, but she had not known to what depths he would sink to obtain his own ends.

"One of my men has been privy to a list of a good portion of the prospective grooms. They average between the ages of seventeen and three-and-forty."

Aloise knew he spoke the truth. Hadn't she already suffered beneath her father's matchmaking attempts?

"They are a hard lot, Aloise. Penniless, they will sell their titles and their freedom for a handful of jewels. Jewels reported to bless their owner and curse his enemies." His voice grew low and silky. "Is that what you want? To be wed to such a man?"

She gazed wildly about her, feeling the light dim, the walls shrink to suffocate her. She couldn't go back to that kind of life. She would rather die than return to her father's bruising reign.

Rushing toward Slater she allowed him to see a portion of her panic. "Please, let me go! I won't tell anyone that I've been here. I'll disappear, leave the country, vanish as if I'd never been. My father will never find me, I assure you, and you can avenge yourself of whatever wrongs my father has committed against you." When he did not respond, she added, "Please." Slowly sinking to the floor, she hugged his knees. "Please, I beg of you!"

The answering silence was so long, so fraught with tension, she feared he had not heard her. But when she glanced up, she found a startling look on his face. His skin had grown white, his normally inscrutable mien haunted. As if he had seen a specter and could not reckon with the fact. He brushed at the hair that tumbled over her forehead, and if Aloise had not known better, she would have said he trembled.

"Will you let me go?" she asked when he did not speak for some time.

He slowly inhaled, as if to clear his mind of his own brand of demons. "No." His voice was curiously garbled.

"No?" She had bared herself to him. She'd dropped all walls of pride and let him see the aching little girl within, and for that he had refused her.

Angry, she bounded to her feet, but he caught her by the wrist, pulling her back. She struggled, but he held her fast, finally bringing her so tightly against him that she forgot to fight.

His expression was sad. Aching. "If it were only you or I who must deal with the consequences, I would let you go, Aloise. I would take you away myself." When his voice grew husky, he visibly swallowed. "But there are other people your father has hurt. Their ghosts cry out for reprisal."

"You, I suppose, must hear their pleas," she added scathingly.

Rather than commenting on her sarcasm, he took her challenge seriously. "I cannot ignore them." He cupped her face. "I tried—dear heaven, how I tried." His thumb teased the corner of her lips. "For that, I unknowingly allowed an innocent to be hurt for my own insensitivity."

She grew brittle, still, somehow sensing he was speaking of her.

"I should have tried to stop your father years ago, but until now, I haven't had the means available to do such a thing."

"No one can stop him."

"You can. You have a great power at your disposal. I can show you how. I can help you defeat him."

"By disappearing," she insisted.

"By staying."

"He won't find me if I leave."

"He would track you to hell and beyond. He'll never let you go."

Aloise could hardly breathe. He was right. She knew he was right.

"There is only one way to prevent him from continuing to hurt you, Aloise. One way." He stepped closer, so close that the scent of male musk inundated her senses. His thighs crowded her own, burning through the fragile weave of her gown. His hands splayed over her back, urging her to lift toward him, even as his head bent.

"Marry me."

14

SLATER HAD STUNNED HER, HE KNEW THAT BY THE WAY her eyes widened and her heart pounded so hard he could see the fluttering of her gown.

"No." Slater sensed the word was a denial of the idea, not the proposition.

"He will see you married to a man of his choice, Aloise. He will use force or trickery, but he will have his way."

She shook her head, looking altogether too young, too vulnerable.

"He will wait until you bear a child. A boy. Then he'll kill you too."

He thought she would resist such a statement, but a curious acceptance spread over her features.

"I know."

For an instant, he thought he'd imagined the words. But she wrapped her arms around his back and held him close.

"I know. He has already tried."

Slater felt an iciness enter his veins. Then an anger. An overwhelming fear.

"He's tried?"

She ducked her head. "My father does not care for my independence, nor for my attempts to escape. The last time, he took me to Loire, locked me away from society, and fed me nothing but bread and water."

If only Slater had known. The omnipresent guilt and remorse he'd felt for fifteen years threatened to choke him. Why hadn't he scoured the countryside for her? Why hadn't he tried harder to find Aloise? She'd told him earlier that she'd been imprisoned in Loire. He'd spent enough time in France that he could have found her had he known where to begin.

She backed away, inch by inch by inch. Once out of his arms, she reached for the fastenings to her dressing gown. She did not speak, she did not look at him. Slater found he couldn't move as the garment dropped to the floor.

Her fingers moved to the tiny satin-covered buttons at the neck of her night rail. They served as little more than a decoration due to the billowing style of the gown, but she loosed them to a point near her navel. A V of delicate, velvet flesh appeared to his gaze, bringing an inappropriate wave of need, of incredible want. Holding the fabric to her breasts to shield at least a portion of her modesty, she bunched the fabric up so that the yoke fell from her shoulders and draped to her hips.

"My father has a walking stick," she said, yanking his thoughts away from her delectable shape, then confusing him with the abrupt change in subject.

"It is a lovely piece, carved of mahogany with a silver tip at one end and the head of a snake at the other. I always thought his choice in animals particularly fitting." She watched him, clearly debating whether or not to continue. Something she saw must have convinced her that she could trust him.

"The cane disguises a riding quirt inside. But since injuring his knee a dozen years ago, my father does not ride. Still, he manages to use the piece with great regularity."

She turned then, exposing the breadth of her back.

Slater felt a sickness seep into his stomach, a

heaviness into his chest. He'd seen her several times dressed in little more than a chemise or the wrapping of a comforter. But he'd never seen her bare back. Her skin had been defiled by crisscrossing scars. The welts covered her shoulder blades and extended as far as her hips, colors of ivory to pale pink attesting to the passage of years, the extent of her punishment.

"I receive one strike for each hour of freedom."

"Dear God."

A bile rose in his throat as Slater realized he was partially responsible for her plight. *Damnit!* Why hadn't he helped Jeanne? Why hadn't he helped Aloise?

He went to her then, enfolding her in his embrace, tucking her head beneath his chin. An overwhelming sense of responsibility nearly took his breath away. He should have moved heaven and earth to come to Aloise's aid. He should have known when Crawford left her injured and bleeding that her childhood would have been a cruel one.

He would avenge the wrongs that had been done against her.

As God was his witness, he would see Crawford paid in kind.

Her voice grew choked. "I always thought there was something wanting in me. Something so horrible, that my father couldn't bear to be near me. I knew it was my fault. Mine. But over the years, I learned that he was the one in need. He'd been born without heart, without conscience."

Slater held her closer, closer, wanting to absorb the pain, the ache. He opened his mouth to refute such a statement; but how could he deny the truth?

Footsteps thundered down the hall, followed by a pounding at the door. "Slater? Slater!"

Slater's arm tightened automatically. "Damnit, Will. Not now."

"He's here. Crawford is here."

Both Slater and Aloise turned to stone. Then she twisted to look at him, a fear such as he had never seen glazing her face.

"The man's hopping mad. Evidently, the spy we discovered on the ridge returned to tell him that a woman tried to escape through the ballroom window. Crawford is sure it was his daughter. He has enough men with him to storm a castle and he's bound and determined to search every inch of Ashenleigh."

Slater grasped her arm. "Come with me." Unlocking the door, he threw it open, confronting Will Curry and a concerned Georgette still clad in her nightclothes.

"Tell the men to assemble downstairs. They are to appear as dissolute as their reputations—gaming, drinking, cards."

Will nodded.

"Georgette, if you would be so kind as to play a jest with me." Slater motioned to the bed behind him.

Georgette smiled in delight. "If eet eez Ollie Crawford you intend to dupe, eet will be my pleasure." She sauntered toward the bed and settled on it like the grandest of paramours.

Curry grinned and threw her a smacking kiss of approval.

"Will, allow Crawford to ring two or three times, then let him in. Give him free rein of the house. Let him search to his heart's content. Just see to it that he doesn't break anything. Then see to it that Miss Nibbs brings up that bathwater she tried to deliver earlier."

Will nodded and hurried to the stairs.

Slater caught the pallor of Aloise's skin. She shook uncontrollably, so much so, the fabric of her gown rustled in warning. After all she'd been through, she was near to breaking and the thought caused him to feel a pang of protectiveness. Fastening her night rail and securing the buttons to her robe, he tenderly grasped her shoulders.

"I won't let him take you. Will you trust me in that?"

She nodded, but it was obvious that she didn't think him capable of fulfilling such a vow.

"Please, Aloise. Believe in me." He framed her face, then bent to place a kiss on her forehead, her cheeks, and finally her lips. The caress was short, but telling, conveying to them both that emotions other than anger boiled beneath the surface. But at the pounding of the door in the vestibule below, Slater knew he hadn't the time to decipher such an incredible experience.

Taking Aloise's hand, he led her to a panel next to the mantel of the fireplace. Twisting the mask above, he released the latch of a door hidden to the side.

"You'll be safe here. As long as you don't make a sound."

She nodded, failing to choke back a small whimper of fear as he began to shut her inside.

"You'll be safe," he promised again, kissing his finger and easing it through the sliver of space to press it against her lips. "Trust me."

Then he closed the door and hurriedly stripped off his shirt, jacket, and hose. Purposely, he scattered the garments about the floor as if he had indulged in a night of passion, then slid beneath the covers just as the shattering sound of the front portal jarring loose resounded through the house.

"Where is my *daughter?"*

The words carried easily, said with overt disdain and fury.

Slater heard Will's muttered reply, then listened intently as it became quite obvious that Oliver Crawford had begun his search.

It took little less than five minutes for Crawford to make his way upstairs, slamming doors, bumping furniture, until at long last, he entered the Rose Room.

Seeing Slater ensconced on the bed with a tousled maiden, his beefy features grew red in fury, so much so that Slater thought the beads of sweat on his powdered forehead must fairly sizzle.

"Daughter!"

He fairly barked the word. Slater heard a slight stirring from behind the wall, but Georgette turned to face her accuser, obviously startling Crawford with the fact that she was a stranger.

"I don't believe we've had the pleasure of an introduction," Slater drawled, painfully schooling his features into a mask of indifference as he found himself face-to-face with his enemy.

Each muscle in his body coiled in anticipation. This was the man who had so callously murdered Jeanne. This was the man who had killed two of the witnesses to such an event. Would he remember the third? Would he look at Slater and see Matthew Waterton?

"Where is she?"

Using every ounce of control he possessed, Slater lifted a single brow in inquiry. "Who?"

"My daughter."

He didn't recognize him. Crawford didn't remember the young man he'd threatened.

The thought brought a burst of anger. Had Jeanne meant so little to him? Had Matthew Waterton's identity been considered so paltry a trade for Crawford's freedom?

"Well, man! Speak up! Where is my daughter?"

"I have positively no idea what you're talking about."

Crawford stamped into the room, the rust satin of his breeches slithering in displeasure. "Don't play games with me, sir. I've had enough of those already."

"Indeed."

"It was your phaeton that took my daughter; your coach I followed through the whole blasted countryside. Your men admitted as much days ago."

"I'm dreadfully sorry you thought the conveyance held your daughter, but I believe my assistant told you at the time that my coach and four were stolen by one of the hostlers and a cheeky housemaid. Do you remember her name, Georgette?"

She shook her head.

"So sorry."

Oliver Crawford scowled. "Who are you?"

"The name is McKendrick." Slater leaned back against the headboard, lazily crossing his arms behind his head. But there was nothing lazy about the tension that coiled inside him. "Slater McKendrick. I'm sorry I haven't seen to introductions until now, but I've been so busy organizing the estates, you know."

"Your bathwater and your tea, sir."

Slater grew even more still as Miss Nibbs stepped into the room. Setting an elaborate tray on the table by the fire, she motioned for the footmen to fill the tub. Through it all, Slater watched Crawford, looking for the slightest hint of recognition on the man's behalf. Did he remember the old woman he'd terrorized? Did he remember Miss Nibbs?

He couldn't be sure, but he thought a slight frown of confusion touched the man's brow. As if his memory had been pricked ever so slightly.

After the woman had left the room, Slater waited a beat of silence before asking, "Tell me, Mr. Crawford . . . do you like my house?"

The question itself caused Crawford's cheeks to flush in fury.

"I hope you will forgive me for the frightful liberties I took in copying your own design."

"There is nothing to forgive."

But it was quite obvious that Slater had peeved the man immeasurably in the process of building his home. Crawford's hand tightened over the head of his cane. The same cane that had savaged his daughter and scarred her for life. It took all the control Slater could muster not to lunge from the bed and throw the man against the wall.

"Your methods of decoration are very unusual," the man grudgingly offered. "So much black."

Slater affected a knowing smile. "Yes. It suits me, I think. I am often being accused of being a dark sort of character." He took Georgette's wrist and kissed the inside of her palm. "Isn't that right, my love?"

She purred and rubbed his chest.

"So, tell me, Crawford . . . what is all this fuss about your daughter?"

Crawford's jaw visibly ground together. "She disappeared. In *your* coach, despite what you might say."

Slater made a *tsk*ing noise. "What a pity that you are so distraught you would think me capable of such connivery." Releasing Georgette, he rose, wearing nothing but half-buttoned breeches, and padded toward Crawford. "You must be at your wit's end to even consider I would waylay your daughter."

He could see by the cunning glint in Crawford's eyes that the man suspected he was being baited, but couldn't prove such a thing conclusively. Continuing past him, Slater stepped behind the privacy screen, reached into the armoire, and removed a black dressing gown that had been hung in the far corner. Belting it about his waist, he returned.

"Would you care for some tea?"

"No. Thank you."

"I cannot tempt you?"

"No."

Slater settled into the chair by the fire. "Then we must focus our attention on your problem." Watching the man with the single-mindedness of a hawk he added, "Finding your daughter."

Crawford's jowled chin quivered in anger and forced control.

"I'm most embarrassed if my runaway servants are to blame for her disappearance. For that, I shall have to help you."

"I doubt there is much, sir, that you could do which has not already been done."

"Possibly, possibly." He steepled his fingers together. "But you see, I have friends. Friends in high places."

There was a rhythmic padding sound of footsteps in the hall. A low growl. "Ahh," Slater exclaimed in pleasure. "Sonja has awakened from her nap." Uttering a chirping sound, he waited, eyeing Crawford as the huge tiger ambled into the room.

Oliver started, cringing ever so slightly toward the fireplace as the animal approached. After it veered toward Slater, Crawford turned to assess Slater more carefully.

"McKendrick, you say? The name sounds familiar."

Slater shrugged, knowing full well that Crawford had tried to investigate his past and had determined nothing of any value. Sonja sprawled at his feet, her eyelids opening, closing, opening as she assessed the stranger. Her claws dug into the carpet, then retreating in a potent reminder that she may appear tamed, but she was ultimately a thing of the wild.

"You are employed by the French king," Crawford finally murmured, obviously speaking his thoughts aloud. "I've heard of you through a friend who has attended the court of Louis the Sixteenth. I believe you furnished the king with the animals for the royal menagerie."

"Louis has a great fondness for unusual things. I indulge that fondness." Slater sighed. "But once again, we have forgotten the gist of our discussion." He added pointedly, "What are we to do about your daughter? I understand that you have guests arriving in the next day or so."

Crawford's brows creased, as if he were suddenly beginning to fathom the intent of Slater's games.

"Yes. To see my daughter."

"She is of marriageable age?"

"Correct."

"And you, being the doting father, are attempting to find a mate for her?"

"It is my duty."

"Come now, isn't she a bit on the shelf?"

"She is but twenty."

"She should have been married years ago."

Crawford's cheeks held a tinge of red. "She has been betrothed on several occasions, but, alas, each of her grooms met with tragedy."

"How unfortunate."

"More than you will ever know," Crawford muttered. "She has been rightfully distraught by such misfortunes."

"As a father, you must be worried about her future."

Crawford shrugged.

"So much so that you now search for the perfect spouse."

Crawford's gaze didn't waver. "Perhaps I will have that tea."

Slater didn't take his eyes from his foe. "Georgette, would you be so kind?"

He saw her draw the robe she wore more firmly about her body and cross to the table. Circling the idle tiger and the tail that thumped impatiently against the floor, she poured a cup of the brew and gave it to their guest.

"Milk, lemon, sugar?"

"No. Thank you." Crawford did not break Slater's regard, but accepted the cup nonetheless. "I prefer it straightforward and undiluted. As I suspect you do, Mr. McKendrick."

"Personally, I have never been overly fond of tea."

Crawford studied him for some time. "You have returned from one of your exploits, I presume."

"Africa."

"Then you intend to stay in England for a time?"

"Until His Majesty needs me again. For now, he is entertained by the gifts I brought him."

The mention of royal influence caused an obvious greed to tinge Crawford's expression. "Are you happy here in Cornwall, Mr. McKendrick?"

Slater could nearly hear the jaws of his trap snapping shut. "I confess I find myself a trifle bored."

"Would you consider becoming my guest this week? I believe your adventures would prove a scintillating subject at dinner."

"I would be delighted. Such an event might prove amusing."

"Providing my daughter were to return."

"Indeed."

Crawford thrust the cup and saucer, untouched, back into Georgette's hands. "Very well, Mr. McKendrick. Contact your friends, your friends in *high places.* If you can locate my daughter . . ." the words were said slowly, as if he still did not believe the story of the stolen coach ". . . then you may consider yourself—"

"A candidate?"

"A guest."

"Ahh, then you would not wish to have a favorite of Louis the Sixteenth as a son-in-law?"

Crawford's suspicion was open now, but it was tempered by a shred of interest.

"If you had been a favorite of George the Third, such a fact might have proved impressive. As things stand, I shall make a few pointed inquiries with some of my guests. If the extent of your influence proves to be as comprehensive as you claim, you may be considered." He took two steps toward the door, turned, and lifted his walking stick, tapping Slater in the chest with the tip. "But, Mr. McKendrick . . . first, you must find my daughter."

The tiger growled in warning and Crawford nearly dropped his cane.

"I shall do my best," Slater replied, his lips twitching.

Crawford managed to summon a stiff, "See that you do." With that, he stepped from the room, slamming the door behind him. "Four days," he called as he stamped down the hall. "I will give you no more, no less. See that you do not fail me. When my daughter has been found, see to it that she is returned, virtue and reputation intact, or even your 'friends' will not be able to help you."

15

You *lied* to me!"

Aloise scarcely waited for the panel to open before storming at Slater, nails drawn. "You fairly gave me to him on a silver platter."

She tried to claw at his face, but he took her wrists and snapped them around his waist, drawing her flush against his hips so that she couldn't move so much as a muscle.

"How dare you?" she cried, an anguish she had never known nearly choking off the words. She had momentarily trusted him. She'd thought he was sincere in his willingness to help her. To offer her a marriage of convenience. But she'd judged him incorrectly and he'd betrayed her.

"I promised you would be safe, and you are."

His placating tone had little effect in tempering her fury. "For how long? Tell me, when do you intend to surrender me? Today? Next week?"

"Aloise, listen to me."

"No! I won't hear any more of your lies!"

"I won't let your father gain control of you again."

"You just promised to return me to him!"

He regarded her seriously, before saying, "You will have to go back. Eventually."

"Damn you!" Tears rose, unbidden, unwanted, but there nevertheless. A thick desperation tightened her throat. All too well, she remembered how her father had treated her for her last attempts at freedom. His retribution had been swift and cruel. This time, she'd managed to escape him for over a week. He would punish her tenfold for that.

She had to get away!

As if sensing her panic, Slater held her in her place. "Aloise, you can't escape a final confrontation with your father. Once and for all, you need to break the ties that bind you to him. Now or later. Wouldn't you rather have it over soon?"

"No."

"Aloise—"

"No! You lied to me before. You're lying to me now!"

"I wouldn't do that to you, Aloise."

His hands moved from her wrists to splay across her back, urging her to credit his words. But she couldn't. She wouldn't. To believe in a man's words was to open the gates of heartache. Hadn't she learned that lesson already?

"Let me go."

"I want to help you."

"No!" She shook her head in derision. "You've done nothing but manipulate me since the moment we met. You have no regard for my feelings, no sense of respect for my dreams."

His features became grave. "That might have been the case at one time. But not anymore. I swear to you."

"You tricked me into coming to this house."

"Because I didn't know you then. I didn't know if I could trust you not to go to your father."

"So what have you discovered to make you believe in me now?"

He cradled her face, holding her still. "That you are kind and beautiful and strong. That you have a great capacity for love—one that has never been indulged."

His words shocked her into silence, but only for a moment. She would not allow him to see how they had affected her.

"I suppose *you* wish to indulge me."

He bent to graze the corner of her eye with his lips. A fleeting, heart-tugging kiss. "I would like to try."

She grasped his wrists with the intent of pushing him away, but found that the moment she touched him, felt the warmth of his skin, the strength of his bones, she was powerless to do such a thing. A need blossomed inside her. The same need he had instilled in her so many times. She'd tried every method she possessed to banish such a traitorous response. But now, still trembling and bitterly afraid of being sent back to her father, she discovered that she longed to feel this man's strength and reassurance. She wanted him to prove to her that he truly cared. Even if he only pretended.

"You haven't answered my question, Aloise."

Her eyes flickered, and she met the burning brand of his gaze.

"Will you do me the honor of becoming my wife?"

"Are you trying to tell me you love me?"

He shifted. "No."

She huffed in indignation and he reminded her, "You asked me to tell the truth. This is to be a marriage mutually beneficial to both." His voice grew softer, more tender. "I'm sure that deeper feelings will develop one day. But those things take time."

"My father will not let such a marriage happen."

"He will not be able to stop it."

"As soon as he discovers that you are my husband, he will punish me for rebelling against his wishes." The fear she felt was very real. Very powerful. "He will kill me, I know."

"Not if I'm with you. We'll tell him together. Then he won't be able to hurt you. Ever again."

"But you want to send me back!"

"I only want you to meet with your father so that he'll know you are legally married."

The idea was tempting, incredibly tempting. But this man underestimated her father's strength of will.

"He will annul the match."

"Not if it has been consummated."

Consummated. The word alone sent a burst of warmth to her loins. Aloise was not a total innocent. She knew a man's needs and she knew that it was a woman's duty to submit to those needs.

"Trust me, Aloise. Trust me to help you, take care of you. Trust me to make things right once and for all. Your father wanted a son. Instead, he was given a rare gift. A beautiful and charming daughter."

Her chest ached at the words. Her throat grew tight with the tears she refused to shed.

"Now he seeks a grandson. An heir." Slater's voice became husky, rich. "Best him at his own game, Aloise. Thwart him in all things. Reject the hand-picked lot of suitors and marry me, a rogue, a rake, and a thoroughly unsuitable match. Then beat him again . . ." his palm lowered, cupping the flatness of her abdomen, bunching the fabric of her nightclothes. "Bear me a daughter. I vow that I will cherish her as you should have been cherished. She will become her father's jewel. More valuable to him than—"

"Rubies?" she inserted bitterly, suddenly understanding. "Is that what you seek? The Bengal Rubies?"

His eyes wavered slightly, dropped.

"You told me there would be no more lies."

A heavy silence cloaked them before he finally spoke. "I cannot deny that the rubies hold a certain appeal."

"Because of the curse?"

"Because of their history."

She gasped in realization. "You must have recognized the piece you said I'd stolen. You never really thought I was a thief, did you? It was all part of your plan."

"Yes."

He offered no other explanation, no apology.

"I don't know where my father obtained the jewels. I have always wondered if he stole them."

Slater's countenance grew enigmatic. "There is always that possibility."

"I doubt my father will give them up if the marriage is not to his choosing."

"He will have no choice if word of a broken promise is spread through London."

"There might be rightful heirs who would claim the jewels. If so, would you give them back?"

He chose his words carefully. "If, as you say, your father took them wrongfully, they should be returned to their proper owners."

"Then, what of me? What will you do with me once you've lost my dowry and gained your child?"

"We apparently have a misunderstanding of sorts. I'm not bartering for your breeding services, Aloise."

She felt a flush of embarrassment at his blunt words. "I hadn't thought—"

"Hadn't you? When I spoke of a daughter, I spoke only of our first. There will be many more after that."

"More?" she breathed.

Winding his arms around her waist, he took her weight, drawing her up to him so that they were eye to eye. "The marriage I suggest is not a temporary proposition. If you accept, you accept to spend the rest of your days with me—and your nights. You agree to bear my children, tolerate my moods, and make my home a happy place."

"Oh." It was the only response she could summon. The air locked in her body, so much so, she feared she would swoon in surprise, but his next words instantly revived her.

"In return, I'm afraid I cannot offer you an easy life, so you must think carefully. You will be required to travel, visit far-off lands, endure primitive facilities and unusual cultures."

Adventure. He was offering her the adventure of a lifetime, and he felt it necessary to apologize.

"I accept."

"I know you will need time to adjust, so we'll stay here for a month or two—"

"I accept."

"But I fear I have been assigned to an expedition to Brazil—"

"I accept."

"—come Christmas. His Majesty is very eager . . . to . . ."

His words trailed away and he finally met her sparkling gaze.

"I . . . *accept,*" she stated slowly and distinctly.

A boyish look of disbelief tugged at his lips, his brows. "Really?"

"Really."

He uttered a short bark of laughter, then scooped her close. "You accept!"

"I accept."

Whirling her in a circle, he buried his head in her shoulder. "You accept."

Weaving her fingers in his hair, Aloise savored the moment, the heady exhilaration. Perhaps she was fooling herself. Perhaps this man had merely strung her another set of pretty tales. But for now, she banished the doubts, banished the fears, banished all thought of her father's wrath. For now, she reveled in what this man had made her feel. Beautiful. Whole.

Cherished.

She could only pray that such emotions could withstand her father's wrath.

They were married in a small rock church on the land bordering Ashenleigh. The ceremony took place at dawn, just as the sun was beginning to paint the sky with brush strokes of gold.

Aloise wore one of Georgette LeBeau's creations, a heavy gown of rose and ivory satin studded with pearls and lace. A half-dozen petticoats rested over her cane panniers, causing her skirts to rustle and drift about her ankles like the foam of a wind-tossed wave. As a finishing touch, one of Georgette's assistants arranged her hair in a riot of ringlets, then inserted a score of diamond-tipped hairpins into the silken tresses.

Until joining Slater, Aloise had never known how beautiful garments made to her measurements could make her feel like royalty. As she walked down the aisle to join her waiting groom, she could have been a queen.

A suspiciously misty-eyed Miss Nibbs and a beaming Georgette had come to the ceremony as her attendants while Slater's men served the dual purpose of witnesses and guards. Taking her place, Aloise gripped the nosegay of pink roses that Slater had sent to her room. A room that had still been firmly locked for two days—as if he did not trust her to remain fast in her decision.

Aloise had not changed her mind. Although most of the previous evenings had been spent pacing her room, it had not been because of her impending marriage. Slater had been right in saying this was the only way to beat her father at his own game. She was valuable to Oliver Crawford as long as she was an unwed virgin.

Staring at the man who stood beside her, so tall, so dark, so serious, she realized that within minutes she would have destroyed the first valuable qualification. By eveningfall, she would have destroyed the second. Then her father would never be able to hurt her again.

The thought of being enclosed in his arms, of surrendering her virtue, caused a weakness to invade her limbs. She had to make love to this man. *Had* to. It was the only way to escape her present predicament.

As the vicar's words droned on, she realized that

her motives were not entirely so simple. There was a part of her that wanted him to take her. Just once, she longed to feel important. Loved. But, come morning, she would have to remind herself that such thoughts were a sham. Their marriage was one of retribution toward her father, nothing more.

Returning her attention to the ceremony, Aloise stifled her impatience. She wanted this day over. Done. She wanted all of her unpleasant tasks behind her.

If the vicar was surprised by the early hour of the nuptials, he made no comment. In fact, the old man was so feeble and nearsighted that Aloise was astonished that he had the energy to deliver the words in a booming voice. Yet, when he uttered the words "What God has brought together, let no man put asunder," Aloise felt a small kernel of hope. Of elation. What she was doing felt right. More right than anything she had ever done before. Their union must surely be blessed by some holy intervention. A higher power that even her father could not defeat. This time—*this time*—she would have emerged victorious in her battle to assert her will.

It began to rain as they walked from the chapel. Miss Nibbs clucked in distress, muttering something about unlucky superstitions dealing with brides and storms, but Aloise knew differently. For once, the inclement weather brought no ill memories. Aloise chose to think the slight shower was a good sign, a cleansing of the past. A chance for new beginnings.

And now . . .

The evening storm continued, the splatter of moisture hissing against the windowpanes, softly, gently. The noise soothed Aloise's nerves and she laid her forehead against the cool glass, knowing that tonight she would irrevocably change. Before the hour was through, she would truly become a bride.

Wild horses could not have dragged the admission from her, but she'd lived the last few days in a constant state of fear. Having had no luck with prospective spouses in the past, she'd held her breath and mentally crossed her fingers, praying that her new groom would live to see the ceremony. To her infinite relief, he had. All that remained was to consummate their union.

She was swiftly discovering that she was not quite as immured to the idea as she might have believed. She found herself tensely waiting for Slater. She started at each strange sound. She trembled. She . . . yearned.

Aloise knew she should dread the next few hours. After all, she was about to indulge in the most intimate of acts with a man she hardly knew. But she found the thought didn't frighten her. In fact, for the first time she could remember, she felt . . .

Safe.

The door from the hallway had been left ajar, and Aloise heard the imperceptible whisper of the door over carpet. Steeling herself, she turned.

It was not her husband who had come to greet her, but Sonja. The tiger stood in the middle of the threshold, eyeing Aloise in careful concern.

"Hello, Sonja." Aloise hoped her voice did not sound as tremulous to the tiger as it did to her. She watched in great trepidation as the animal's tail swished from side to side. Not a good sign from the barnyard variety of cats. Aloise could only hope it meant something different to Sonja.

The cat padded forward, offering a warning grumble. She circled Aloise once, twice, sniffing and growling to herself. Aloise was beginning to wonder if she should back away or call for help when the animal dropped to the floor, rolled to its back, and began to purr.

How astonishing and how completely unexpected! Moving warily, Aloise bent and placed a tentative hand to the animal's stomach. The purring increased.

"You're just a big kitten at heart, aren't you?"

Aloise murmured, stroking the silky fur. "You're nothing to be feared at all."

"On the contrary."

The dark voice melted from the shadows and she started, looking up. "Sonja has been with me on my travels since soon after her birth, but she is still a wild thing at heart."

The cat yowled in protest at having its petting disturbed and Aloise renewed her efforts, stroking the pale white fur of her stomach.

"Over the years, she has learned to choose those whom she can trust."

The words were so carefully spoken that Aloise knew Slater referred to more than the tiger.

"She is wise to do so. There are many who would seek to hurt her."

"Yet she has given her trust to you, Aloise."

"As well as to you."

"Will you believe she won't hurt you?"

"As long as I can gauge her moods."

"And what about me, Aloise?"

She thought carefully before responding. "I shall have to learn to gauge your moods as well."

The tiger, miffed at being placed in the periphery of attention, huffed, yawned, and rolled to her feet. Grumbling deep in her throat, she padded from the room. Slater followed the animal far enough to close the door behind her striped tail.

When he turned, the light of the single taper next to the bed cast a weak glow of light over his features. Such blunt, rough-hewn, bearded features.

"However did you come by such coloring?" Aloise asked. "Such black eyes and hair—very unusual."

"My mother was French."

"Ahh." Aloise toyed with the lace at one cuff. "Do you miss her?"

"My mother?"

"Mmm."

He shrugged. "She died when I was an infant."

"I see." The idle conversation was having no effect against the mounting tension of the room. None at all. But Aloise preferred the meaningless flow of words to the silence. "I missed the influence of a mother."

The statement was made without thought, but it brought with it a shivering expectancy. The man at the opposite end of the room grew still, so still.

"But then, you know that," she murmured. "You were the one to ask me if I yearned for such a thing." Tilting her chin, she wondered if she would rue the question she must ask.

"Did you know her . . . intimately?"

"I knew her quite well."

"How well?" Her fingers trembled and she clenched them together. "You said you were at my birthday party. Why?"

She knew that he had absorbed the slant of her questioning, that he understood the intent of her queries even though Aloise could not bear to utter the words.

Had he been her mother's lover?

16

How close was your friendship, Slater?" Aloise asked again, knowing that he assessed each thought, each emotion that flitted across her face.

When he hesitated, she felt a deep sense of loss. She'd been conscious of the fact that their union held little romance, but Slater hadn't married her for the reasons he'd given. He hadn't wanted to help her, protect her, or care for her. He'd wanted a substitute. A ghost of her mother.

She started when he took her shoulders.

"You're thinking far too much again, Aloise."

He smoothed the small crease of worry between her brows.

"I am not my mother," she stated fiercely, angry at having been so easily duped, so easily used.

"No. You're not."

She grew quiet.

"She was gentle, sweet, and refined—with only a touch of your temper."

Aloise folded her arms in pique at his words, but her mood evaporated upon his next statement.

"I can't deny that I loved your mother, but merely as a friend. A very close and dear friend. A sister. When you and I met on the beach, I thought you were her ghost. Now, I realize you are Aloise. A woman in her own right. Jeanne would have been very proud of you. Of the person you have become." He rubbed her cheek, peering at her thoughtfully. "Rest assured that I did not marry you because of your resemblance to your mother."

"Didn't you?" There. Her suspicions were out in the open. Naked.

"No."

"Then why?"

He didn't answer immediately. Aloise saw the way he considered his words carefully, then eased away.

"I gave you my reasons."

"You told me you wished to gain your revenge on my father. Why?"

He touched her cheek. "Oliver Crawford stole a portion of my youth, just as he stole yours." He turned away, blatantly changing the subject. "You've had a long and exhausting day." He gestured to the tray by the fireplace. "Have you had enough to eat?"

He wasn't going to elaborate and any amount of prompting would not aid her cause. Of that she was sure. But one day, she would discover the extent of his motives. One day soon. "Yes, thank you."

"Is there anything more you require?"

She shook her head, then reconsidered. "One thing."

"Yes?"

"There will be no more locked doors between us. I wed you to be your helpmate, not chattel. You asked of my trust, now I demand yours."

His head dipped. "Very well. You have my word." He walked toward her, silently, effortlessly, clad all in black from his boots to his breeches while above, a snowy white shirt billowed about the width of his shoulders. "But what, in return, will you give me, Aloise?"

"I know what this night will bring," she said with

forced bravado when he grew so near she could barely breathe.

"Do you?"

"You will take your pleasure."

"What about you, Aloise?"

She gazed at him in confusion.

"Have you no wish to share in that pleasure?"

She didn't know what he meant. There could be no pleasure on the woman's part. It went beyond all the laws of nature.

Didn't it?

"Perhaps you do not know all there is to know." He touched her cheek, her jaw. "Perhaps you have much to learn this eve."

Tipping her chin, he lowered his head for a kiss. One so soft and sweet that Aloise found her eyes fluttering closed, her breath locked in her throat.

"Relax, *chérie.*" He brushed his lips against her cheek, her temple, her ear. "We have this night, and many more to come. You will grow to enjoy the time spent together. Of that, I promise. But first, I have brought you a gift."

Her brow arched in surprise as he reached inside his shirt and withdrew a flat gold box tied with a black velvet ribbon. "A gift?"

"It is customary to exchange presents on the eve of one's nuptials."

Her fingers toyed with the velvet band, her limbs flooding with shame. "I've nothing for you."

"On the contrary." Again he touched her face, then trailed a finger to the dipping neckline of her wedding gown. "You offer me a great gift. The most valuable thing a woman can give a man."

The reverence of his words were her undoing.

"Come, love, open the box. 'Tis but a trifle in honor of the occasion. When you took my name, I awarded you the rights to everything I own. My house, my fortune, my security."

"What of your heart?" The words slipped free before she could retrieve them.

He eyed her long and hard then admitted, "Most men would attest that I have no heart to give."

"What of the women?"

"None have been able to find it." Relenting somewhat, he took her hand. "But you are at liberty to try."

"What if I discover this uncharted territory?"

"Then it is yours to claim. In return, you may find that I will demand that you allow me a similar prize."

He had given her more than she had expected. He had at least offered her the hope that their future together would not be completely without caring.

Setting the box unopened on the table beside the bed, she kissed him softly on the chin.

"Thank you, Slater. For all you have done."

Her gratitude made him uncomfortable, and he paced to the far window. "The dress was to your liking?"

"Yes." Fingering the delicate ivory lace, she turned to give him full vantage of her gown. "It is beautiful, don't you think?"

He did not answer, and when she looked at him, it was to find that he stared her way in open hunger.

"Slater?"

Without speaking, he moved to her. "*You* are beautiful." His hands spread wide, rubbing over her shoulder, the taut line of her torso, her tiny waist. "The gown is but the setting for the jewel."

Aloise's heart leapt in pleasure at the unexpected compliment.

Slater pulled her against his hips so that her skirts bunched between them. Whispered. Caressed.

"You will not regret having trusted me, Aloise." He found the laces at the back of her bodice and tugged at the bow. "I will do everything in my power to see this situation to its rightful end."

When she would have spoken, he covered her

mouth with his, softly at first, then deeply, hungrily, kissing her with the appetites of a man starved. She responded—how could she not? But deep down, she wondered. She wondered . . .

When he drew free, she could not prevent the words. "How many women have heard such a statement?"

Anger clouded his features, then resignation, then thoughtfulness.

"None before you, Aloise. None that mattered as you do." The admission surprised him as much as it did her.

"Then why *me?*" she asked fiercely, disbelieving that a man who had traveled the globe, charted unknown lands, discovered exotic beasts, could want her. *Her.* "You could have obtained the same end without a lifetime commitment."

He didn't wish to speak. He didn't wish to disclose his thoughts, but when she refused to relent, he finally said, "Because you have fire. Spirit. Something I never knew I needed. Until now."

Nimble fingers loosened her ties, then tugged the gown over her shoulders. With an uncanny accuracy, he found each fastener of her petticoats and the buckle of her panniers, allowing them to drop to a heap at her feet.

Without pause, he scooped her into his arms and placed her on the bed. Then he stared at her, the way she wore nothing but a sheer silk chemise, rose satin stays, delicate hose, ribbon garters, and petite brocade slippers.

Kneeling beside the bed, he freed her of her shoes and paused to caress her feet, her ankles. He paid special attention to the sensitive nerves, the delicate bones. Aloise gasped, her toes curling in delight. Who would have thought such a place to be so sensitive? So . . . erotic.

Grinning at her expression, he moved upward ever

upward. His hands splayed wide, kneading the curve of her calves, gripping her knee, then inching to her thighs. There, he unfastened the first garter with a delicious sense of delay, tugging ever so slowly on the ribbon, and drawing it free. After dropping the frothy confection of satin and lace to the floor, he moved to the opposite side, repeating the procedure.

She shifted, attempting to right the hem of her chemise when it rode nearly to her hips in the process, but he stopped her.

"Tell me, Aloise. Do you like the feel of silk against your skin?" He rubbed the length of her leg, causing a delicious tickling sensation since only the faint layer of her hose separated his flesh from hers. "As a man, I can assure you that it is very becoming. Very . . . arousing."

Discovering the hem of her stocking, he drew it free with a leisurely pace. A tingling permeated each inch of the limb he exposed, then its mate, until her stockings joined the garters in an untidy puddle on the floor.

When he lifted her slightly from the pillows to unlace her stays, removing them so her breasts were freed of their constraints, she did not demur. A fire settled deep in her loins, and with each of his subtle ministrations she became more and more impatient.

Why didn't he join her? Why didn't he settle his weight on her? Why? She wanted him, now, held fast against her.

Sensing a portion of the chaos storming her body, he stood and tugged his shirt over his head, exposing a chest that was wide, well defined, and beautiful. Dark hair delineated each muscle and the pink hearts of his nipples, then swept down, ever down, to disappear beneath the waist of his breeches.

"Do I frighten you?"

Aloise shook her head. He'd asked that question several times. Now, she could honestly answer, "No."

"Good." Sinking onto the mattress at her side, he

bracketed her body with his arms. "I never want you to be afraid again."

Then he bent to kiss her. Not restrained delicate kisses, but a kiss of passion. Overwhelming desire.

The intensity of his caress summoned more of a response from Aloise than had he been gentle. The spark of need, of want, she'd felt so distinctly burst into an inferno, and she discovered that she didn't care what had happened earlier, what he'd said, what she'd done. There was only this moment. This night.

Wrapping her arms around his shoulders, she drew him down, needing to feel his flesh against her. Needing his strength.

He responded, the kiss deepening, becoming savage, deliberate.

Her heart pounded with such fury, she felt sure he could hear each stroke. A whimpering noise came from her throat, her body arched.

"Easy, easy. We should take things slow."

She grabbed his hair and forced him to look at her. "No. All my life I've been told what to do. This time, I want to do it my way."

He eyed her consideringly, then freed himself from her embrace. Standing by the side of the bed, he stripped free from his boots, his hose, then began on the buttons of his breeches.

Aloise watched in avid fascination as each inch of flesh was bared to her view. She had never seen a naked man. Finally, her curiosity would be slaked.

What she saw, however, soon caused her to pause. "Oh." The word slipped unbidden from her lips. The man she had married was completely and utterly aroused. Swollen. Large.

"Oh," she sighed again as he settled beside her and began to unfasten the ties of her chemise. One by one by one.

He worked slowly, savoring each morsel of flesh disclosed to his view. Aloise found herself unable to hold still on the bed. She wanted him to finish with such unimportant details and kiss her again. She wanted him stretched heavily above her. She wanted this night to be over. She wanted . . .

Him.

Impatient, she reached for the bottom of the garment and swept it over her head. Before she could lower her arms, he had drawn her close, his mouth closing over one taut nipple.

She cried out as a burst of lightning exploded in her loins. When his teeth closed about her, she writhed against him. He'd given her a hint of this untold pleasure, but she'd never dreamed—never *dreamed*—that it could become even more powerful and enduring.

Panting, she drew his head up, staring at him in confusion.

"So you see, madam, there are things your husband can teach you that cannot be found in books."

And teach her, he did.

Pressing her back against the pillows, he kissed and explored each inch of her body from the tiny shells of her ears, to the hollow of her collarbone, to her navel, her knees, and the sensitive indentations of her ankles. He soothed and tickled and caressed, bringing her to a frenzy of need, an aching, intolerable want.

She gripped his shoulders, his back. Felt him straining toward her, his body heated and slick with sweat. Pulling free, he ran the tip of his tongue from her sternum, to her navel, then lower to her hips.

"No." Grasping his hair, she pulled him away. He merely grinned, murmuring, "Next time. Or the time after that. After you have grown accustomed to what you are feeling, *chérie.*"

Still he continued, until Aloise feared she would not be able to endure a second longer. She bucked against him, writhed. She became a pagan thing. A tight aching ball of need. Then finally, he stretched his body above her own, fully. The weight of him felt pleasant. Right.

Poised there, he stared deep into her eyes, searching for . . . who knew what?

"I will always protect you," he murmured. "Remember that. Just as you will always remember this night."

"I know." She could barely force the words free. Her body throbbed, ached. She wanted, needed . . .

More.

"Slater . . ."

He kissed her again, magically, completely. She felt him shift, his hand slide down her ribs, her hips, then between her legs.

Reaching for that low, delicate, womanly place, he found her moist, ready. She whimpered at his touch, sure he meant to inflict some torment to continue to arouse her thus. But Slater deepened their kiss, positioned his body over hers, and thrust into her willing flesh.

Aloise gasped, trying to push him away, but he lay still, so still, until she adjusted to the weight of him, the length of him, the heat. Slowly, he withdrew, and her brow knit in confusion.

That was all? That was what such fuss had been made about in the whispered conversations at Sacre Coeur?

Slater arched into her. Again, again, again. Back and forth. In and out. The rhythm caused her to gasp, her nails digging into his shoulders. Her eyes closed and the room about her disappeared. She could only center around the feelings. The exquisite, indescribable rush of feelings that tumbled through her. She had never dreamed. In all her wildest imaginings, she had never dreamed!

The motions increased, grew more forceful, more demanding, more intoxicating. The tight knot of need in her belly grew achingly heavy, so much so she feared she would scream or expire on the spot. Then, just when she became certain such a thing would actually happen, something deep in her loins shattered and contracted, shuddering, spilling through her like the scattering of stars. Squeezing her eyes shut, she held on to the sensation, trying to memorize it, sure it would never come again.

The man above her began to tremble. He thrust one last time, causing a renewed flurry of reaction in her exhausted body, then spilled his seed into her womb.

The following minutes floated by, indistinguishable in their passing. Aloise didn't know how long she lay there, absorbing each nuance of the lovemaking she had just experienced. His weight. His scent. The way his body relaxed on her bit by bit, not uncomfortably so, but soothing her, warming her.

Aloise smiled against his shoulder. No wonder the art of love was such a closely guarded secret in society. If the young women at Sacre Coeur had guessed the half of what it entailed, none of them would have remained virgins for long, of that she was certain.

She didn't know how much time passed when Slater lifted away from her, rolled to her side, and wrapped his arms about her waist so that her back pressed against his chest.

"Are you sore?" he asked some time later.

"Not anymore."

Her answer must have startled him, because she felt him grow still, then chuckle against the back of her neck.

"You enjoyed your first taste of true passion?"

"Mmm-hmm," she purred, snuggling sleepily against him.

She had nearly drifted into slumber when she smiled to herself, roused, and asked. "Slater? Must we wait many days before we can do it again?"

17

"MR. CRAWFORD?"

"What is it, Humphreys?"

"Your daughter, sir. She's been seen."

Those two statements brought Crawford's gaze away from the papers he'd been studying to spear the slight form of his secretary with an iron gaze.

"Where?"

"She briefly left Ashenleigh, then returned again. Early this morning."

The mention of the neighboring estate caused Crawford's heart to beat a little harder. "No doubt, it was that Frenchwoman."

"No, sir. It was Aloise. I saw her myself when she returned."

Crawford's jaw tightened and his hand clenched about his quill. "Where did she go?"

Mr. Humphreys shifted nervously. "I-I don't know, sir. The guard you assigned followed them as far as the village then came to retrieve me so that the woman could be properly identified."

"You're sure it was my daughter?"

"Positive."

"She was with that man?"

"Yes, sir." He tugged at the band of his cravat, admitting, "They were holding hands."

A wave of fury settled in his breast and Crawford slammed his fist against the desk. "Just as I suspected, that girl is trying to form a scandal, trying to create enough gossip so that I won't be able to bribe any titled gentleman enough to take her."

Jumping to his feet, he strode to the window, staring into the gloomy afternoon as if he could see beyond the next ridge. "Where is she now?"

"Ashenleigh."

"You're sure."

"Yes, sir. Nearly everyone else left."

That comment caused Crawford to turn. "Left?"

"Yes, sir. I saw them go myself: the housekeeper, the Frenchwoman, her friends, McKendrick's men. All but one. A rather swarthy looking fellow was left as a guard by the boarded-up window."

Crawford's jaw clenched, then he strode across the room to retrieve his jacket and his walking stick. "Come with me."

"Are we going to retrieve your daughter?"

Crawford whipped the door to his office open, his buried fury barely contained. "All in good time, Humphreys. All in good time."

"So what did you give me?"

Aloise rolled on her stomach and reached for the wedding gift that still lay unopened on the night table. Confronted with the lithe line of her back, Slater took the opportunity to kiss her at the base of her spine. He felt her shivering reaction and was surprised at the way it pleased him immeasurably. She was beautiful. So passionate.

And she was *his*.

She pressed her face into the pillows, then peered at him over her shoulder, her eyes dark, slumberous, and sultry. "Slater, if you continue thus, I won't have a chance to see my present."

"I haven't finished with mine yet," he growled, clasping her thighs, and pulling her irretrievably toward him. He couldn't get enough of her.

Aloise giggled at his words. The first genuine laughter he'd heard without the benefit of rum. Shifting to her back, she lapped her arms around his shoulders. "You are an evil man," she teased. "An evil, awful man."

"I consider that a compliment."

"You would."

He kissed her stomach, then trailed a string of similar caresses over her ribs. When he reached the fullness of her breasts, he murmured, "Come, let me love you."

Her fingers wound in his hair, drawing him closer to her lips. "You've done quite enough of that already."

He could not prevent his grin of pleasure. "You enjoyed it?"

"The first time. As well as the second. And the third."

"We could make the experience an even dozen."

Her eyes smoldered. "I suppose. But I believe I am entitled to a gift of my own."

Offering her a heated look, he pressed her firmly on her back, stretching her arms above her head. Straddling her hips, he remained thus for some time then finally reached beyond her to snare the package. Returning to her side, he placed the box in her hand, purposely rubbing his chest against her sensitive nipples.

Her lashes flickered closed. "You are cruel."

"Only to be kind."

"Hardly."

Chuckling, he relented, leaning against the headboard. He gestured to the box held in her lax fingers. "I'll have you know I obtained this through great labor and expense."

Her brows lifted.

"I sent Clayton all the way to London to retrieve it."

"London . . ."

She sat up, barely managing to juggle the drape of the sheets and the box at the same time. To his infinite delight, she lost the battle with the linens and they dipped to allow him a peek of her nipple. One pink, luscious nipple.

"None of that, Slater."

But she was not looking at him, she had given her attention to the package, shaking it to analyze the thumping rattle, testing its size, its weight.

"Open it."

She shot him a coy look, delaying one minute longer to prolong the suspense. Licking her lips, she tugged at the bow with an inestimably slow pace that nearly drove Slater to distraction. He wanted to see her reaction.

"I do hope it's not jewelry."

"It's not."

"Oh."

Slater couldn't tell if she were relieved by the news or somewhat disappointed.

"Then what?"

"*Open* it and see."

Still, she hesitated. One last instant.

"Very well." She removed the lid, slowly, carefully. A delicate piece of parchment had been placed on top of the contents, obscuring what rested inside. Slater noted the way her fingers trembled slightly as she lifted the covering away.

"Oh, Slater . . ." she sighed. "Chocolate."

He waited until her gaze clashed with his own. "Truffles. Just as you once requested, my dear. Sweet and rich and thick."

She took one of the candies from the box with the reverence of a fanatic. As if it were the most precious of diamonds, she studied its shape, its weight, its color. She waved it beneath her nose to savor the bouquet, then closed her eyes in delight. "I have surely died and been sent to heaven."

"Indeed, madam, I should hope not. I still have a few designs to enact on your body."

She opened her lashes just a slit and peered at him in a way that made him suddenly wary of her intentions. Yet, infinitely aroused.

"Tell me, Slater . . . would you like a taste?"

He could not force himself to speak. Her expression brimmed with mischief. And more. So much more.

The rich truffle had begun to melt against the heat of her skin. Transferring the chocolate to her opposite hand, she held the finger to his lips in an offering. Taking the digit into his mouth, he sucked, licked, tasting not only the sweet candy, but Aloise's distinctive flavor.

"Now, it is my turn."

She rubbed the treat over his nipple, then bent, taking the sensitive tip into her mouth.

Slater's hands gripped her skull in reflex and his head arched back at the pleasure. His body surged to life. His heart pounded. The heavy ache in his groin could only be assuaged in one manner.

Aloise had no time to think or to resist. The truffle dropped to the floor as he dragged her over his body. Her lithe limbs settled easily over his hips, but it wasn't enough. Not nearly enough. He had to have her. Now. Reaching low, he found her wet. Warm. Without a word of warning, he grasped her hips, then impaled her.

Aloise gasped, her knees tightening, her eyes opening. Obviously she had never dreamed that a woman could take the upper position.

"But how . . ."

Slater could barely speak, let alone think. "You've sat upon a horse, Aloise." His voice became husky as he enjoyed the sheathing of her body. "Ride me."

So she did, willingly, eagerly, her face flushed with the unexpected intensification of the sensations gripping her body. She became utterly wanton, adorably absorbed. When she climaxed, he quickly followed, holding her tightly, vowing he would die before he let her go. She was his now.

His . . .

Later, much, much later, Slater McKendrick yawned, watching as his bride grappled with the too-long sleeves of his shirt and struggled to return to the rumpled bed without spilling a drop of the tea she carried. Finally, she handed both cups to Slater and slid beneath the linens. The folds of the garment she'd borrowed drowned her, making her appear even more petite and even more desirable.

She retrieved her china, sipped, sighed, and closed her eyes in pleasure. "This is good. Quite good. But chocolate is my favorite. Chocolate and a particular mixture of blackberry tea."

He took a tentative taste, wondering how he was going to manage to swallow the brew. Slater had tumbled many a woman. He had initiated more than his fair share of virgins, but he had never felt for one of them what he felt for this imp, this temptress.

His bride.

Aloise eyed him over the rim of her teacup.

"Have I a smudge on my cheek?"

"No."

"Then why do you persist in staring at me?" she asked in obvious embarrassment.

"I stare, because you are beautiful."

His compliment took her unaware just as similar remarks had in the past. Such simple kindnesses must have been few and far between for her.

"Slater?" she asked tentatively. "Why did you decide to marry me? The truth. We simply could have done . . . this." She waved at the rumpled bed.

So, she found herself returning to that subject again. Slater did not immediately answer. What could he possibly say? That he had done so out of necessity? After the night they'd shared, he realized that answer was not totally true. Slater had managed his own life for so long, he brooked no interference. Just as she'd said, if he hadn't wanted to commit himself to this woman, there would have been other ways to enact his revenge.

But he *had* married her. He had taken her virginity. With each second that passed, he found himself anticipating all their tomorrows.

Such a proposition held its own set of dangers. They might have exchanged vows, they might have bonded in the most intimate of marital rituals, but there were so many unresolved issues that could tear them apart. Oliver Crawford waited to be dealt with; Jeanne's death to be avenged. All of which could prove to be powerful tools to drive this woman away unless his plans were handled skillfully. Carefully.

In order to do that, Slater would have to tell her the truth. All of it. Things he had told no one but his closest friends. There could be no secrets between his wife and him. Slater had discovered long ago that such knowledge could be used to injure. He would have to broach the subjects that needed to be expressed. Using all of the tact and diplomacy he possessed, he would have to admit that he was Matthew Waterton and thereby expose her father's treachery.

For that, she may choose to leave. He'd seen enough of her moods to know her childhood had not been a happy one. Nor had the last few years been particularly pleasant. But that would be her right, her decision.

Setting his cup aside, Slater stood and crossed to a Chinese chest in the corner of the room, unlocking the door with a key he'd hidden under the leg. Knowing the risk he took, he withdrew the bundle that Aloise had so carefully packed for her original escape.

As he carried it back to the bed, the weight of the bulky shawl seemed as heavy as his own heart. "I believe these are yours."

Aloise smiled in genuine delight when he placed her things in front of her.

"Oh, Slater, I thought you'd thrown it all away."

"No." He settled on the feather bed as she opened

the fabric and sifted through the contents. Her actions held a distinct wonder and nostalgia—as if she and the paltry collection of items were old friends long kept apart.

When she paused over the woolen gown, he offered, "You will not need the clothing again."

She smiled shyly. "Of that I thank you. I have never been fond of black wool." She tossed it to the floor.

"These as well," he muttered, discarding the awful undergarments.

"You must accept another heartfelt thanks for that."

Slater sought each flicker of emotion, each germ of thought he might find flitting across her face. "What of the coins? What will you buy with them?"

Aloise weighed the bag in her hand. "There's but twenty pounds here."

"Twenty pounds?"

"It was all I could manage to . . . liberate from Sacre Coeur. I was supposed to receive five pounds a month allowance from my father. But the headmistress had a penchant for drinking. Since I was not permitted outside the school's walls, she thought I would have no need of money."

She dropped the bag back into the shawl and continued her search. "My books are ruined, I'm afraid."

"I've a whole library downstairs. Next to the ballroom."

Her eyes sparked with interest. "Really?"

"You may help yourself at any time."

Her excitement was unmistakable. "Thank you." She poked at the sack of jewels that had served to imprison her in this man's home. "These *are* mine, you know?"

"Your father gave them to you?"

She snorted at that unlikely idea. "I took them. I was to wear them when my father retrieved me at Tippington."

"And this?" Slater touched the locket.

"That is the only portrait I have of my mother." She opened the delicate piece. "She was very beautiful, wasn't she?"

"Very."

His hand closed around the medallion suspended around his own neck and he opened the catch. Aloise gasped when she saw the same small portrait nestled inside. "But how—"

"Your mother gave them to us both the Christmas before she was killed."

Aloise reverently touched the cold metal of his locket then that of her own. In that instant, Slater felt an emotional connection with this woman, a subtle bond.

"Come with me."

Taking her hand, he helped her to dress in her robe then drew her behind him, ushering her into his office. Papers and charts littered a huge battered desk. Empty glasses testified that he'd met with his men here some time in the none-too-distant past. Leading her farther inside, Slater released her, then drew back a set of heavy brocade curtains to reveal a life-size portrait.

"This was your mother, Aloise. This was Jeanne Alexander Crawford."

He watched as she slowly approached, reaching out to touch the canvas as if she would encounter flesh and blood.

"I remember how she doted on you. Never have I seen a mother more loving of her own child."

"She looks a little . . . "

"Like you."

She eyed him in disbelief. "Where did you get such a painting?"

"It was made years ago, to remind me of things I had tried to forget. Things I should have remembered." His hands closed over her shoulders. The time had come to tell her the truth, to expose his true identity, to risk her anger at his betrayal. "Aloise, there are things you don't know about me. Things I need to tell you."

But she wasn't listening. Her gaze was caught and held by those of her mother. Memories seemed to stir in the depths of her eyes.

"Aloise?" She didn't seem to hear him. "Aloise!"

She roused with some effort, staring unseeingly in his direction. Her skin grew pale, her breathing increasing to such an alarming rate that Slater eyed her in concern.

The memories had knocked at the door of her consciousness and with them, they'd brought the pain. Swearing, Slater realized that now wasn't the time for confessions. Seeing her mother's portrait had done something to her, perhaps jogged some image.

"Aloise!"

She touched a hand to her brow, slowly meeting his gaze. "Wh-what were you . . . saying?"

Her voice emerged so lost, so forlorn, he drew her close to his chest. "Nothing." A rock's weight settled in his chest as the truth lay dammed there once again. "We will speak of such matters at another time."

When he would have led her from the office, Aloise peered over her shoulder. "She should not have died."

Slater grew still. "No."

"My father would have been kinder if she'd lived."

Her words struck him to the very heart, but not as much as her following statement.

"He would not have beaten me."

Beaten. The word lodged in his brain. A horror such as he had never known rose to choke him. Unable to bear her anguish or his own, he wrapped Aloise in his arms and drew her against him. Her shoulders shook. Hot tears dripped to his chest.

"I never cry," she insisted, sobbing.

"Sometimes it is good to cry," he reassured her, tracing the welts on her back and wishing he could take her pain as his own.

She hiccuped and rubbed at her cheeks, lifting her face to confront him, the evidence of her grief gleaming on her velvety skin. "Have you ever cried, Slater?"

Aloise had a way of cutting bluntly to the heart of things. Of opening his soul and peering inside.

"Yes."

"When?"

"Upon the news that my father had died. When I was forced to leave my home." His thumb swiped at the moisture that still dripped from her lashes. Looking at her, he also realized that his emotions had never been so true, so fine-edged as they were now, when she stood in his arms.

She rested against him again, holding him closely, imparting her own brand of comfort. As the seconds piled into minutes, Slater could not suppress his own pointed question. "Tell me, Aloise, do you regret what has happened between us? Do you regret having married me? In any way?"

She became quiet. Unmoving.

"Do *you* regret it, Slater?"

He shook his head. "Not for an instant."

"My answer . . . would be much the same," she hesitantly admitted.

Her reply should not have touched him so deeply. But it did.

Bending his head, he kissed her, gently, then passionately. When her body yielded, when his control had run out, he carried her back to the bedroom. There they consummated their union again. But this time, Slater could not deny that—for him—their lovemaking held something special, something unique. Something wonderful that soothed his battered soul.

He could only pray that one day he could inspire a similar emotion in Aloise. Otherwise, she may never forgive him for the man he was . . .

As well as the man he had once been.

* * *

Something awakened her. A subtle sound that infringed on her dreams. The whispering of her name.

Blinking, Aloise yawned and stretched, rolling toward the heat easing into her back. Slater slept like the dead, his face free from its accustomed tension. A slight smile lifting his lips.

She was responsible for that smile, Aloise realized with pleasure. Just as she was partly responsible for his heavy slumber. Their lovemaking had filled most of the night, fiercely passionate, then tender, interspersed with gentle nonsense talk when their energy flagged and they rested half in sleep, half out, until the next burst of desire persuaded them to rouse.

Aloise smoothed a lock of black hair from Slater's cheek, amazed at the rush of tenderness she felt. A deep, soul-touching warmth. He was a wonderful man. Oh, he might prove gruff and blustery, he might brood and pierce her with one of those dark stares now and again. But deep down in her heart of hearts, where such feelings mattered, she knew he would be good to her. She knew they would be happy.

Suddenly, she found herself contemplating dreams that she had never allowed herself to entertain. She imagined long winter evenings in a man's embrace. A home filled with laughter. Children.

The thought brought a sharp yearning that startled her in its intensity. She had never really thought herself the type to wish for domestic scenes. Yet, curiously, she wanted to see Slater's features stamped on a younger version of himself. She wanted to hold the infant in her arms, cuddle it, nurture it.

How grand a future could appear when one had hope. How filled with infinite possibilities. Especially when one knew they would not be spending such years alone.

Softly, so she would not awaken him, she teased his shoulder, the indentation of his sternum, the medallion she had once mistaken for a friar's crucifix. A tender smile curved her lips. This man had claimed to be her mother's special friend and she believed him. Come morning, she would demand that he satisfy her curiosity concerning Jeanne Crawford.

The odd whispering came again, softly, barely disturbing the quiet. Sighing, Aloise supposed she would have to investigate. Slater had dismissed Miss Nibbs and most of his men for the evening, wanting the house to be theirs alone. The low tone sounded suspiciously like William Curry. He must have forgotten something in his move to the inn for the night, and not wanting to embarrass her, now called to see if she were awake.

Tracing the scar on her husband's cheekbone, Aloise yawned again in complete satisfaction, then slipped from the bed, donning Slater's shirt and her own moire dressing gown. Taking the gutted candle from the bedside, she crept to the door.

It had not been locked, just as Slater had promised. The thought caused a rush of pleasure. He had trusted her. He had known she would keep her word as well as the vows she'd repeated in the church. Such trust was more valuable to her than gold.

Aloise crept into the hall. Touching the wick of the candle to one of those left burning in the corridor, she hummed softly to herself, holding her hems safely away from her feet as she tiptoed down the front staircase.

She felt no fear in wandering through such a gloomy house at this hour. Indeed, there was something about Ashenleigh that had begun to make her feel inordinately safe. As if nothing could harm her here.

"Aloise."

"I'm coming," she whispered in return, hoping that her husband had not been disturbed.

Clutching the robe more tightly to her neck, she made her way along the hall, following the faint sound of her name. The cool night still clung to the house in ebony pools and the feeble light of her candle proved welcome as she made her way through the house.

"A-lo-ise." The cry came from the west wing. The library?

Exchanging the nub of her candle for one of the fresh tapers in the wall sconce, she eagerly made her way down the hall with its wealth of *objects d'art.* Reclining nudes, painted sylphs, and carved masks watched her progress.

Passing the open door of the game room, she sniffed at the faint smell of liquor, smiling at the mess Slater's men had left behind after their own nuptial celebration. She would have to speak to them about that, she decided as she saw the gleaming tables scattered with crumbs and spilt snuff. Miss Nibbs had quite enough to do. These men really must learn to pick up after themselves.

"Aloise."

"I'm coming as fast as I can!" Impatient now, she moved to the door at the far wall. The panel swung wide on well-oiled hinges. The light of her candle eased in, illuminating a desk, a couch. Bookcases.

"Curry?"

No one answered and she stepped more fully inside. The sight that met her eyes caused her to gasp in delight. Aloise placed the taper on one of the small tables. Her fingertips skimmed the spines of the books—so many books! There were novels and diaries, volumes of poems and philosophical essays, tomes of history and copies of historical manuscripts. Sweet heaven, she'd stumbled into paradise. By marrying Slater McKendrick, she had indeed found her own little piece of heaven.

"Curry, I'm in the library. Since I can't find you in this dark house, you must come to me."

While she waited, she tugged one of the volumes free, opening the pages, reading a snatch of Shakespeare's *Macbeth.* Putting it back on the shelf, she scanned another, and another, reaching for each new selection with an addict's greed. How marvelous! How bloody marvelous to have such a variety of literature free for her perusal. She had only to close her eyes and reach out in order to select another tasty morsel, verse or prose.

She had married wisely, of that she was sure. The man she'd chosen loved adventure and travel, chocolate and books. How could the next few years prove to be anything but happy?

Footsteps thumped on the marble floors behind her, reminding her that Curry had been trying to find her. Selecting a thin volume of Pope, she turned. "Curry, how in the world did Slater manage to collect so . . . many . . ."

The question withered on her lips as the man who had followed her entered the library and stepped into the light.

Oliver Crawford glowered in barely restrained rage. His walking stick pounded against the marble floor. "So, Daughter. I have found you at last."

18

ALOISE HUDDLED INTO THE CORNER OF THE COACH AND shivered. She was quite certain that she had never been so miserable or so cold. The dressing gown she wore had been fashioned more for beauty than for warmth. Its minimum of coverage, combined with the less than adequate layer of Slater's shirt, provided no barrier to the cool morning air that rushed through the open window of the phaeton.

She knew that Oliver Crawford must have seen the way she wrapped her arms about her body and chafed her bared skin. But her father remained remote, unmoved. Although he sat on a woolen rug, he didn't bother to extend it in her direction. Instead, he remained firmly entrenched on the bulk of the blanket in order to keep it from her grasp. It was a subtle form of punishment. One that did not necessarily surprise her.

They had been traveling now for the better part of ten minutes, but Crawford refused to speak. His disapproval hovered like a palpable shroud, smothering her, but Aloise had grown accustomed to that emotion long ago. What disturbed her now was the added essence of distaste. It hadn't been enough that he'd isolated her, imprisoned her, and beaten her. It hadn't been enough for him to refuse to answer her letters or heed her pleas to be released. No, her father had wanted to subdue her, break her, make her as biddable and meek as a doormouse.

In that respect, Aloise had disappointed him yet again.

Her jaw lifted ever so slightly and a subtle strength began to infuse her limbs. She refused to let him intimidate her. She refused to let him wound her. Years of neglect had tempered her self-will and made her into a woman who knew what she wanted and how to get it. To her utter amazement, she discovered that her values had shifted. Staring at her father, she realized that somewhere in the last few weeks, he had lost his power to threaten her. Aloise had changed. She didn't need this man's approval to enhance her feelings of worth. She was no longer quite so naive. She knew things about this man—things he had kept secret for decades. Knowledge, she had learned in the past, was a powerful thing.

"You look well, Papa." Risking his wrath she added, "I'm pleased you have not succumbed to the fevers and accidents which seem prone to this climate."

Crawford's eyes narrowed in suspicion; his jowls trembled in barely concealed fury. His hands curled around the silver tip of his walking stick with such force, Aloise was quite sure he wished it were her neck he throttled. But even though he might beat her, he could not break her.

"I assume you are about to deliver me to my next matrimonial prospect—or should I say *prospects.* That appears to be the only time we see each other." The fact that she was already married, already protected by Slater's name gave her an added bravado. "Tell me, who have you decided should serve as my groom this time?" She continued before he could speak, "An escapee from a debtor's prison? A—"

"Enough!" Oliver Crawford's voice grew garbled with the effort he exerted to control his emotions. "You have shamed me, Daughter. *Shamed* me!"

Daughter. Until tonight, when he had lured her through the depths of Slater's house, he had never used her name. He referred to her as *Daughter.* More often than not, the tone he used for that single word of address emerged more like a curse than an endearment.

"I'd thought that the expensive school you attended would have beaten the insolence from you, but I can see now that I was sadly mistaken." Lifting his cane, he whacked the seat next to her thigh.

Aloise jumped, but did not cry out.

"You allowed a man—a stranger—to abduct you, to imprison you, to sully your reputation, to attempt to force me to accept his offer for your hand, but you have yet to apologize for your behavior. Even though it is obvious that your virtue is no longer an issue."

Her cheeks flamed but she managed to utter, "Apologize? To you? For what? When have you ever cared what happened to me?"

"Don't get impertinent with me. I am still your—"

"Father? I do believe this is the first time you've claimed the relationship."

She'd gone a step too far. Aloise knew that instantly. Her father's face grew red with fury. He lunged forward, viciously slapping her cheek. Pointing a finger at her, he whispered, "I gave you life. For that you will show me the respect I deserve."

Aloise didn't speak. She couldn't. A rage was bubbling inside of her. An anger like she had never known. One that had been building for years, that she had tucked away but never forgotten until it had condensed and now enveloped her entire being.

This man might have given her life. But he had tried to squelch all semblance of happiness and peace. He had thrived on her unhappiness. He had attempted to mold her into a vacuous, simpering fool, and after failing that objective, had been bent upon thrashing her into submission. He deserved none of her honor, none of her loyalty.

"I trust that you will remember something of your lessons in deportment once we've reached Briarwood."

"Why?" Aloise asked carefully, tamping down her desire to rant and rave at her father, to pummel his chest until he listened, to make him look at her. Really look at *her* instead of a point over her left shoulder.

"We shall be entertaining a number of . . . guests within the next few days."

The statement fell into the blackness between them, but this time, Aloise was prepared. She knew what her father had intended by inviting these people to Briarwood. Slater had told her. Her skin crawled in shame at the idea. If not for the fact that she was already wed, she would have been paraded in front of a score of men, rated, then auctioned to the highest bidder.

She opened her mouth to tell her father that he was too late for such attempts, but he interrupted by saying, "After what has occurred, I can see that I will have to alter my arrangements before the scandal of your actions can reach their ears." Cruelly clasping her chin, he whispered, "We will never speak of this again, do you understand? This night never happened, whatever . . . *liaison* you entertained never occurred. If one word contrary to that fact leaves your lips, I will see your lover killed. I will arrange with the local authorities to see him drawn and quartered for raping my beloved child—and *you,* my dear, will watch the proceedings."

The words were said with such venom, Aloise knew her father would see them through—and he had the power to do so. Everyone knew the local constable had been accepting bribes from this man for years.

A chill raced down her spine. She would have to remain silent about her marriage, she would have to wait and hope and pray that Slater would realize what had happened and come for her in time. Otherwise she may be forced to stoop to bigamy in order to protect his very life.

Looking at her father, Aloise knew her husband had been right when he'd warned her that her father intended to use her as a pawn to further his own ends. Her *husband.* The very thought brought a kind of peace. He would come for her, sometime, some way. Of that she was certain.

Dear heaven, he had already become a part of her. He had already woven his way into the very fiber of her thoughts.

"How did you know where to find me?"

Oliver snorted. "That man thought to extort an invitation to the festivities by stealing you away, seducing you, then returning you to me as if he'd found you like a babe in a basket. He was sadly mistaken. I am not such a fool. I don't like his kind. Liars, cheats. Just because he's a confidante of that blasted French king, he thinks he owns the world."

Crawford's gaze raked over her tousled hair and rumpled form. "He left the single guard by the broken window, foolish man. I had only to bash him over the head then call and wait for you to appear."

"Slater might have been the one to answer."

"I was willing to take that chance."

"What do you intend to do with me?"

"Never you mind. You will do as you're told." His lips lifted in a sneer. "First, I suppose I will have to pretty you up a bit, fix your hair, put you in a proper dress." He snarled in remembered frustration. "Luckily for you, Daughter, I was able to delay your prospective grooms until you could be found."

Prospective *grooms.*

"Does that mean I'm to be married by the week's end?"

"There will be no more unfortunate incidents, no more stains on your virtue until you are safely wed."

"What if I refuse?"

Crawford gripped his walking stick, sliding the quirt from its hiding place.

"If you leave fresh marks, no man will take me," Aloise baited him softly. "Those on my back can be hidden for a time, but new ones . . ."

His gaze became menacing as he snapped the cane together again. Leaning toward her, he captured her chin in a bruising grip, his voice growing low and harsh. "You listen to me, Daughter, and you listen well. I will not lose face on your behalf again. You will follow my instructions to the letter. You will speak when spoken to. You will dress as I request. You will be charming, witty, and above reproach, damn your hide!" Each word was punctuated with a rise in inflection and volume. "If you don't, I'll have you whipped and sent to a nunnery—and it won't be for schooling. *Do . . . you . . . understand?"*

Aloise had never seen her father so livid—granted, she hadn't seen him at all for quite some time—but the man was not to be taunted. She might defy him in her heart, but open rebellion would serve no purpose.

At least for now.

She needed time to formulate a plan, to somehow notify Slater. He would help her. She knew he would.

"Yes, Papa."

He seemed somewhat mollified by her docile obedience, but still stared at her as if she were some unpleasant creature that had crawled from beneath a rock. "You should have been a boy."

There it was. Her father's favorite means of putting Aloise entirely in her place.

"You should have been a *boy,"* he said again, as if once had not been enough.

But this time, to Aloise's infinite amazement, the phrase held no sting.

Slater McKendrick slammed into the main hall of the Bull and Finch Tavern. The door crashed against the opposite wall, then shuddered for several seconds as if cowed.

Marco, who followed him somewhat unsteadily, glared at his friend, clasping his bandaged skull between his hands.

Curry lifted his head from one of the tables. "Damn it, Slater. Quietly, quietly. The boys and I thought that since you could not join us . . . in our drinking . . . we should absorb your share."

In response to his claim, there was a moan. A grunt. Louis kept his forehead pillowed in his arms, but lifted a finger in a weak salute, while Rudy, stretched full-length on one of the tables, snored to wake the dead.

Feeling little pity for himself or his companions, Slater slammed his fists on the planks. The five men sat bolt upright, their eyes bugging.

"She's gone."

"Who?" Curry breathed.

"Aloise."

"Maybe you should have taken more time . . . to woo her."

One of the men snickered. Slater could not tell which, but he continued on, knowing there wasn't a second to waste. "Damnit, man, she didn't leave of her own free will. She was taken!"

At that, his men managed a bleary-eyed batch of stares.

"Who?"

"Her father."

"Hell." Curry struggled to his feet. "What do you plan to do?"

"How in the bloody blazes do I know? The whole plan we concocted involved sending her back for a confrontation."

Will shrugged. "So? She's back. I see no problem in that."

No problem? *No problem!* At that instant, Slater could have cheerfully broken Curry's neck. Didn't he know that things had changed? Didn't he know that Slater had decided not to exploit Aloise, but to protect her? Last evening, just as he'd fallen asleep, he'd determined that the inherent danger of his plans was not worth the possible rewards, that he would send word to Manuel to prepare his ship so that Slater could spirit Aloise away. Once free of England, he could see to her safety, hide her on some island, some distant coast.

But Crawford had outsmarted him. He'd skulked into Slater's house, completely destroyed the library and all its contents, then had left a note saying that he had taken Aloise home where she belonged. As an added insult, he had included an invitation for Slater to attend Aloise's wedding.

Her *wedding,* damnit!

His blood fairly boiled in fury and frustration. Slater knew Crawford meant to outsmart him. The old man's position was tenuous at best. If Slater were to proclaim loud and clear where Aloise had been the last few days, Crawford's hopes of a good match would be dashed. Therefore, he planned to marry her off within the next forty-eight hours, blunting the effects of any sort of scandal.

"What . . . do you want us to do?" Curry asked.

Slater considered his options for a moment. "Some of the penniless aristocrats Crawford invited have already arrived in the hopes of a free meal. Do we still have a schedule of the estimated arrivals of each prospective groom?"

"Clayton has it."

"*I* don't have it."

"Louis—"

"No."

"*I* have the blasted thing," Hans whispered. "There's no need to shout."

Since the fractured conversation had been uttered at little more than a murmur, Slater frowned.

"How long will it be until all of you can become sober?"

Curry waved his hand in dismissal. "An hour."

"Two," Louis groaned.

"Three," Clayton corrected.

Hans groaned.

Rudy merely continued to snore.

"Then get on your feet and weave to your horses. I want half of the possible grooms weeded out long before they can reach Briarwood."

"How . . . do you propose that?"

Slater leaned over the table. "How do you think? Lie to them, ambush them, throw them in the stables and tie them to a post. Do whatever is necessary. But do it *today.*"

"I suppose that will have to do."

Aloise nearly rolled her eyes at her father's grudging compliment. He had ordered her to dress in one of the gowns he had provided, then meet him in his office. She'd complied. Not because he had told her to do so, but because she'd thought she ought to be clothed in case Slater came to get her.

Passing through the doorway into the dim interior of her father's sanctuary, she noted that the gentlemen's haven was not as intriguing as the one at Ashenleigh. Her father had decorated the chamber with the proper society-prescribed furniture—a desk, three chairs, and a small table for the liquor decanters—but there was no intimacy. No pictures on the wall, no loving knickknacks of fond remembrances. No charm.

"The first of your prospective mates will arrive this morning," Crawford said, stepping around the desk. "From the moment he enters this house, you will be on your best behavior."

"Yes, Father."

"You will be charming and witty."

"Yes, Papa."

"And you will not speak unless asked a direct question."

"Very well, Father."

Her biddable replies held just enough of a sting to needle him, but not enough for him to call her for her impertinence.

Stalking toward the far wall, he lifted aside a gloomy Dutch portrait to reveal an iron safe. He carefully withdrew a set of keys from his waistcoat, unlocking the series of latches, then twisting the handle.

The stream of sunlight spilling through the window illuminated the metal cell as if it were a pirate's treasure chest. Loose jewels, strings of pearls, chalices, and goblets had been heaped inside. Stacks of coins, bonds, and contracts crowded the corners. But in the middle of it all lay a huge gold tiger, its mouth opened in a perpetual snarl, its eyes glowing ruby red.

The Bengal Rubies.

Horror settled into the pit of her stomach. No. No! Had her father discovered the missing necklace? Did he mean to punish her for her thievery?

Aloise could feel the blood drain from her face. If only she had the necklace now. If only it weren't still lying on the floor of the Rose Room amid the other belongings Slater had returned to her.

Her father lifted the vessel from the safe and carried it to Aloise, holding it tightly against his chest.

"You will take these with you. I want you to wear them when I introduce you to your first suitor."

Her mouth grew dry, her muscles tense. But judging by her father's actions, he couldn't possibly know about the missing piece. Not yet.

When she took the case from Crawford, she had to rack her brain to summon one token protest about wearing the jewels, a way to delay the inevitable. If she appeared without the intricate collar, he would know immediately who had taken it. He would punish her unmercifully for that. Then she would have to claim that she had lost it. She couldn't let him challenge Slater for its return.

"I don't think I should wear the rubies. They will clash with my gown," she offered hastily. It was the only excuse she could think of as she gestured to the garnet silk her father had ordered made for her. She had no doubts that the dress had been designed to finalize a purchase of sorts. The square neckline plunged to the very edge of her stays and had been trimmed with little more than a velvet cord. The waist had been fashioned excruciatingly tight, while the skirts billowed over her panniers to fall to the floor in a rustle of fabric. A row of delicate silk lace nearly a yard wide had been sewn just above the point of her knees and fell to skim the floor with a whispered caress.

"You will do as you're told."

The panic in her breast intensified. "Yes, Father."

"Now go to your room and wait. Within the hour, I will summon you to the salon."

"Is that where you plan to hold the auction?"

His lips pursed in anger. "Go!"

"Yes, Father."

As she exited the room, she heard Crawford say behind her, "Take great care, Daughter."

"Or what, Father?" Glancing at him, Aloise allowed herself one last taunt. After all, Oliver Crawford was but a man. A petty, cruel little man.

"I could wed you to a diseased invalid."

One of her brows lifted. "I believe you have already tried to do so."

Slater sat rigidly on his horse, his silhouette edged against the dull onslaught of dusk. Below him, nestled in a valley of emerald green grass and clover lay Briarwood. And his bride.

The coming evening tinged the air with a russet hue. The last beams of sunlight trickled through the clouds, causing a flurry of delicate rays to shimmer and dance in the misty breeze so that the white marble building gleamed like an oasis.

"What has you scowling so fiercely now? You look as if you'd like to tear the place apart stone by stone. Our plans are set and the men are ready to ride."

Slater didn't comment. Why hadn't he been more careful? More wary? Damn, he'd been so stupid to think he was beyond Crawford's reach. For one night, he'd lowered his guard and Aloise had been stolen away. He had failed her again, just as he'd failed her fifteen years ago, and he had no one to blame but himself. After all the planning, the plotting, the careful strategy, he'd endangered her through his own carelessness. If anything happened to her . . .

His hands clenched and he fought the panic settling in his breast. Nothing would happen. Dear God, please let it be so. Hadn't he atoned sufficiently for past mistakes? Hadn't he tried to make amends? If Aloise were harmed this night, he would never forgive himself. He may not have been able to prevent Jeanne's ultimate fate, but he had vowed to himself that he would protect her daughter at all costs. Sweet Aloise. His wife. Crawford must not succeed in destroying her too. Slater would never be able to live with himself if such a thing occurred.

Pushing his fears resolutely away, Slater tried to reassure himself that Aloise was still protected by his name, his ultimate possession. Matters were not completely unsalvageable.

The galloping of hooves tumbled into the quiet as Marco rushed to meet them. Drawing his mount to a shuddering halt, he put a hand to his head then offered without prompting, "Crawford has been in a snit for hours about the fact that none of his prospective grooms has arrived. He's locked Aloise in her bedchamber and ordered her to prepare for the evening meal. He's stated that she will be wed to the first man to appear. The wedding is set for tomorrow evening."

"Doesn't he know that she spent an entire evening with me? In my bed?"

Marco's eyes became somber. "*Si.* But he doesn't care. He will barter her body for a title. The coachman told me that he heard Crawford threaten her on the way to Briarwood. If she breathes a word of scandal to anyone, Crawford will see to it that you are killed in front of her very eyes."

Slater felt a black rage fill his body. How could a father be so cruel, so heartless? Aloise was flesh of his flesh, blood of his blood.

"Where will the ceremony take place?"

"The folly near the pond."

"Who will officiate?"

Marco grinned. "The same vicar who wed her to you."

"What of the candidates?"

"We've snared a good portion of them and sent them on their way—either through force or blatant knavery. Two have yet to arrive. Crawford will not wait much longer for a match. He has already delayed his plans for nearly a fortnight."

Had it only been that long since Slater had encountered Aloise on the beach? He felt as if he'd known her for a lifetime. As if she had been a missing piece to his heart.

His heart . . .

Slater's hands tightened around the reins, and he became suddenly oblivious to his companions. Staring down at that house, he realized his priorities had changed. It wasn't the rubies he sought. Or even vengeance.

Aloise had purged him of that need. She had offered him her trust. She had offered him her hope. She had offered him a tiny corner of her affections.

Grappling with the unfamiliar whirl of panic, desperation, and concern that threatened to inundate him, Slater realized he wanted more than a sliver of her devotion. He wanted it all. He wanted to wake to her each morning and dream with her each night. He wanted to see his children clinging to her skirts. He wanted to be by her side as they both grew old.

He had only known her a short time. Two weeks. But she had woven her way into his soul. She had taught him so much. That tenderness was not a curse. That even in the safety of the shadows one needed the glimmer of hope to light the way. That love was not a bolt of lightning, but a seed to be nurtured and allowed to grow toward the sun.

"We will retrieve her, Slater."

Something of his emotions must have shown on his face, because Curry's statement was filled with quiet reassurance.

"Such feelings cannot happen so fast," he murmured, not realizing he'd said the words aloud.

"They can if one is lucky enough to circle the globe, search hither and yon, and return home to find his heart-mate but thirty miles away from where he was born."

"She is a riddle, isn't she?"

"You have always enjoyed a puzzle."

"She has endured so much."

"Yet, when you walk into the room, her smile cannot be dimmed."

Slater eyed Will in surprise.

"Trust me, my friend. You may have been too blind to notice, but the rest of us have seen it. Haven't we, Marco?"

The Spaniard nodded solemnly. "In matters of the heart, you have found your equal."

Slater straightened in the saddle, still not entirely comfortable with having his emotions so easily dissected. "Then we must do our best to retrieve her."

Marco and Curry grinned.

"I take it you have a plan?" Curry inquired.

Touching his heels to his horse's flanks, Slater drawled, "Indeed," then galloped away from the knoll.

It took only a few minutes to join the upper road. Turning from the rutted path into the foliage bordering either side, he led his mount toward the rendezvous point. Slater prayed that he could keep a clear head on his shoulders to see the next few days through.

Seeing Clayton and Louis waiting in the assigned location, Slater came to a halt asking, "Any news?"

Louis abandoned the study of his cravat. *"Mais oui.* Hans and Rudy are behind us a bit, seeing to things, but we thought we'd best warn you that we encountered a specific nuptial bidder midway through his journey and detained him just as you asked."

"Which one?"

Clayton brushed at the dust clinging to his coat, all to no avail. Compared to the eternally impeccable dress of his partner, he never ceased to look rumpled. But his brown eyes sparkled with fun and a pair of dimples winked in his cheeks. "I do believe it's the one you've been waiting for most of the day. That damned bilge-assed naval officer, Peter Torbidson."

"You're sure?"

Clayton and Louis exchanged knowing glances, but it was Clayton who spoke. "Quite, quite sure. We boys met up with him at the Bull and Finch of all places. We plied him with brandy—"

"Ale—"

"Was it ale first?"

"It was ale."

"Then brandy—"

"Wine."

"Really?"

"Wine."

"Well, whatever the order of the spirits, we made sure he was well and snockered. Meantime, we delved for certain delectable bits of information."

"And . . ." Slater prompted.

"Nobody from the Crawford household has ever seen the man. All of the arrangements were made through a courier."

"What about Percival Humphreys, Crawford's personal secretary?"

"He has never met him either," Louis supplied. "In fact, Torbidson acted most put out that Humphreys had not come to meet him at the docks." He and Clayton exchanged indecipherable looks. "I fear the man has set too much store on a hero's welcome. No one really appears to give a damn that he's returned at all."

"Then he's the one we want." Slater's posture became stiff, determined. His eyes hardened and deepened to the color of obsidian. "We'll take his place and see to it that Torbidson is the man selected to marry Aloise. Only when her father believes a title is within his grasp will he lower his guard."

Curry nudged his horse closer, speaking lowly to keep his advice in confidence. "I think you should wait and consider all your options. This isn't the only means available to disrupt the wedding ceremony."

"What else do you suggest?"

Clayton's brows lifted. "Slater could disguise himself as a priest—"

"A friar," Louis corrected.

"—and perform the ceremony himself."

Slater shot a scowl in their direction. "This is our chance. Take Torbidson before anyone can get a good look at his face."

Clayton nodded. "This is indeed our chance. Actually, I'm quite sure that Providence has put a hand in the whole affair."

Staring at Slater, Will objected, "You can't be serious. You aren't thinking of masquerading as that chap."

"Not at all," Slater drawled.

"Thank heavens."

"I have left that honor to you."

"What?"

"It's settled," Slater said, ignoring Will's outburst.

"Damn it, why impersonate anyone. Why don't you just ride in and claim the woman?"

"In order for Crawford's downfall to be complete, it must occur in the company of the people he strives so diligently to impress. His precious collection of penniless aristocracy and powerful government officials. Once the truth has been uncovered, he will never be admitted into society again. The wealth and influence he has courted for years will be shattered."

Slater gestured to the other men. "Take your positions as outlined." He tied a black scrap of fabric around the top half of his face and settled the ragged holes that had been burned into the weave over his eyes.

Clayton and Louis followed suit with a great deal of glee, but Will was much more reluctant. "Slater, I don't think this is wise. I've no talent for playacting—you know I speak the truth."

"Relax, Will. I trust your limited talents."

"But . . ."

"Come, Curry. You've always enjoyed a lark in the past. Consider this the grandest of all."

Only after Slater had thundered away in the direction of the ambush site did Curry speak again. "Damnation, that man has lost his wits."

"Now, Curry," Louis soothed. "It will be fun. You'll see. Don't you think, Clayton?"

Clayton eyed Louis.

Louis eyed Clayton.

Both men grinned.

"What has the two of you looking like a pair of retired priests locked in a brothel?"

The pair laughed out loud.

"Wait until you see the chap," Clayton said, spurring his horse into a gallop.

Louis chortled. "Wait until you see the hats."

19

DOES EVERYONE UNDERSTAND THE PLAN?"

Slater looked at each of his men one by one, seeing that—despite the unusual nature of their tasks—they would not fail him.

"Good. Assume your position in Crawford's household—quietly, carefully. Remember . . . one wrong step and the entire situation will fall like a house of cards." He eyed Clayton gravely. "Your timing is especially critical. You must return with the proper authorities listed in your instructions—those not being bribed by Crawford."

The men nodded and began to disperse until only Miss Nibbs was left in the office. Miss Nibbs and the portrait of Jeanne Alexander Crawford.

"You will not fail, Master Waterton."

Slater eyed her in surprise. It had been years since anyone had called him by his real name. In all of England, there was only Miss Nibbs to remember who he'd once been. A simple schoolmaster. A naive young boy.

"I am proud of you," Miss Nibbs whispered. Then, gazing up at the woman in the portrait, she added, "Miss Jeanne would be too."

The old lady was nearly to the door before Slater stopped her. "Miss Nibbs?"

Her brows lifted.

"You've been a true and loyal friend."

"I missed you, my boy."

"I'm sorry you were inadvertently dragged into this affair."

"My only regret is the time that has been wasted. The lives." Her voice became low and fervent. "See that he pays. See that he pays for what he has done."

Her lips tilted in a rare, encouraging smile, and then she was gone.

Slater slowly turned to eye the portrait that had witnessed the interchange. "So . . . we have come full circle. Fifteen years ago, you asked for my help and I refused it. For that, we were all damned to a hell of one sort or another. But tonight . . . tonight I will see to it that all debts are paid in full." His hand closed around the locket. "That I swear to you."

Then, turning, he made his way to the bowl and pitcher waiting beside his shaving kit. The time had come for Slater McKendrick to step from behind the man he'd created.

"Get in there—and don't be trying to take any trips by night, either!"

Aloise stumbled as her father threw her into the bedchamber at the end of the hall. The hems of her skirts tangled about her ankles, causing her to fall, but she did not miss the snarled instructions he added. "Be ready by the stroke of seven tomorrow evening, or you will answer to me, Daughter. This time . . . you will wear the rubies. All of them."

The door slammed shut, the key turned in the lock, and Aloise was alone.

No. Not quite alone.

Something had changed since she'd donned the elaborate earrings and bracelet. Something had . . .

She rose somewhat unsteadily. Her eyes skipped to

the top of the bureau, tarried, then widened in disbelief. There, gleaming on the dressing table was the necklace she had left at Ashenleigh. But how . . .

Even as the thought raced through her head, Aloise became aware of a presence. A warmth that seeped into her soul long before she turned.

A hand appeared through the slit of her bed curtains, drawing back the heavy brocade and exposing the one face, the one form, she had longed to see the entire day.

Slater smiled at her from a face shaved free of the dark brooding whiskers. Her eyes widened as the blunt planes and angles of his face revealed a private humor and open desire that she had grown accustomed to seeing during their brief night of passion. "In your hasty relocation of sleeping arrangements, you left something behind." He gestured to the necklace and grinned. "I thought you might need it."

"Slater?"

Ignoring her breathy query, he gazed about him and clucked in disapproval. "Personally, I like my taste in furnishings far above those of your father. He has no essence of style. None whatsoever."

"Slater," she breathed again, staring at him as if he were a mirage. But he continued to sprawl on her bed, lacing his hands behind his head, resting his back against the frame, and crossing his legs at the ankles. He looked thoroughly relaxed, thoroughly devil-may-care.

And thoroughly wonderful.

"Is that all you can say after I scaled a wall, risked life and limb, then—"

Before he could finish his teasing remark, she had scooped her skirts to her knees, bounded to her feet, and rushed to him. She fell full-length on his body, grasped his head with her hands, and began scattering kisses over his face. That lean, angular, heart-stopping face.

When at last she paused for breath, he uttered a low,

self-satisfied, "Now, that's what I like. A wifely welcome after a difficult day tending to business."

His teasing remark had barely been uttered before she snared his mouth for a more thorough caress, one that dissolved in seconds into a fierce joining of lips, of tongues, of minds.

When at last she drew back, his smile was somewhat sober, self-deprecating. "I have not had much luck in keeping my promise to see you safe."

"You're here now." She soothed his brow, touched the scar creasing his cheek. "I knew you would come."

Her statement caused him to eye her in wonder. "Why would you think such a thing when I failed you?"

She shook her head. "You've done nothing of the sort. It is my father who has failed me." Rising, she sat on the edge of the bed. "Failed me and humiliated me."

"What happened, Aloise?"

Her lips grew tight in remembered anger and disgust. "He took me to meet his candidates. Only two of the six arrived by supper, and my father decided against waiting any longer. He had me stand on a dais and circle beneath their avid gaze as if I were a slave to be bought. The men—Lord Ravenaugh and a certain naval officer—even demanded to look at my teeth."

Slater pulled her fast against his chest, tucking her head beneath his chin.

"They tried to buy me, Slater. They shouted out what they would give my father, the favors, the money, the influence. Then my father decided on a match and the deal was sealed."

Groaning in fury, she leapt to her feet and paced the width of the room. A bare, empty room. "He even dressed me to his advantage," she cried, holding her arms out to display the garnet gown with its severe tailoring and black lace. "He dressed me in this awful dress"—her hand lifted to the earrings dangling against her neck—"then ordered me to don his jewels. The Bengal Rubies. No man can resist them," she said sorrowfully. "They might not want *me,* but they all want these gems. You can't imagine how terrified I was knowing that it was only a matter of time before he discovered the missing necklace."

Slater's gaze dropped to the piece on the bureau. "The collection is very beautiful."

Aloise felt a sting of uncertainty. Her relationship with Slater was so new, so untried, that she wondered if he, too, placed a great deal of importance on the rubies.

Her thoughts must have been written on her face because Slater stood and prowled toward the necklace. As he reached to touch them, Aloise felt a pang of hurt as his fingers traced the golden birds, the tigers, the ostriches, the antelope. Like a blind man given sight, he examined each link, each gleaming stone.

When he moved to take them, her eyes closed in defeat and she realized the ultimate extent of her folly. She, who had vowed to live her life alone, she, who had reassured herself she would never need, had broken her own promises. Somehow, between that instant when she'd washed ashore to find herself confronting a man's boots and those idyllic hours of lovemaking in the Rose Room, she had given away her heart.

She heard the slight rattle of the stones. "Oh, Aloise, do you trust me so little?"

When she looked up, he gazed at her with those dark, licorice eyes, his heart reflected there. His soul.

" 'She is more precious than rubies; and all the things thou canst desire are not to be compared unto her,' " he quoted, his voice low, vibrant. Real. "Never doubt me, Aloise. Never doubt my love."

Love.

The word shimmered in the room, startling them both. But Slater didn't appear upset by his choice of words. His eyes revealed an acceptance, relief, and then an untold joy. One that wrapped her heart in a layer of warmth that could never be dampened.

"Aloise . . . my wife . . . my love. As long as there is breath in this body, I will cherish you above any treasure."

With that, he drew back his arm and hurled the necklace into the night. Aloise heard a faint splash, a gurgle, and knew the jewelry had disappeared somewhere in her father's prized ornamental pond.

"Slater?" she breathed, scarcely able to credit what she had seen, what she had heard.

"I love you, Aloise. I don't deserve you, not after all I've done, all the time I've wasted in helping you. But bastard that I am, I love you."

He took a step, but Aloise was running to meet him halfway, was being clasped in his embrace. His arms closed about her, tacitly offering her all she needed in this world: strength, passion, tenderness, hope.

"You truly love me, Slater?"

"More than life itself."

She held him tightly, burrowing his confession deep in her memory. She would never forget this hour, this moment. The scent of him. The feel of him. The joy that blossomed in her soul.

"And you, Aloise? Have I still a sliver of your heart?"

Kissing his neck, his chin, she said, "You have it all."

They fell on the bed, that narrow, unimaginative bed. To Aloise, it could have been the divan of kings. She had all she needed now. Her home was this man's arms, whether it be the splendor of Ashenleigh or the most primitive surroundings.

It took them only a moment to strip off their clothing. Once they were bare to one another's gazes, their passion adopted a reverence.

"Will you continue to trust me, sweet?" Slater

asked. "No matter what the morning brings, no matter what is said."

She nodded, knowing that there was still her father to contend with. Slater's impulsive gesture would require him to retrieve the necklace again. But not tonight. Tonight belonged to them and them alone.

Drawing him to her, Aloise basked beneath Slater's evident adoration, his gentleness, his passion. With each caress, she grew stronger. With each whispered compliment she grew more self-assured. Emboldened by their mutual feelings, she indulged her wildest fantasies, touching him, tasting him, kissing him. She absorbed each muscle, each valley, each vibrant ridge of his body. When finally he settled on her, joining her, filling her, she closed her eyes and held him tightly, knowing that—in this man—she had found what she'd sought for so long. Adventure, excitement, acceptance.

As well as an everlasting devotion.

20

THE DOOR BURST OPEN, JARRING ALOISE AWAKE.

"So, Daughter. You have purposely shamed me yet again."

Blinking, Aloise focused on the looming shape of her father. Abruptly, she absorbed the weight of her husband's body pressing against her from behind, the band of his arm tightening around her waist, and the way the sheets had been pushed far below their feet. She had no time at all to think before her father stepped aside to reveal a half dozen of his personal guards.

"Take that man out of here. Chain him and lock him in the cellar until I can deal with him."

The liveried servants stormed forward. Automatically, Slater rolled over Aloise, shielding her with his body, but it was not she they were intent upon capturing. Yanking him from the bed, they hauled him outside.

"No!" When Aloise would have run after them, her father slammed his walking stick across the opening, barring her way.

"Ready, yourself," he growled. "You are to be wed this evening. I expect you dressed and biddable. If you please me in your efforts, I may let the man live and serve as your lover on future occasions. If you defy me, I will kill him this instant. Do you understand?"

"But—"

"Do as I say! I will have you wed to Torbidson. Today. Before you can breed with another man's child and ruin my chances altogether." His eyes narrowed, becoming dark and cruel. "And if you are wise, when the man takes you tonight, you will play the virgin. Do I make myself clear?"

This time, Aloise offered no pithy remark. Once again, she thought of telling him she was already wed, but a blatant fury burned in Crawford's eyes. The same emotion that must have been there when he had arranged her mother's death. As well as those of his other wives. If she were to say anything, she had no doubts that Slater would be immediately killed.

Pushing her roughly aside, he slammed the door closed, locking it behind him.

Even so, Aloise tugged at the handle, shouted, begged, pleaded, but to no avail. Her father would have his way. In order to protect the man she loved, she would have to comply.

When Mr. Humphreys came to fetch her, she was dressed in the garnet gown she'd worn the previous day. The timid secretary crept into the room, offering her an apologetic shrug. Aloise didn't bother to invoke his help. He would not defy his master. He would see she was wed.

"Your father wishes you to wear the rubies."

Sighing, she did as she was told, donning the rings, the earrings, the circlet, and bracelet.

"Where is the necklace?"

"I lost it."

Mr. Humphreys's eyebrows soared. "*Lost* it?"

When she did not speak, Mr. Humphreys added, "Your father will be most upset if you don't wear it."

"I threw it away. In the pond."

Mr. Humphreys was obviously scandalized by such a foolish action, but he didn't comment other than to say, "I'll retrieve it immediately. Come, my dear." He led her into the hall where four guards waited to escort her to the ceremony.

Aloise fell into step, following the men to the delicate scrolling staircase. She was midway down the treads when she was greeted by the sound of applause and clapping fans. Looking up from where she'd been watching her dark skirts swish around the toes of her shoes, she discovered that her father had invited a good many people to the ceremony. True, they were not the *crème de la crème* of society, but even if they had little in the way of obvious funds if their worn clothing was any indication, she was sure that they were the sort he wanted to impress. The titled aristocracy.

The muted strains of Mozart greeted her arrival, filling the air with sounds of lilting sophistication. The mixed aromas of powder and perfume, candles and leather teased her nostrils, becoming heady, overpowering, bringing memories half-remembered and still frightening. Her head swam with them all, ache, throb, so much so that she contemplated bursting away from her envoy and running into the darkness to take deep draughts of the cool evening air. But just when she would have taken her first step, Oliver Crawford melted from the crowd to take her hand. His grip was bruising; his eyes glittered. As if somehow he had sensed a portion of her thoughts.

"How lovely you look, Daughter."

Daughter. Evidently, he still couldn't bring himself to call her by name. He had bent her to his will, and now meant to break her heart. Yet, she had not atoned sufficiently for him to forgive her gender.

As he led her through the throng, Aloise wracked her brain for some way to avoid her dilemma. She did not want to marry—she was *already* married. Drat it all! She was about to commit bigamy!

But her father's hold tightened painfully, as if to

remind her that he held all of the power. She could only submit.

He led her into the garden. The music came louder, jangling her nerves. Distant thunder warned her of an approaching storm. An excruciating tattoo beat in her temples—especially when she saw what awaited her. She had briefly seen her prospective mate, Peter Torbidson, at the "auction" and had found him to be an incurable fop. He wore more ruffles and furbelows than any woman she'd ever seen. His skin was completely obscured by a layer of makeup, two bright spots of color carefully painted on his cheeks. He wore a pair of lavender breeches and a darker lavender waistcoat encrusted with pearls. Above, he wore a wig of palest pink topped by a three-folded hat exploding with a riot of ostrich plumes.

Blast and bother. Her father wanted her to marry that? That!

"Here you are, Aloise." Mr. Humphreys hustled to their side, holding the dripping necklace. When her father scowled, he hurriedly explained, "They were in need of cleaning, but I hadn't the time to dry them off."

"Put it on, Aloise."

She opened her mouth to refuse, to proclaim she would not be bought, but what was the use? In the clash of wits, her father had emerged the victor.

Fastening the elaborate piece around her neck, she ignored the way the remaining droplets dribbled down her chest and beneath the facing of her gown.

"Smile, my dear. We wouldn't want people to think you're anything but an ecstatic bride."

She couldn't; she wouldn't. But when her father's fingers dug into her skin, Aloise discovered she could.

The yards to the folly where her groom and the vicar waited seemed an interminable distance, but not nearly long enough. Before Aloise could think of a way—any way—to extricate herself from this situation, Torbidson had taken her hand in his, winked lewdly in her direction, then turned to the vicar.

"Lud, man, marry us so that I don't ravish her on the spot."

Aloise's eyes squeezed closed in denial, but when she opened them again, the vicar still squinted at her in confusion, her father glowered, and Torbidson leered.

"Dearly beloved . . ."

Her pulse pounded. Her head ached. This could not be happening to her. It couldn't. She had found her heart-mate, they had confessed their love. Such avowals were supposed to result in some sort of happily-ever-after. That's what she had discovered in the novels she'd read.

But this marriage ceremony was not fiction. It was a horrible, terrible fact.

Closing her eyes, she prayed for a miracle, prayed for some sort of deliverance. When it did not come, when the dipping sun became obscured by the clouds and the night air chilled the gold about her neck, she steeled herself. She had done what she'd had to do. Slater would understand.

". . . if any man can show just cause—"

"I can." The words were dark, molten, filled with a potent possession. "She is already wed to me."

Aloise whirled to find Slater, Hans, and Marco striding up the aisle, swords drawn. Clayton and several other gentlemen in uniform waited beyond. Ladies squealed and dodged aside, gentlemen sat with their mouths agape.

Leveling his weapon toward her father, Slater demanded, "Release her."

"Damn you, how—"

"In your haste to see your daughter wed, you and your men failed to take a good look at your guards, Crawford. A pair of them belong to me."

On cue, the two men stripped the elegant wigs of

their livery away to reveal the grinning features of a beefy Rudy and a rumpled Louis.

"Come, Aloise." Slater held out his hand. "Come to me."

"Damn it, Torbidson," her father snarled. "Are you just going to stand there gaping?"

"I think not, old chap."

To Aloise's infinite amazement, Peter Torbidson tore off his hat and his wig, then removed a kerchief from his pocket and swiped at the thick makeup. She gasped, recognizing Will Curry.

Curry also drew his sword free. "This match does not prove to my taste. So sorry."

"Come, Aloise," Slater beckoned again.

She tried to run, but her father snagged her arm, dragging her back against his chest and lifting a pistol to her temple.

Aloise felt the breath lock in her body, a surge of pain swell inside her head. From far away, she heard the clamor of voices but she couldn't think. A woman was screaming. The cries echoed in her brain.

Aloise. Aloise, hold tightly to me. We mustn't let your father find us.

Mama?

Come along, Missy. The master has asked us pretty like t' bring ye home.

No.

Aloise? Aloise!

"Get back, McKendrick. You and your men!" This time the shout came from her father, but the words brought another instance to mind. Another night.

"Mama!" The cry wrenched from Aloise's throat. In an instant, as if floodgates had been released, she was inundated with a thousand memories. They flew through her head, leaving her with a host of impressions and one overwhelming set of images.

A stormy bluff.

Her mother's body broken and bloody.

Her father surveying the scene with cool dispassion.

Then the pain. The overwhelming pain.

"No!" She fought against her father's grip with all her might, filled with a remembered panic. *"You* are responsible for my mother's death. *You!"*

Her father's skin grew deathly pale and his mouth gaped in disbelief. "Daughter? What—"

Before she could think of the consequences of her actions, she wrenched the pistol from his hand, then whirled to level it in his direction.

"Damn you! *Why?* I *needed* her."

Her father uttered a short laugh, glancing at his guests, then his daughter. "Aloise, listen. You're mistaken. I don't know what this man has told you, but—"

"He hasn't told me anything. I remember. I *remember."*

"That isn't possible. You were only a child. After your fall, when you didn't recall what had happened, I saw to it that you were drugged for a time, so that you . . ."

Her father's eyes widened as he realized what he'd said.

"You drugged me? You *drugged* me?" Aloise stared at him in fury. "I was only five years old!"

"You shouldn't have been there."

"My mother was trying to protect me."

"She shouldn't have left."

"Even if she hadn't died that night, you would have killed her."

"No. I loved her. I loved *you."*

"Quiet!" The word was sharp and slightly desperate. Because, in her heart of hearts, she knew the avowals of devotion were simply lies. "It's too late for that. Fifteen years too late." She held the pistol with both hands and sighted down the barrel. "Don't you see? I *remember.* I know who you are, what you are. I know what you've done. You hired those men to bring my mother and me back to Briarwood. There was a fight, a scuffle. One of them took out a knife." Her voice became hoarse, the pounding of her head excruciating. "I was frightened . . . so I ran . . . I ran toward . . . I . . ."

She struggled to recall something, some dim image that refused to focus.

"I saw the knife. Mother ran to help me . . . and he killed her."

"Silence!"

"Why? Don't you want this auspicious crowd to know the truth? How you arrived minutes later and looked down on her body as if it were a broken toy flung onto the rocks? You were glad she was gone. You said as much. I was there! I tried to stop it all, but I couldn't. Instead, I saw what you did . . . I tried to get to . . ." Her eyes widened. "Brannigan?" A horror swelled and the bile rose to her throat. "You killed him. He was the man you hired and you stabbed him in the throat. Then you tried to kill . . ." She grew still, so very still, turned.

Slater stood a mere foot away, watching her with sad, quiet eyes. Eyes she knew. Eyes she remembered. A thunder of images swam over her, a library, books, climbing on a kind man's knee.

"You?" she whispered, trembling, so cold.

With his hair tied back in a queue, she realized that she knew him. He too had changed, had become darker, more dramatic. But she *knew* him.

"*This* man," she whispered. "You tried to kill *this* man. Matthew Waterton. My . . . betrothed."

A hush settled over the onlookers, then a rumble of murmurs.

Wrenching away from her astonishing discovery and the wealth of unanswered questions it brought, she turned again to the man in her sights. Crawford had grown still pale. She thought she saw a glimmer of fear. "What else do you plan to hide, Father? Your own impotence? The nefarious plots you hatched to sell your only daughter? Or the way you masterminded the deaths of five other women?"

"Damn you, stop it. Stop!"

"I know everything, Papa. Everything. You should have killed me too. You should have known I would remember someday."

Crawford blanched. "You showed no signs . . . I thought I had succeeded in wiping that night completely away."

She shook her head in disgust. "No doubt, you also feared the scandal my death might bring so close on the heels of my mother's. After all, the demise of each of your following wives was carefully planned to prevent any talk."

He glared at her, his face growing red in fury.

"You failed, Papa. You failed to best me. And you failed to defeat this man as well." Glancing at Slater—Matthew, Matthew Waterton—she felt a great pity rush through her, imagining what the intervening years must have been like for him. "You might have stolen his past, his true identity, but he became a man in his own right. In fact, I would hazard a guess that you made him stronger. More honorable."

Aloise saw the way her father trembled. His own daughter had exposed the awful truth. She had brought Crawford's crimes to the light in front of the very people he had hoped to impress. His reputation was in ruins. His pride destroyed. She hated him for the fact that such facts seemed far more important to him than the way he had affected so many lives.

Her finger tightened over the trigger.

A hand curled over her shoulder. "Let him go, Aloise," Slater urged.

"No."

"He's your father. Your blood."

"No!" This time, the cry came from her father. "No, damn it! She can't do this to me! She's a girl. A *girl!*"

Aloise closed one eye, her finger tightening, tightening, the metal biting into her skin. The throbbing of her head made it hard to think. She only knew that fathers were supposed to love their daughters. They weren't supposed to hurt them.

The hand at her shoulder squeezed ever so slightly. "Don't stoop to his level, Aloise."

He was right. So very right.

Taking a deep breath, Aloise lowered the weapon and turned to her husband.

Crawford lunged toward her, wrestling the pistol free. There was a scuffle, shouting, then she was being thrown to the ground as the gun discharged.

Some minutes passed. Minutes where she waited for the pain, the sensation of oozing blood. It never came.

"Have you fainted on me again?" Aloise blinked as Slater rolled her to face him. "There isn't a drop of blood, I assure you."

She managed to peek over his shoulder, saw that the uniformed men who had been with Clayton had taken the pistol away and now dragged Crawford bodily to the house.

He couldn't hurt her. Not now. Not ever again.

"What will they do to him?" she asked, curiously saddened by the fact that he would have to pay for all he had done.

"For now, he'll be locked in the cellar."

"And then?"

Slater drew her into his arms, sensing her ambivalent emotions, the way her body had been drained of its anger thereby leaving it curiously purged of the need for retribution.

"He must be punished, Aloise. The families of his late wives will demand it."

She supposed he was right. But even after all the heinous things he had done, Aloise discovered she still felt a shred of pity. The man they spoke of was, after all, her father.

Rolling to his feet, Slater reached for her hand. Drawing her to his side, he turned to the bewildered guests. "As the true husband to this beautiful woman, I invite all of you to celebrate the exchange of vows between me"—he withdrew a ruby encrusted band from his pocket and slipped it over Aloise's finger—"and my beloved bride."

The cheers that resulted were caused by the impetus of his men, but the stunning turn in events did not prevent the curious onlookers from drinking and dancing in the hours to come. In fact, what had started as a dull evening soon became a rollicking party. After all, the night had provided enough scandal for a dozen years. There were murders to discuss, secrets to disclose, suspicions to share.

Through it all, Slater watched as his wife was drawn into the tight-knit circle of select society. The titillating circumstances surrounding her introduction to the aristocracy had made her a coveted prize. He knew it was only a matter of time before the *grande dames* began inviting her to tea, to fancy-dress balls, and intimate salons. There she would find her niche and the friends she had been denied for so long.

Slater could have watched her for hours, days. But as the light grew dim and the lanterns were lit, he began to feel the taut expectancy brought on by evening. He was tired. His wife was tired. There were still so many things to discuss . . .

Filled with a purpose, he waited until those around them had become slightly inebriated and no longer watched him with such avid attention. Seeing Aloise near the gate that led into the formal gardens, he began to make his way toward her.

"Excuse me, Baroness," he murmured to a dowager who had once hired him to instruct her niece. "But I am about to abduct my new bride." Taking Aloise's hand, he ignored the nostalgic twinkle in the baroness's eyes and drew his wife into the darkness.

"Where are we going?"

"Away."

Leading her to where his stallion had been tethered, he lifted Aloise into the saddle, then swung behind her. Swiftly, he urged the animal far from the incessant din and into the quiet of the night. The ebony shadows seeped into his soul, offering him comfort, but more than that, offering him hope that all would be well.

"Are you angry with me for not warning you what to anticipate this evening?" he asked some time later when Aloise made no attempt at conversation. "I knew your father would find us this morn. I planned the events, my capture."

"Why would you do such a thing?"

He could tell by the slight hurt buried in her voice that she was still disturbed by his methods.

"Once Crawford discovered I had . . . ravished you, I knew he would watch my every move. If I tried to get close to you, he would be there, waiting. So I decided to give him a chance to find me, lock me up, then twist that fact to my advantage. Once he thought I was safely incarcerated, my men freed me and we prepared to confront your father when he was most vulnerable. When all eyes were on you both."

"Your plan worked."

"Nearly." His arms tightened, remembering the pistol being held to her head.

Despite her confusion, Aloise soothed his sudden tension by sliding her hand down his knee. The action caused his body to grow tight in an altogether different way, but he couldn't think about that now. Not until he knew that Aloise could forgive him for all he had done.

Slater drew the horse to a stop once they'd reached the grounds of Ashenleigh. The house gleamed in the darkness, looking much more inviting to him than it ever had. This place had sprouted from the sweat of his labors. It was here he'd brought his treasures. Here he'd claimed his bride.

He swung from the stallion, needing to see her face. "I think we should talk."

She nodded, her expression difficult to read in the darkness.

He took her hand, twining their fingers together, and led her into the privet maze where he knew no one would inadvertently interrupt their privacy. He took them through the shadows, winding his way through the familiar paths toward the middle, where most of the restoration had occurred. There, the walkway widened and became easier to follow. He continued past the spot where Aloise had hidden that night she'd escaped from the ballroom, deeper and deeper inside, until he finally reached its center where a fountain and ornamental pool gurgled in delight.

Standing in indecision, he wondered where he should start his explanations. Aloise looked so small, so fragile, but he knew explanations had to be made tonight.

"Your mother loved this maze," he began quietly, softly, instantly capturing her attention. "She was the one who ordered it built. So she chose a spot just beyond Briarwood knowing that your father would forbid her to build anything so frivolous on his own property. That was how I met her the first time. The cottage we visited was my house—there, just down the valley." He saw by the softening of her face that she remembered the cottage, this place and probably more—Miss Nibbs, her mother. A man named Matthew. "I was on my way to teach school in the village when I rounded the path to see this diminutive woman ordering a host of gardeners to plant a mountain of privet bushes." His lips twitched in remembrance. "She'd sketched her design on the back of an old letter. Sitting beneath a canopy erected to shield her from the sun, she oversaw the entire construction while at her side, a wide-eyed little girl played in the dirt with a battered trowel."

Aloise's eyes gleamed suspicious in the darkness. Slater did not wish to make her cry, but now that he had begun his tale, he discovered he could not stop.

"At first, I would pause to greet Jeanne on my way each morning. From their, our friendship grew when we discovered a mutual love of books and the arts. There was something about her. Something so familiar. As if I had known her all my life. We soon knew each other's secrets and dreams as intimately as our own."

He sat on the bench and took Aloise's hand. "When she came to me with a proposition, to marry her daughter and see to her happiness, the entire situation seemed far from strange."

Aloise's fingers tightened ever so slightly.

"You were an inquisitive child. I saw you each week when Jeanne came to visit me. Yet, I must confess that I never really saw you as a future wife, only as a little girl. Jeanne's curious daughter."

He took a deep breath wishing that he could avoid the events of that night so long ago, but the words had been locked in him for too many years.

"Your mother had been sent to Briarwood because she was to give birth to a child. Your father told her he thought it would be healthier for her in the country, but everyone knew he simply wanted her out of his way. When the baby—a little girl—was stillborn, Jeanne was beside herself with grief and despair. She came to me soon after, still weak and sick, and begged me to help her escape, to take you away." His voice grew husky as the years of guilt and responsibility threatened to crush him. "I . . . refused."

Aloise gripped his hand. Whether to offer him strength or in disappointment, he did not know. He only knew that the words could not be stopped.

"That night, there were lights on the sea road, signs

of a struggle. In my heart of hearts, I knew that your mother had decided to take you away. I tried to reach you in time, but when I arrived at the scene of the scuffle, your mother was already backed onto the ledge. She kept you shielded behind her skirts but Brannigan was insistent that you both return with him."

He saw Aloise's eyes squeeze closed and knew that she fought her own memories of that night.

"You know now what happened," he said gently. "You tried to run to me and were caught. Your mother dodged to protect you—"

"And Brannigan killed her."

He nodded.

"Then my father arrived."

"Yes."

"He was so cold, so distant."

"He never truly knew her. Never loved her. Or you."

She blinked at the tears gathering in her eyes. "He killed Brannigan with the man's own knife."

"You tried to run away and that was when he knocked you down." Slater touched her temple and felt encouraged when she leaned into the gesture as if she drew comfort from the contact. "You struck your head on a rock, otherwise you would have seen the rest. How he shot the second man he'd hired, then retrieved the blade to come for me."

Taking a deep draft of the cool night air, he said quickly, "I was a coward. I should have stayed."

"No." She pressed her fingers to his lips. "He would have killed you too."

"I should have tried harder to take you with me."

"My father was a powerful man—even then. He never would have allowed such a thing."

Slater stared at her in amazement, feeling an infinitesimal lightening of the heavy emotional burdens he'd carried for so long.

Aloise released his hand and stood. For some time, she kept her head bowed as if carefully choosing her words. "I can see why you could not help me then."

"But?" he prompted when she grew silent.

She turned to face him and he was struck to the core by the misery of her expression. "Why didn't you come for me?"

He sighed, having asked himself that question a hundred times in the past few weeks. "At first, I *couldn't.* As you said, your father was a powerful man with at least a dozen of the local authorities under his control. I was forced to flee from Cornwall, change my name, my appearance, and obtain passage on the first vessel needing seamen. In time, I was able to make your father believe I had died, thus giving me a little more freedom. For years, I scrimped and saved, barely able to eke out a living. That was no life for a child."

Sighing, he stood. "I soon developed enough of a reputation to attract the attention of a captain who would be journeying on an exploring expedition. He hired me as his assistant, but then, after he grew too sick to lead the men, I took over his duties for a time before obtaining my own clipper. That was when I drew the attention of the French king. He offered me a position as one of his cartographers. Year by year, I traveled more, learned more, gained more responsibility, more influence, until I was leading my own missions and gathering my own men."

"Rakes and roués."

"Men unjustly accused."

She stared at him with wide, dark eyes. Eyes filled with hurt. "Why didn't you come for me?"

"I couldn't find you."

"You must have known I was sent directly to Sacre Coeur."

"No."

"What of the farmhouse in Loire? Didn't anyone tell you how my father tried to control me by imprisoning me? By hiring a host of guards to keep me from escaping? Guards who cared more for the village women they chased and seduced beneath my very eyes than the girl they were hired to keep in tow?"

He took her hands. "Had I known, I would have moved heaven and earth to retrieve you."

He drew her close, unable to bear the wounded betrayal he saw in her eyes. "Several years ago, I hired a man in London to try and locate you. He was able to determine nothing other than you had been sent to school. We began watching your father's ship, knowing that would probably be the best way to trace you. Luckily, fate stepped in and you were seen in Calais being taken aboard *The Sea Sprite.* Within days, a bedraggled maid was washed ashore at my feet."

He tipped her chin, forcing her to look at him. "I was instantly charmed. You were like nothing I had ever imagined you would be."

"You thought I was my mother."

"I knew you were Aloise. My betrothed." He drew her hand to his cheek, laying it against the scar Jeanne had caused so long ago when she had grappled to save herself. He saw by the widening of Aloise's eyes that she understood its significance.

"There is but one scar on my body that has the power to testify to all that occurred that night. But we both have scars much deeper, unseen, barely healed. Please, Aloise." He slowly sank to his knees hugging her about the waist. "Will you forgive me?"

He waited tensely for her answer, knowing that whatever she said, he would have to abide by her wishes. If she told him she never wanted to see him again, he couldn't blame her.

The silence of the night flowed about them like a dark sea. Then she lowered herself to the ground and held him close. "There is nothing to forgive."

Wrapping her arms around his body, she hugged him close, offering a balm to his battered spirit that he had feared he would never obtain. His chest grew tight with emotion and he clung to her, knowing she was his life, his destiny.

His soul mate.

He could have stayed that way for hours, but Aloise wriggled free and offered him a tremulous smile. Standing, she drew him to his feet and took his hand.

"Where are you leading me, mistress?"

She shot him a knowing look. "This is my wedding night."

"Not really. Not technically speaking."

"What do we care for technicalities?"

Once at the marble bench, Aloise stopped, staring at him for long, wonderful moments. Her expression changed slowly. From serenity, to wonder, to adoration. Hunger. Then, as if the horror and trials of the past few years melted into the night, she dropped his hand and tugged at the laces of her gown, plucking them free, then her petticoats, her panniers. Pushing them all to her feet, she kicked them away.

Slater quickly followed suit, divesting himself of his waistcoat, his shirt, his boots, hose, and breeches. When at long last, he stood bare, wanting, he looked up to find her standing in the moonlight, wearing nothing but the Bengal Rubies.

He gestured to the jewels. "Didn't I rid you of those once?"

She touched them lovingly. "Yes, but you will not rid me of them again."

"Of that you are sure. They were given to my father, you know. As his only heir . . ."

"They are mine now, not yours."

"How so?"

"You threw them away." She offered him a coy shrug. "Therefore, I stake my claim and decree that they shall be passed to our daughter, and our daughter's daughter."

Slater's throat grew tight with a very powerful mixture of emotion. Love, devotion, and unmeasurable joy.

Seeing him thus, Aloise smiled, her own happiness radiating from her lovely face. So much so, he knew he would remember this moment until his dying day.

As he drew her into his arms, the Bengal Rubies glinted with a molten fire, and Matthew Waterton—alias Slater McKendrick, explorer and adventurer—knew the jewels had found a way to fulfill their promise. They had finally obtained an owner who was completely pure at heart.